The Voodoo Go

Walter Walden

Alpha Editions

This edition published in 2024

ISBN : 9789364736954

Design and Setting By
Alpha Editions
www.alphaedis.com
Email - info@alphaedis.com

As per information held with us this book is in Public Domain.
This book is a reproduction of an important historical work. Alpha Editions uses the best technology to reproduce historical work in the same manner it was first published to preserve its original nature. Any marks or number seen are left intentionally to preserve its true form.

Contents

CHAPTER I .... - 1 -
CHAPTER II .... - 5 -
CHAPTER III .... - 10 -
CHAPTER IV .... - 14 -
CHAPTER V .... - 23 -
CHAPTER VI .... - 31 -
CHAPTER VII .... - 36 -
CHAPTER VIII .... - 43 -
CHAPTER IX .... - 52 -
CHAPTER X .... - 56 -
CHAPTER XI .... - 64 -
CHAPTER XII .... - 70 -
CHAPTER XIII .... - 76 -
CHAPTER XIV .... - 80 -
CHAPTER XV .... - 84 -
CHAPTER XVI .... - 89 -
CHAPTER XVII .... - 96 -
CHAPTER XVIII .... - 102 -
CHAPTER XIX .... - 107 -
CHAPTER XX .... - 113 -
CHAPTER XXI .... - 116 -
CHAPTER XXII .... - 121 -
CHAPTER XXIII .... - 131 -
CHAPTER XXIV .... - 137 -
CHAPTER XXV .... - 143 -
CHAPTER XXVI .... - 149 -

CHAPTER XXVII ....- 156 -
CHAPTER XXVIII ....- 162 -
CHAPTER XXIX ....- 170 -
CHAPTER XXX..- 177 -
CHAPTER XXXI ....- 183 -

CHAPTER I

WE GET INTERESTING NEWS

It was on a tropic sea, and night, that I heard a little scrap of a tale that had in it that which was destined to preserve my life. The waning moon had not yet risen; the stars were all out, the Milky Way more than commonly near. The schooner's sails were barely drawing, and flapped idly at times. I leaned on the rail, listening to the purling of the sea against the vessel's side, and watching the phosphorescence where the water broke. The bell had just sounded a double stroke—two bells. Near by, the taciturn black fellow—who was our guide, and who alone (as shall appear) knew our course and destination—was in talk with Rufe, our black cook.

Heretofore, this man—black he was, but having hair straight as an Indian's—had been steadfastly mum on the subject of his past; this manifestly being but part and parcel of his policy to avoid any hint of the place to which he was piloting us. But now, I gathered, he was reciting to Rufe an episode set in this far away land to the south; and I cocked my ear. He was telling of something that had happened in his grandfather's experience, who, as he said, was in the service of the king of that land. It was one day when this king was set upon by his enemies, who came thundering on the doors; and the king employed the narrator's grandfather to assist him in his escape. The king collected his jewels and much gold which he put in a bag, and set it on the back of his servant. Then he led the way to a dungeon in the palace. Set in the thick rock wall of this dark cell was a shrine, a carved Calvary—Christ on the cross and figures at the foot.

"The king," the black narrator was saying, "horrify my gran'father, when he put his hand right on the Virgin, and pull that piece out. Then the sacrarium swing open, and there is one big hole, and the king push my gran'father through, and come after."

And he went on to tell how the king had led on, groping down the steps of this secret passage, and presently out into the forest; and how they two finally came to a fortress, and found safety.

It is this circumstance that (for the very good reason indicated) stands most forward, as I look back over the early days of that voyage. And you are to hear more of that.

Sailing the seas in search of adventure was not altogether a new thing for me. Nor was it to be quite a novelty—the drifting into mysterious places, and the poking into hornets' nests. Indeed, my friend, Ray Reid, declared that it seemed like I was picked out to drag poor, inoffensive young innocents (meaning himself) into all kinds of scrapes—and that every little while. But it was with neither a light heart nor an indifferent purpose that I, for one, set forth on this new enterprise, of which it has been given me to tell the tale. I had been orphaned of my dear mother two years before, when I was barely sixteen; and recently my father, who was a builder of houses, had variously suffered, in pocket and in health, and had journeyed far to the west, in the hope to recuperate both. And I lay awake nights, trying to hatch schemes for earning money, and that in considerable amount. It was mortgages harassed us; one on our home, and more on other property.

It was then there came the letter from Julian Lamartine, a good friend, far south in New Orleans, and in whose company my comrades and I had sailed in a former voyage. He now proposed—in fact he had long planned—another adventure. This time it was to seek certain gold fields in the tropics, his letter said, of which he had had some private news. The real mainspring of his enterprise, I allege, was to seek to make some return to my comrades and myself for certain services we had rendered him on this former voyage. For it was on this occasion he came into his wealth; and he maintained he owed it all to us. Thus, it was Julian Lamartine, who was finding the ship and all the equipment—in short paying the whole shot.

Most of our original crew were either scattered or hopelessly entangled in some employment or other, so that there remained only three to make that journey from Illinois to the point of departure in the southland: Ray Reid, Robert Murtry, and myself (Wayne Scott, to give you my name). Two old friends met us in the station in New Orleans. They were Julian and our former sailing master, Jean Marat.

"I am so ver' glad to see you once again," said Jean Marat, as with his beaming smile he took our hands. "We go some more an' fight thee pirates, eh?" he continued.

"Say now!" broke in Ray, "I want you to let me get my full growth before you steer me among any more of that crew." Ray often told how he had been scared out of two years' growth in a minute, that he never would be able to raise a moustache, and that the reason he hadn't lost his hair was because he had had his hat on. I don't believe Ray ever knew what it was to be really scared. An earthquake wouldn't disconcert him; he'd make sport while the ground was shaking him off his feet.

When greetings were over, Julian spoke up, "Madame Marat has insisted that we take supper with her. The carriage is outside, and it's time we were going."

Madame Marat was the mother of Jean Marat. She was a handsome, sympathetic, motherly soul, and we had all sampled her cookery. When we were bowling along behind the horses, Julian put his hand on my knee.

"Wayne," he said, "You ought to have seen how she took on when I told her you had lost your mother. If it hadn't been winter she would have taken the train next day, and gone to you. But she declared she would never have lived to reach there in the cold."

When we had climbed the stairs and gone into the little parlor, Madame Marat held forth her hands to me, "*Ah, mon chere!*" she said. And she had me in her motherly clasp—only a mother knows how.

Madame pushed us in, to a table steaming and savory with her French things, dishes she knew so well how to concoct. And there was grinning black Rufe, who had been all his life in the service of Julian Lamartine's family. And then, when the meal was well under way, and we had all had our fill of comparing notes, Julian opened the business of our projected voyage.

"You probably noticed that I hadn't much to say in my letter regarding details," he said, "where we're going and so on. The fact is, I don't know."

We showed our interest.

"It was Rufe, here, that picked up the information," went on Julian. "I'm going to let him tell you how it was. Rufe," he turned to the black fellow, "tell the boys how you found the man."

"Well," began Rufe, "you sees I got some kin living up Tchoupetoulas way, an' I hadn' been to see um fo' a right smart long time. So I goes. An' dere I meets up wid a niggah I ain't seed befo', whose name is Amos. He ben in town moh dan a week, an' he was low down sick—lef' by some ship he been a' sailin' on. He's home way off some'ere, he don' say where. Well, I dopes him up on calomel and quinine, like ol' Mistah Lamartine use ter do, an' he soon gets well, an' he kinder tuck a shine to me. An' after a while he tells me how he an' a brother of hisn has got a gol' mine some'eres, an' as how his father discover dat gol' mine. Amos was a little pickaninny then, an' his father tells him as how he is goin' to show him dat gol' mine when he gits big 'nuff. But when he try to sell the gol' wat he take fum de mine, a ornery debbil of a white man gits in wid Amos' father in de mine, an' murder him. Amos say he know dat, 'cause he's father nebber come back, and dat white man, he jis' is swimmin' in gol' fum dat time on.

"Amos plumb refuse to tell whar dat place is, 'cept hit on an islan' down South America way. But he say ef I got some sure 'nuff hones' folks dat'll go, he take 'em to dat island and divide up fair an' square, w'en de gol' mine is foun'. He say he an' his brother ain't nebber foun' de mine, cause dat white man tol' 'em dat ef dey come nosin' roun' dey is goin' to get shot. And Amos showed me in his leg where he once did git shot."

"Well say," broke in Ray, "did this Amos ever show you what kind of stuff he burns in his pipe?"

"Yes, perhaps he's just yarning," spoke up Robert, "so as to get somebody to take him back home."

Julian shook his head.

"No," he said. "That's what I thought when Rufe first told me the story. But I've talked with him enough times to feel satisfied he's in earnest. He tells a straight story, so far as he will tell. And he refuses to say where the island is, but agrees to take us there."

We all saw this black fellow, Amos, the next day, and we came to Julian's conviction of the fellow's truthfulness; though I will not avouch that our willingness to believe had not something to do with it. He was rather a taciturn, sober-featured being. His hair was not crinkly like the average negro, and his nose resembled an Indian's. Though illiterate, he showed intelligence, and he would add nothing to the tale he had told to Rufe, except that the islands of Cuba and Jamaica might be considered to lie in the path to this island of his nativity and our goal.

CHAPTER II

WE MEET WITH A SERIOUS REVERSE

I shall not dwell on our preparations for the voyage; nor shall I attempt a lengthy description of the schooner *Pearl* which lay in the Basin. Jean Marat's eyes sparkled, when first we came in view of her. She was of one hundred and twenty-one tons burden, and sported a flying-jib, jib, fore mainsail, foresail, fore gaff top-sail, mainsail, and main gaff top-sail. Forward, a companionway led down to the men's quarters; after, the cabin roof, with its grated skylight, was raised but a little above the deck. Two small boats hung in davits. The cabin was sufficiently spacious, and there were four staterooms, and then there was the galley—the jolly Rufe's domain. And he took great pride in exhibiting its treasures.

A day early in August saw us out in the broad Gulf of Mexico, all of the *Pearl's* sails set to the westerly breeze. Madame Marat mothered our party. In fair weather when she was engineering Rufe's activities in the galley, she sat with her lace-work on the deck. Even the roughest of the sailors would put himself in the way of her smile.

And then, late one afternoon there gradually rose out of the sea the higher peaks of Jamaica. And on the following day we made the harbor of Kingston, a beautiful city, with its fringe of cocoa palms at the front, and at its back the mountains clad in tropical vegetation. It was here events were brewing that were to set a kink in our plans. It was here, too, that Madame Marat had old friends expecting her arrival. Indeed, we had not long been at anchor till they had found us out; Monsieur Paul Duchanel and Madame Duchanel.

But a real shock, too, awaited us. I had no sooner made my bow to the Duchanels than I turned, directed by Ray's grinning look, to see an old friend of our former voyage, Grant Norris, whom we had believed to be in England. He had come over the other rail.

"Thought you were going to slip away on another ramble without me, did you?" was his greeting.

Julian and Marat had kept this thing a surprise for Ray, Robert and myself. They had been in correspondence with Norris, and he had found it convenient to join us here. He explained that his sister's husband had been sent by his London employers to represent them in Jamaica.

What with entertainment in the home of the Duchanels and in that of Norris's sister, and the drives over the wonderful roads, among groves of palms, mahogany, and multi-colored tropical vegetation, three days had soon gone. It was on the fourth day that we three boys found the cherished opportunity to turn a little trick at the expense of Jean Marat and Grant

Norris. These two were crack shots with the rifle; we had witnessed samples of their shooting years back. On this day we six drove out of Kingston some miles, to a mountain stream to fish. Robert and I carried what purported to be cases holding fancy fishing rods. Ray was to manage the show.

"Now, gentlemen," he began, when we had settled down on a grassy slope beside the stream, "now, gentlemen, I want to show you the trick of the disappearing mangoes." He produced two small green mangoes and set one each on the ends of two long bamboo fishing rods. These he handed to Marat and Norris. "Now, gentlemen," he again began his speech, "wave them slowly from side to side. Watch the mangoes very carefully and see them disappear. Watch very carefully or you will miss it."

Robert and I had slipped away behind the bushes to a distance of about sixty yards. Marat and Norris smilingly watched the mangoes, as they waved them far above their heads. Then suddenly their faces changed, as the mangoes shattered, as if from an internal explosion.

Robert and I sped back, as the two astounded men were scratching their heads over Ray's trick. And we exhibited our .22 caliber rifles, fitted with *silencers*.

"Ah, that was ver' clever," said Marat, as he slapped us on the back.

Norris rolled Robert in the grass in playful punishment. "To think," said Norris, "that these kids would play a trick like that on us!—and to put *silencers* on their guns."

Robert and I had worked long, and expended very much ammunition, in our ambition to emulate these two rifle-men, and now we had our reward.

When we arrived back in Kingston with our basket of fish that evening, it was to hear startling news. There was great excitement in the home of the Duchanels. A family of close friends and neighbors had this day been bereft of their little seven-year-old daughter, Marie Cambon. She had been last seen before noon at play in the yard of the Cambon home, where there was much growth of flowers and decorative bushes, at the back. The city and surrounding country was being carefully searched, we were told.

Our party was making preparations to join in the search when black Rufe appeared. His usual jovial face was a picture of terror.

"Amos, he done daid," he announced.

"Amos dead!" said Julian, "What, how—what do you mean?" he stammered.

Rufe told the story. He and Amos had been on board the *Pearl* when the news of the disappearance of the Cambon child came to them. "It's the voodoo," Amos had said. And thereupon he became restless, and presently was for rowing ashore. He wanted to get a nearer view of a certain sailing vessel he pointed out; but insisted on getting that view from some place up the shore; he would not go near it in a boat. So the two rowed to shore and made their way toward the desired spot. It was a sheltered region amongst the trees and brush. Amos was well in advance of Rufe. Suddenly a group of two blacks and one white man appeared in an open space.

"Dat white man an' Amos on a suddent stopped," said Rufe, "like two high stumps, de white man wid his han' to his face. Den Amos turn 'roun' an' say, 'Run!' And he run one way, an' I run anoder. I run nigh half a mile, an' den I gets ashame' o' myse'f an' stop. I run jes' 'cause he sayed 'run.' I sayed to myse'f, 'Dis ain't no way fo' you to do,' an' den I goes back. I goes de way I seen Amos run—I picked up a club, not a knowin' jis' what hits all about. I didn' go fur till I see Amos lyin' on de groun', an' a puddle o' blood. An' he was plumb daid."

"Did you hear a shot?" said Norris.

"No, dar warn't no shot; hit was a knife dat did it," declared Rufe. "Now you-all know, Julian," continued the poor black, "it ain't my way to run; I run jes' 'cause he sayed run."

We reassured him, telling him we knew him too well to doubt. And then we took steps to recover the body.

Darkness had spread over the city and harbor by this time. With Rufe's help effort was made to identify the vessel that had excited Amos's curiosity; and it was learned, finally, that a sailing vessel had moved out of the harbor soon after darkness had fallen; and before the return of day it became possible to identify the vessel. It was the schooner *Josephine*, owned by a Monsieur Mordaunt, that had thus stolen away in the murk.

It was then the parents of the missing little Marie Cambon made known to us certain facts that had apparently strong bearing on these events. For a year past this M. Mordaunt had been a suitor for the hand of their elder daughter, Josephine. He had come to Kingston in his handsome yacht; and had almost taken the society of Kingston by storm. He appeared well educated, accomplished, and apparently possessed vast riches, expending money with astounding lavishness. He professed to come from France, but balked all efforts to induce him to be particular as to his antecedents; till finally it became whispered about that this Mordaunt bore an assumed name, and that he not only was of mixed blood, but that some of it was ignoble blood.

It was then Cambon forbade him the house. For the past several weeks he had sought an interview with Miss Josephine, who had been dutifully guided by her parents, though she was slow to accept the unfavorable reports.

The next day following the tragedy there came news of a mysterious ship's boat having put in in the night beyond Portland Point, and taken on a pair of black men who had with them a huge hamper.

Madame Cambon's condition was pitiable. Not a tear did she shed; she was dazed and all but dumb of the shock. She would not rest, but must go with the others in the search. She walked until her limbs gave way, then she must continue in a carriage. In the morning her strength failed, and blessed unconsciousness came. It was Madame Marat took her in hand.

Our party joined in the hunt, and it was not till noon of the day following the disappearance, that all came together again. We had been guided by people of Kingston in the search. Now we of the *Pearl* had all come to experience a desire to put our heads together to some purpose as a separate party. It quickly developed that all minds were as one on several particulars. Even had we not lost our guide in the quest for gold, that lure had been pushed aside by this new, humane call.

"And now," said Norris, "We've got to decide what's to be our line."

"And you all know as well as I do," began Ray, "who it is that's got it all figured out."

And they all turned their eyes on myself. It was always Ray's way, when in the old days our little troop of boys met problems, he usually contrived to put the solution up to me. During our former voyage, whenever an enigma presented, he discouraged all efforts of the others by assuring them that Wayne would work it out without half trying; just leave it all to him! And there was the inevitable result. Ray was always incorrigible.

A number of circumstances were significant: This M. Mordaunt held a grievance against the Cambon family; his character is at least under suspicion; the time and manner of his sailing away is also suspicious; the close association between Amos's getting the news of the child's disappearance and his suddenly awakened interest in that vessel in the harbor was a suspicious circumstance; it developed that Mordaunt's yacht lay opposite to that point to which Amos went to obtain a nearer view of the vessel of his interest; it is very probable that the white man seen by Rufe was Mordaunt, and that he it was caused Amos's death; that it must have been that Amos had some knowledge of him the publishing of which he had some reason to fear; this Mordaunt then must be a very fiend; on learning of the child's disappearance Amos had declared that it was the voodoo, and according to Rufe's account he talked like he knew—this is a thing Madame Cambon must not hear of—

"Jus' so," agreed Marat. "She could not stand to think that."

"Now then," I said, "we are agreed on one thing. We must seek Mordaunt's schooner yacht *Josephine*, and not forget voodoo for a guide."

"Of course we're agreed on it," said Ray, in his tantalizing manner, mingling sport with earnest.

CHAPTER III

WE SAIL ON A DIFFERENT QUEST

There were none among us who had not heard stories of the voodoo, of that strange snake worship of the negroes; how at night the devotees came together secretly in the forest; and how they got themselves into a frenzy of excitement with the music of the drum and the drinking of rum, which they mixed with the blood of fowls, or better that of a goat; how at times they were not satisfied with anything less than the blood of a human (*the goat without horns*). It was more often a child, black or white, which was sacrificed to the voodoo god, which was incarnate in the form of a small green snake, kept in a basket on a platform, on which appeared the *papaloi* or *mamaloi* who presided at the horrid ceremony. Then it became an orgie—dancing—cannibalism, for after the warm blood had been drunk, the flesh was boiled and eaten.

Thus you can imagine our horror at the thought of sweet little Marie Cambon falling into such hands; and so too you will understand our easy abandonment of every other ambition that we might turn our zeal toward the rescue of this poor innocent.

Monsieur Cambon's suspicions, too, had turned to this Mordaunt, when the report of the schooner's flight in the dark had come to him, and particularly so when the news came of the mysterious landing of a boat to take off the black men with the great basket. But we of the *Pearl* were very careful not to repeat to Cambon anything of Amos's mention of the voodoo. Such a blow to let strike a parent, we felt, would serve no purpose.

Let us pass over those hours of preparation for the sailing in pursuit of the schooner *Josephine*.

Monsieur Cambon, accompanied by his daughter, Josephine, came with us to the boat, to give last expression of gratitude and God speed. Miss Josephine pulled me aside for a word. Her face was pale, and a wild look was in her eyes as they gazed into mine.

"You go after him!" She meant it for a question, though she gave it the form of an accusation.

I made no denial.

"He did not steal Marie!" she said, her tone expressing a wish rather than a conviction. I could see that she, even, now had begun to doubt, for she knew, too, that Mordaunt had stolen away under cover of night.

"I am convinced he did," I asserted.

Her face became more pale. "Oh, tell me!" she said.

I considered a moment; then decided that it would be a kindness, if I could cure her of her belief in this man. Pledging her to secrecy I then told her Rufe's story of Amos, though carefully omitting any mention of the voodoo. I believe she matched other circumstances with what I had to say, to the end that conviction was stealing into her heart. Finally she spoke.

"Oh, I didn't want to believe!" she said. "Oh, I hope he will die!"

And she turned away.

It was at four bells of the morning watch (ten o'clock) that we sailed out of Kingston harbor. We set our course to the east in spite of the fact that the mysterious boat had landed to the west, beyond Portland Point; the home of the voodoo was to the east, not to the west. He who was our guide living, was still our guide, though dead. Indeed there seemed almost ground for believing that his spirit continued to direct us, on a number of occasions, when we were completely at a loss.

Madame Marat had remained in Kingston; so the *Pearl* company consisted of Grant Norris, Jean Marat, Julian Lamartine, Rufe, Ray Reid, Robert Murtry, and myself, not to mention the sailors, forward.

When we had passed Morant Point, Captain Marat set the course east northeast. We aimed for the home of the voodoo. It was the only clue we had. At midnight we sighted the white flash of an island light; it was day when we passed the towering rock. Then at last the peaks of the great island we sought began to creep up out of the sea. The great jumbled mass of rocks came even nearer, spreading out as if to engulf us, till, on the following day we dropped anchor off the city.

It was not a cheerful passage, this from island to island. Even Ray had been caught in the general gloom. We had time, each severally, during these two days, to come, by reflection, to a realization of the apparent hopelessness of our task. Beyond the almost haphazard selection of this one large port as our first point of contact, we had no plan. While the query,—what next? was uppermost in the minds of each, he dreaded to hear another—every other— confess that he did not know. For of necessity he *could* not know. And so, when we moved in, in that late afternoon, seeking a suitable anchorage, every eye—independently—sought out every sail within view, only half daring to hope for a sight of a vessel that should appear to be the *Josephine*.

When everything had been made snug above deck, and the harbor officials had made their visit, dusk was on. No move could be made until morning. And then came supper. All lingered at the table, knowing that the time had come for a council of war. It was Norris who volunteered to open the ball.

"Well comrades," he began, seeking to be cheerful, "I suppose we'll now have to decide on a fresh start. How are we going to find out if the *Josephine* is here?"

"Well," said Captain Marat, "If she have not change her name, that will be easy."

Captain Marat had hit on the thing that was troubling us all. The man Mordaunt, we knew, had at one time changed the name of his vessel to honor her whom he had hoped to make his wife, and now he might have two reasons for making another change in name: He had been disappointed in his hope, and there was the criminal reason—for concealment. None had taken any note of the schooner, and Monsieur Cambon's description of the vessel made a picture that answered for almost any schooner yacht of dimensions a little greater than the *Pearl*.

It was also unfortunate that none of us had set eyes on this man Mordaunt. But Monsieur Cambon had been able to give us one characteristic of the man that might go far toward identifying him, should we be fortunate enough to encounter him under favorable conditions. Cambon described him as of medium though strong build; of finely chiseled, rather handsome features; black eyes, black hair, which he wore a little long and which was disposed to curl. His manners Cambon described as studiously polished, if self-assertive. But the single characteristic that interested me most was a certain mannerism.

"Sometimes," M. Cambon had said, "when he is unconscious of his surroundings, deeply cogitating on something, he will take the lobe of his ear between thumb and finger, pulling or stroking—like when others scratch the head when they are puzzled."

It took us but a short time to determine on a course. Some were to go in a small boat among the many ships of the harbor, while others should visit the city. We spent an hour on deck, breathing the balmy air, and watching the many lights of the ships and the city. There, too, was the revolving red light on Point Lomentin, and the green light, set in by the city.

We were early astir, all eager to be doing. Ray and Julian went with Grant Norris to sail about the harbor, to seek news of the *Josephine*; Robert and myself, with Captain Marat, rowed to a wharf of the city. It was verily a city of blacks. Mulattoes were few, and we walked up and down numerous streets before we found a white man whose appearance encouraged us. He was a Frenchman, seated before an apothecary shop. The smile on his thin smooth-shaven face invited us to stop. He and Captain Marat were directly in conversation, in the tongue they knew best.

The Frenchman gave us his name—Jules Sevier—and had us into his shop, with its many bottles of patent medicines, in rows. He and Marat sipped

French wine while they continued their talk. At last the apothecary turned to Robert and myself.

"Ah," he said, "I am 'fraid you have one ver' deeficult task. But I am glad you fin' your way to me. I will help you all I can."

It developed that he knew nothing of either the schooner *Josephine* or M. Mordaunt, or anyone to fit the description Marat was able to give him. But after listening to the recital of the circumstances (set about the disappearance of little Marie Cambon) he said,—"Oui, oui! it was thad man. Such things like thad have happen more times than the world think. You have come to the right place."

Jules Sevier at the last told us that he would make some private inquiries, and advised that we come back on the following day to learn the results.

We were soon in our boat, somewhat cheered by the bit of encouragement we'd got, alloyed as it was.

"I think it's a good sign," declared Robert, "that we went so straight to that man. He can help us if anybody can."

Robert was something of a fatalist you see.

"Yes, he know ver' much about the voodoo," said Jean Marat.

We boarded the *Pearl*, to wait several hours before the others showed up. When they drew near we could see that they had been unsuccessful. They had found no schooner of the name sought, nor any with a newly painted name.

"Of course," said Norris, "she might be lying hid behind some small island, or point, miles away, and it will take anyway a week to find out."

CHAPTER IV

WE PICK UP THE TRAIL

In the morning all but Rufe went to shore. Rufe would have none of it.

"Say," he said, when Ray offered to remain aboard in his place, "say, you-all, you ain't guine git dis niggah in dat town to be voodooed by dem heathen niggahs. Hum-n! An' I ain't got no rabbit-fut, nor nuthing."

Julian, Ray, and Norris went sight-seeing, while Marat, Robert, and I made our way to the apothecary shop.

Jules Sevier greeted us.

"I ver' sorry I have no news for you," he said. "There is one, I could not find, who have a son who carry the mail, and know ver' much of thees country. Maybe tomorrow she weel be home, and we can learn sometheeng."

He ushered us into the shop, where there awaited us a black woman of middle age, who, Sevier said, would tell us a tale that we would travel far to find a match for. She could speak only in the French; so Jean Marat got her tale, which he interpreted for Robert and myself.

Her husband had been a voodoo devotee; but twelve years ago he had been induced to renounce the worship, and turn to one of the Christian denominations. One of his old associates contrived to introduce into his food one of the poisons so well known to the voodoo.

The man died.

The authorities insisted on his immediate burial. The poor widow had gone to visit his grave on the following day, only to find his empty coffin, beside the opened grave. The body was gone. The remains were found, however, hours later, with the heart and lungs removed. She said she then was convinced poison had been given him to put him in a trance, and that the voodoo worshipers had exhumed him a few hours after burial, and resuscitated him, to obtain the living blood for admixture with the rum, and to take the heart for a voodoo feast.

When the woman had gone, Jules Sevier told us that he was prepared to escort some one of us to witness an actual voodoo ceremonial that very night. He assured us that by reason of the nearness of the locality to the city, our sensibilities would be subjected to no greater shock than to witness the sacrifice of fowls. We none of us confessed to over much curiosity, even for so mild a show; but in this quest we were on, some more actual knowledge of these practices might stand us in good stead.

It fell to me to be Sevier's companion on the excursion; and I returned alone, at dusk, to take supper with him, and prepare for the show. The apothecary assured me that if we were to go as white men, we should see little to our purpose, since it would then be necessary to depart before any important part of the ceremonial should begin. So he brought into a back-room certain grease-paints, and a pair of black, woolly wigs, and two outfits—jackets, trousers, and hats,—of the same nondescript style that I had seen on the streets of the city.

He set to work to help me to smear and rig myself first; and when the operation was complete he set a glass before me. I was shocked at the spectacle, and I set to, to rubbing my wrist, to see if this black stain might not be permanent, so natural did it appear. It refused to rub off. Sevier saw my embarrassment, and laughingly assured me that any tallow would take it off.

We passed out at the back, into the dark, and made our way through the streets. The rows of unattractive buildings with their second story balconies, shallow and overhanging, were like the pictures I'd seen of the Chinatown of a great city. The stench from the gutters was nauseating, the heat stifling. We had presently passed the outskirts of the city, and were treading a rough road.

For some time I had been cocking my ear to a distant sound. It began as a scarcely discernible rumble; then it would swell to a roar, as of an approaching storm, and die away, and then swell again, and then fall away again, in a most improper and bewildering fashion. The blackened apothecary at my side informed me that it was the *Ka*—the voodoo drum, and that I should presently see the drummer. When we had covered some above a mile of this road, the drummer seemed to have taken his instrument and gone some considerable distance away, for the rumble had now become scarce audible. But my conductor informed me it was a peculiarity of the thing that it was heard with greater distinctness at a distance than when near by; and so the lesser sound was evidence that we were drawing near our goal. The skin over my spine was becoming a bit creepy. The ghostly palms looked down on us, and seemed to whisper things. If I had been alone I am quite sure I should have turned back. In an interval between the rumblings of the drum I heard a cricket, and that familiar sound gave me some comfort.

Then at last we made out a great fire ahead, and between us and the leaping flames were many dusky figures, grotesquely capering. As we approached we saw that one or two were already in a frenzy of excitement, and there was constant drinking. Then I made out the drummer. He was sitting astride of what appeared to be a cask, his fingers playing upon the end. The dancers seemed as if they would fly into the tree-tops with ecstacy, at each swelling of the sound.

We two kept well out in the shadows, till all of that hundred or more of blacks seemed to have reached the height of intoxication; then we moved in. Finally the dancing ceased, and an old crone in a red robe mounted a rude platform, taking her place beside the snake-box.

She first addressed the mob; and then each worshiper in turn came forward, spoke words, and lay some offering before the box. My companion whispered me the explanation that they were asking favors. The old crone—the *mamaloi*—set her ear to the box, and gave out the answers, one by one.

All now crowded close, as the *mamaloi* seized a white rooster by the head in the one hand, flashing a knife in the other. A sweep of the blade, and the black devotees directly were mixing blood with the rum in their cups, which they drank. Fowl after fowl followed the first, and all presently found their way into pots for cooking. And the wild caperings recommenced with the drinking, and the shouting, and all.

I began to sicken of the spectacle; and then I noted suspicious eyes taking us in. It was then Jules Sevier whispered me—"Come, it is time we go now." And so we slipped off in the shadows.

The drum ceased its rumble, and the tree-frogs began their warble; to which music I trod the dark road with a lighter step. "They will keep on," said Sevier, "till they be exhaust', or ver' drunk, and then they fall, and sleep all the day."

Certain odors of the dank vegetation filled my nostrils; similar odors ever after have served to recall the spectacle I had witnessed that night.

The city was quiet; the populace seemed all to be sleeping. The howling of some cats was all the sound we heard as we threaded the streets.

Soon we were busied with removing the black stain from our skins. The operation consumed nearly an hour—with the fats, the soap, and the rubbing. And then I was lighted to my bed by Sevier.

We were at breakfast, when there arrived at the back door the mother of the mail carrier, that Sevier had told us of. The apothecary had her in, and questioned her while we ate. She had no knowledge of any Monsieur Mordaunt, but her son had often made mention of one Duran, a white man, of the north coast, who was much abroad in his schooner yacht, and who had, many years back, come suddenly into untold wealth. It was said the source was wealthy connections in France.

"Ah, thad is your man!" said Jules Sevier, when he had repeated to me what the woman told. "Thad is your man. Duran he is on this island, Mordaunt w'en he is in Jamaica, or where not."

In an hour, appeared Captain Marat and Robert. While they were not a little entertained by the account of my last night's experiences, they found greater interest in the news of the morning.

"We're on his trail now," declared Robert.

"Yes," agreed Marat. "Now it weel not be hard to find heem, I theenk."

But Jules Sevier had a word to say. He spoke rapidly in French with Jean Marat for some minutes; then he turned to Robert and myself.

"I have explain' to Captain Marat," he said, "thad eet will not do to spik weeth the authorities about thees matter. The authorities are too much in the voodoo themselv'. You weel have to keep quiet about thees business, except w'en you know with whom you spik. The voodoo are ver' strong in thee government here."

Sevier left his shop in the care of an assistant, and accompanied us to the shore. He gave us much valuable information about the region to which we were going, and advice as to our dealing with the natives. Before we stepped into the boat he held out a small parcel to me.

"Here is some supply of the paint," he said, "and the two black wigs. They may be of use to you, if you go back in the country. Remember these people ver' suspicious of white men."

It was with some relish that we up anchor and away from that city of stenches. The heat was oppressive, of which we got some relief when well out to sea.

What with squalls, followed by dead calms, which in turn flung us about, and then held us much off our course, it was some days before the *Pearl* finally approached the land again, this time on the north coast of this island of towering peaks.

We delayed the noon meal until we had cast our anchor within the sheltering reefs. Our first care was to search the harbor for some vessel answering the description of the *Josephine*, owner M. Duran. And we were in no doubt that Duran and Mordaunt were one and the same. Both our boats were lowered, and manned by two parties of searchers: Captain Marat, Ray, and Robert went in one, Grant Norris, Julian Lamartine, and myself set off in the other. There were sailing vessels a plenty in the harbor, but not one whose appearance touched our present interest. But when our boat returned to the *Pearl*, the three of us a bit dejected over our non-success, we found the others awaiting us, and having a different story. They had not found the schooner we sought, but they had at any rate come across news of her. Captain Marat had chanced to speak with the first officer of a steamer in from Kingston on the day before.

"This man say," exclaimed Captain Marat, "thad w'en the steamer come in, he see the *Josephine*, which he recognize to have seen in Kingston harbor, and she have a new name painted on—*Orion*. An' ver' soon after, he see the *Orion* sail away out of the harbor."

At this last bit I felt my heart fall.

"Don't cry yet, Wayne," said Ray, "wait till you hear the rest."

And then Jean Marat went on to relate how he had continued his inquiries, with the result that he had found a sailor whose vessel had lain near the *Orion* and who told of seeing a white man of the *Orion* go to shore in a boat, into which had been put a basket of unusual proportions. This sailor had been quite sure that the white man had not returned aboard when the schooner *Orion* had sailed away.

We were all now in a flutter of excitement; it was the recollection of the story of the big basket that had been taken aboard the boat, together with the two blacks, beyond Portland Point, in Jamaica. Whatever doubts we had held of our being on the right track were thus dispelled.

Night had fallen quickly while we talked, all squatting in a circle on the deck. I could hear Rufe mumbling to himself, and rattling pans in the galley. The sailors, leaning on the rail, forward, were watching the lights of the city.

"We have now only to find Mordaunt—or Duran—and the big basket," said Julian. "It looks like everybody notices that basket."

"Yes, that is the first step," agreed Norris. "But that city over there is big, and there's no telling when this Duran will throw the basket aside."

"Yes," said Robert, "when he gets the little one among the voodoo folks he won't have any more use for the basket."

"Say!" broke in Ray, "I don't believe a man can turn over a little kid to the voodoos to be killed that way, unless he's a voodoo himself. This Mordaunt—Duran, or whatever his name is—is just bluffing, to make the Cambons give in to him. All he wants is to set up housekeeping, with Miss Josephine Cambon as Mrs. Duran."

"Ah, no," said Captain Jean Marat, "this man have mix' blood; ver' many of the mulatto' are ver' cruel; and mos' of these men who have ver' near all white blood are the mos' cruel. They like best of anything to have vengeance. The more exquisite they can make the suffering of others, the more exquisite the pleasure they feel."

I had been very late dropping off to sleep, troubled as I was with thoughts of little Marie and her danger. It seemed I had barely closed my eyes, when

Rufe came beating a pan about our ears. "De sun soon up," he said. "Dey ain' no mo' sleep foh de weary."

The light was already on the mountain peaks; and soon the sun leaped into view. Cool breezes came from the hills, carrying the heavy vegetal odors from the forests.

Early the *Pearl* was abandoned by all except Rufe (who refused to go ashore) and two black sailors. We separated into parties of two, to search the city. It was Robert Murtry who paired with me this day.

We passed up one street and down another, hour after hour, in this search for one whom we had never set eyes on. It was much as if we were dependent on instinct to spot our man, should we meet up with him. Unfortunately we were a good deal conspicuous because of our color.

At noon Robert and I munched the lunch we carried, and so continued along street after street of this large but unattractive city, with its uncouth, wooden structures.

At last, far up the street we glimpsed a white man. We hurried after him, but lost him at a second turning.

The afternoon was better than half gone, when there stepped out from a house, almost treading on our toes, a white man who seemed startled at the sight of us. He passed on down the way we had come. We moved on a few steps and looked back, to see that our man had also turned, and was observing us. A few yards more brought us to a tight-board fence. When the man's head was turned, I pulled Robert through a gap and so got us behind the board screen. We contrived to get a peep down the street, and soon observed our man retracing his steps. We were each at a knot-hole when he came near.

And then it was I experienced a thrill of conquest. The man had stopped in an attitude of wonder. At once his hand went to his ear, and he pulled gently and intermittently at the lobe of it, while he continued to puzzle over the thing that was in his mind.

Here was our man at last. How fortunate that he had possessed that mannerism! It was rather a well-formed, swarthy face he had, clear-cut features, and hair that curled. I do not know if it was what I knew of him, but I seemed to see something sinister in his aspect.

He stepped toward that opening in our fence. For the moment I was in panic; there was no time to dodge into the shed at the back. Then I whipped out my pocket-knife, and Robert and I were at a game of "mumble the peg," when we felt the man's eyes upon us. We were careful not to look up. He must have stood there observing us for about the space of a minute, and then we heard his step as he went his way. We sprang to the break in the fence and cautiously peeked. He looked back at frequent intervals as he walked down the street.

"Well, he's spotted us," said Robert. "How can we follow him?"

"We'll just have to do it anyway," I answered. "It's our only chance."

We stepped out boldly, making some effort to reduce the space between the man Duran and ourselves, all the while, endeavoring by playful punches at one another to make it appear that we had no more serious purpose than to pass the time of a holiday.

Presently the man turned off the street, disappearing from our sight.

"There he goes!" said we both together; and we darted off, one after the other. When we reached the place where our quarry had made his turn, we looked in vain down the side street. He was nowhere in view. On each of the two corners stood a two-story house with the usual shallow balcony above the walk.

"He may have gone into one of these houses," suggested Robert.

"Yes," I agreed, "and he may be watching us now."

From a point of vantage we watched for above an hour; but our man did not again appear.

"Well," I finally began, "he's given us the slip. We can't do better than go hunt up the others."

We were anything but dejected, for we had discovered the region of one of Duran's haunts.

We had not long to wait at the wharf, and our friends were much interested in the tale we spun them.

"It's plain enough that fellow suspected you were looking for him," declared Norris. "It wasn't just ordinary curiosity made him go back to see what you were up to."

"We must loose no time," pressed Captain Marat. "Some of us who' have not see' can watch for thees Duran."

And now came the return of Robert and myself to the street of our adventure, accompanied by Jean Marat and Ray, to whom we pointed out the place where we had last seen Duran, by which name I shall now call him. Then, leaving Marat and Ray on the watch, we returned to join the others, and go aboard the schooner. It was considered needful to make some provision for a possible sojourn ashore for some part of our company.

"I sho' is glad you-all is come back," Rufe greeted us, as we climbed aboard. "Some o' dem heathen voodoo niggars has been a' circumvallatin' aroun' dis heah ship."

"What do you mean by that?" demanded Norris.

"Jes' what I say," returned Rufe. "Less'n two hours ago Neb come to me an' says dey's a boat a comin'. I goes out, an' I see four o' dem niggars a rowin' dis way, jes' like dey fixed to come on board. I goes in afte' mah shot-gun, and I lays it on de roof, so's dey kin see it; an' when dey is close, I says: 'I reckon you-all better not come too close to dis heah ship.' Dey seems kin' o' s'prised, an' eyein' dat gun, and hol'n back wid dere oars. Den one o' dem niggars up an' says: 'Whar is you-all from?' And I says—'We's from de good ole U. S., I reckon.' He says—'Ain' you been in Kingston?'

"I begin to smell dat rat, an' I say to myself dat dese here niggars is from dat schooner we is lookin' foh, an' dey's come to git wisdom.

"I scratch my head, an' say—'Kickston—Kickston—if dey is a town in de U. S. by dat name, I ain' heered of it.' He says, 'No, Kickston, dat's in Jamaica.' I say, 'Oh, I reckon you mean de kick dat's in de rum. No we ain' got no Jamaica rum wid no kicks by de ton in it—we ain' got no rum at all; dis here ship is strictly temperance.'"

"Well, did that satisfy him?" laughed Norris.

"Not 'zactly," returned Rufe, "He wanted to know whar we-all was a goin', and I tol' him dat depend on de wind an' how de 'maggot bite'—we ain't got no sailin' orders, 'zactly. And den he seem plumb disgusted, an' dey rows away widout no t'anks foh all de wisdom I give um."

"Well, did you see what way their boat went?" I asked.

"Yes, sah," said Rufe, "I got de glasses, an' I wach um row way up de shore to de east, I reckon way outside de town."

"It's plain enough," began Norris. "That man, Duran, has had his eyes on us, and sent those blacks out to confirm his suspicions that we had followed from Kingston."

"And I'll bet," offered Robert, "that he sent them since Wayne and I saw him, and that he is now a long way from that place where we left Captain Marat and Ray on watch."

Night had come on while we talked. Rufe set a meal before us, and while we supped we had new meat for discussion. It was part of the information we got of Jules Sevier that criminal voodooism was practiced only back in the hills. It was plain, then, that the trail must finally lead us somewhere beyond the city. And what more reasonable than to conclude that Duran's blacks had gone that way in their boat? It was there then, we must seek little Marie Cambon. And it was then I made the suggestion that Robert and I should follow that trail alone, if we found that it pointed inland.

As expected, Marat and Ray had got no news of the man, Duran. Captain Marat, however, had got into talk with a mulatto, of whom he drew the information that the part of the city in which we had come upon Duran was a hot-bed of the city voodoo, whose practices were said to be of a moderate nature. It was well back in the hills that voodooism went full swing.

Captain Marat fell in with Robert's and my plan to take up the trail on land, alone, if occasion should come; and he helped us with our equipment. We would have with us our little rifles and some fishing tackle. If the trail should lead us into the country a dove or two, and some fish, now and then, might prove welcome additions to our grub-sacks.

CHAPTER V

WE GAIN AN ALLY

It was an hour before dawn that we pushed away from the schooner in one of the boats; Captain Marat, Grant Norris, Ray, Robert and myself. We passed among the sleeping vessels with their white night-lights showing aloft.

The harbor light still continued its revolutions, sending bright rays out over the sea. Norris and Ray were at the oars. The land breeze was cool; there was little sound except the swish of the oars. But as we moved on down the shore, presently there came the night sounds from the country, frogs' voices in the ascendent. Then all at once, it seemed, light burst on the high peaks of the mountains; in a few minutes it was full day. The royal palm and cocoanut trees lined the shore, curving out over the sand beach.

We came opposite two boats on the white sand; and a pair of huts showed above the bushy growth. Here we went to shore. Jean Marat entered into talk with some black children who had appeared on the beach at our approach. Did white men ever land there? he asked. No, no white man had been there for ever so long—years. Did black sailors ever land there? Yes, two the evening before. "And oh yes, two days—three days before, some black men came in a boat with—oh, such a big basket! Two men carry the basket and go back in the country." There was but one road or trail, going any distance back. There was a small village a few hours walk toward the hills.

I felt my heart leap with hope at the mention of the basket. And yet I was never destined to hear of it again.

"It looks like we're on the right trail," said Norris, when Jean Marat had interpreted for us the last statement of the little blacks.

"Yes," said Marat. "And now," he added, turning to Robert and me, "you still feel you weesh to go, only you two together?"

"Yes," I answered for us both. "As you have admitted, we two alone won't attract so much attention. And then we have the black wigs and paint. If we get up in the hills and need you we can signal."

Our equipment made but a small pack each. The rifles we bore in their canvas cases.

"Now, boys," cautioned Marat, when we stood among the cocoanut palms at the beginning of the path, "now, boys, go ver' slow and ver' careful. W'en you have find thee place—if you are so fortunate, just come for us."

"Or if you get up on the side of one of those mountains," broke in Ray, "you can signal us at night."

"And look here," began Norris, "if signalling is going to be that easy, you let us know how things are going—before the third day, or by all that's holy! I'll be hiking after you to see what's up."

Grant Norris was not one that was used to holding back while others were doing, he was always eager to be in the forefront of the fray.

"Well you can depend on it, Norris," I assured him, "we'll not delay letting you know, when we've located them."

And so, after a shake of the hand all round, Robert and I plunged into the brush. Cocoanut palms and cabbage palms leaned over our path; the sweet odor of orange blossoms delighted our nostrils. Beyond the second of the cottages—a palm-thatched ajoupa—the ragged leaves of banana plants gave an added touch to the tropic scene. A mile or more back from the beach, the trail took us into open country; here tall grass bordered the way.

Two leisurely hours of tramping had brought us again among the trees. The ground became broken, and we had some stiff climbs. And then at last we came upon a wee bit of a village. There were dwellings of various descriptions; some were of stone, most seemed to be of palm-thatch. And there were numbers of children, though none who could understand two words of English. But they pointed a way toward the hilly side of the hamlet, as if to indicate that that way we should find something in our line. And at last we came upon one who could make something of our speech.

In the midst of a cluster of palms stood a stone cottage, better kept than any we'd passed; and the garden showed straighter rows. While Robert and I stood contemplating the scene, there came from the back, a woman; black, like all the rest, but with superior features and an intelligent eye.

"Yes, sar, I speak the English," she answered our inquiry.

We began with no fuller explanation than that we were strangers; but she invited us to a seat on a bench in a cool arbor at the back, and before we could protest, she had up a small table and dishes of food.

One thing leads to another in talk, and it was not long till it became plain that our hostess was in no sort of sympathy with the voodoo.

"It is very horrible, the things they do," she said. And she told of a neighbor who had lost a child at the hands of the voodoo worshipers less than two months gone. "If it was not for my brother, Carlos, I would leave thees island," she said.

And thus it came about that we finally confided to this woman the purpose of our visit to the region, telling her the story of the kidnapping of the Cambon child, making mention of Mordaunt, alias Duran, and all.

She showed much excitement while she listened, and when we had finished, she spoke with vehemence.

"Oh, thad Duran!" she said. "Ah, my brother, he will help you. Wait till Carlos come. I cannot explain now, but he will be very glad to help you."

Carlos was gone to the city on some marketing errand, and would be back by night, she said.

And so we lay aside our packs, and, to while away the time, set off to explore the region, a mile or so farther inland. Our hostess warned us to keep aloof from an old ruin of a palace we were likely to see on our tramp. The place, she said, had a bad name. The natives had it that the old ruin was now the abode of *zombis* (devils); and there were stories of men who had gone to explore the place and had never returned. Some of the stories were fanciful, she admitted, but she had herself seen one man return nursing a bullet wound, and who had refused to talk of his experience, and had gone away never to return.

Robert and I moved on up the valley, curious for a look at this tabooed ruin. The path for some time led through heavy forest growth, where was a perfect tangle of lianas, running from ground to tree, and tree to tree, in a great network.

Presently we came to an open space. Robert was ahead.

"There she is," he said, pointing.

The ground sloped away, down to the left hand of our path. The forest trees hid the bottom of the valley—a big ravine I prefer to call it—and over there, over-topping the trees on the other side of the valley, a mile away, loomed a wonderful structure—or the ruins of one.

For a minute we gazed in speechless wonder.

The air was clear, and from our high vantage point we could see with unusual distinctness the high walls of each story which seemed to rise a wide step behind that of the story below. Flanking a great arched portal at the ground, either side rose wide stone buttressed terraces, zigzagging in their ascent. The top—the fourth or fifth story of the palace showed only crumbling walls, and trees grew up there, evidently rooted in the crevices. And one tree, I saw, poked its head through a window opening. The grandeur and bizarre beauty of the structure made it seem like a chapter out of "Arabian Nights Entertainments."

"Who'd think to see a thing like that here!" I said.

"I'd like to get inside of it," said Robert. And I saw it was a hope he expressed.

"And what about the devils that live there?" I quizzed him, though I had the same thought as he.

"I don't take any stock in that part of those stories," said Robert—"Any more than you do," he added, studying my face.

"Well, suppose we try getting a little closer," I said.

So we again took up the march, now moving down into the ravine. When we had crossed the open ground, we found a way into the tangled growth. It was apparently an old, though now unused, path, that must have been cut through the forest with much labor. When we reached the stream, it was at a shallow fording; and then we ascended the other side of the ravine by a path, grass overgrown like that of the descent. Seldom would we see more than fifty feet in front, so close was the growth, and winding the path.

We moved silently, the effort of the climb taking all our breath. When we had gone what we judged to be some over half the distance to the palace, we came to a halt, to rest, and to consider. We had hoped that by this time we should have come to a close view of the structure. But there was yet no sign of a break in the trees.

"Perhaps if we go a little farther we'll come to some opening," suggested Robert.

Directly, the slope of ascent became more gentle, and we went with greater ease. But we were soon brought to a sudden halt. We had just made a sharp turn of the path, when we came upon a bleached human skull, fixed in the notch of a tree. Below it were nailed two long bones. They evidently were meant to be crossed, though now they lay almost parallel, doubtless due to the giving way of some rusty support. The skull was small, apparently that of a child; and the sight was not cheerful.

"It's a warning," I whispered.

Robert nodded agreement, and then there was a question in his eyes.

"Better try it a little farther," I said.

And so we moved on cautiously. The trees were very tall and very close set together, making the wood very dark, where not so much as a fly buzzed. I was debating whether to call a halt, when the light of open ground showed ahead. By way of caution I pulled Robert with me off the path to the right; there might be danger in the path; and we crawled through the heavy undergrowth and tangle of lianas to the edge of the forest.

When we looked out across the open it was to find ourselves almost under the walls of that great ruin. The tooth of decay had gnawed big gaps in the top parts, but the lower stories still boasted a sound fabric; and might even be habitable. What a place to play in!

But we got a rough awakening from our dreaming contemplation: There came the sudden crack of a gun, and the ball whizzed close over our heads, causing us to drop flat on the ground and wriggle away lively into the underbrush.

For above a quarter of an hour we crouched in our burrow, not daring to move, or even converse in a whisper. Then, with infinite labor and extreme caution, we finally worked our way back to the path, down which we trotted, half expecting a shot from some ambush.

We had just passed the ford at the bottom of the ravine when we were startled by the sudden appearance of a black directly in our path.

It proved to be Carlos, the brother of our hostess, who had come in search of us. When we had recited our adventure he was inclined to scold.

"Id is ver' danger' to go to thad place," he said, "Melie say she tell you about thad."

The shadows already covered the open spaces and it was night when we came to the cottage of Carlos and Melie Brill.

Carlos told us that he had got it of friends in the city that M. Duran's schooner had been in the harbor.

"And where did the schooner go that he did not go with it?" I asked.

"Oh, the schooner she go not so ver' far," said Carlos. "She hide in one bay not ver' far away, I guess."

We had not spoken long with Carlos Brill, till it became plain that in his mind this man, Duran, was associated with some kind of emotion, and it was equally plain that that emotion could not be given the name of love. The real nature and source of this sentiment he seemed disposed to keep to himself; though he was in no pains to make us believe that his willingness to help us was entirely disinterested.

Melie Brill had a meal prepared. The chief dish was a soup, as she called it; carrots, yams, pumpkins, turnips, bananas, salt pork, and pimentos, boiled all together. Pineapple and bananas made the desert. Our host gave us to understand we were already installed, as of the household. They would listen to no other way of it.

These two, brother and sister, were not much of a kind with their neighbors. It was plain, dark as they were, they were of some mixed blood, it was shown in the features and hair, which was straight, not even deigning to curl.

Before we had finished our supper there appeared the black neighbor who had so recently lost a child to the voodoo. She seemed to have sensed, in some manner, the purpose of our visit, for she wished Robert and me all kinds of success. This was interpreted to us by Melie Brill, for the woman had only the West Indian-French. She gave me a kind of fetish; it was of some very hard wood, the shape of a bird, bill and tail, and the thickness of a marble. She said that within was a drop of blood of a great wizard, and that it would preserve me from a violent death (and so from the attacks of the *zombis*) and would insure success in my undertakings. She was soon gone, for it is the practice among all the natives to retire to bed early.

The desire to press our business was upon Robert and myself, and we put a number of questions. We desired to know who they were who inhabited the ruined palace, and who it could have been who fired the shot at us over there.

"I do not know who it is who stay there," Carlos answered, "an' I do not know who fire' the shot."

"Don't you think it's that man, Duran, who makes that his headquarters?" I pressed.

Carlos exchanged a look with his sister before he spoke. "I have suspect for some time, that Duran he keep there, when he not away in hees schooner," he said. "I have think that for two year."

"Hasn't anyone seen him around there?" queried Robert.

"No," returned Carlos. "No one have seen any white man that way, but I suspect Duran he go there."

"Then," I asked, "do you think that's where he has hidden little Marie Cambon?"

"Yes, ver' like'," said Carlos.

Further talk only strengthened our conviction. Next we required of Carlos to guide us to a barren hillside—some spot in range of the harbor, so many miles below. This Carlos professed to be easy of accomplishment.

We went the way we had been in the afternoon. The forest was of an inky blackness; even the stars could seldom be seen from the path. Carlos had no trouble to keep the road. A perfect hush was over everything until the night birds and frogs tuned up to show that the world was not dead.

When we got out into that open space, instinctively we turned our eyes across the valley in the direction of the mysterious palace. And then, as if for our particular benefit, a light flashed over there. It disappeared in the same moment, only to appear again, perhaps at another point near. Again it went out, and though we waited some minutes, it showed no more.

"There's some one there, sure enough," observed Robert.

"Thee people here have see' the light many times," said Carlos. "They theenk it is the *zombis*."

"I guess Duran is the king Zombi," said Robert.

Carlos laughed. "I theenk you right," he said.

We passed through another patch of forest and climbed to a ledge on the steep hillside. To gather a pile of wood was the work of but five minutes. Then we set it akindle.

Using our jackets for a screen, we began to signal, alternately covering and exposing our fire. Our friends on the *Pearl* must have kept a good watch, for hardly two minutes had passed, till we made out an answering signal.

"Ray is on the job," said Robert.

Then I spelled out, in short and long flashes, the following words:

Good So Far.

Then came from the sea the terse acknowledgment: O.K.

"That ought to hold Norris," said Robert.

"Yes, till tomorrow night," I returned. "If we don't signal them again tomorrow night, Norris will be piling up here hand over foot."

Carlos had been very quiet, taken up with watching our procedure. That mode of communication was far from unknown to him, but it seemed to him marvelous that white folk should use it. But the wonder of it all was that we could spell out any words we pleased in that way.

"An' if you tell your frien's to come, they weel come?" he asked.

"Yes," I answered, "they will come, in a hurry."

That somehow seemed to please Carlos; and he became pensive. We had put out the fire and were already on our way back through the black forest. When we came again to the open space, we stopped for near half an hour, in the hope that we might again have a sight of the mysterious light over at the old ruin.

While we squatted on the ground, watching, my mind was taken up with the problem of how to discover where little Marie Cambon was hid; and would our little handful of men be sufficient to storm the place? I put the questions to Carlos.

"No—No!" declared Carlos, "the voodoos are too many, and they watch ver' careful, as you have find out."

He referred to our being fired on.

"Wait till tomorrow, then maybe I fin' out sometheeng," he said.

Carlos and his sister made us a pallet in the arbor at the back.

CHAPTER VI

WE BREAK UP THE VOODOO CEREMONIAL

Carlos was gone when Robert and I awoke. Melie told us he had gone off early on our business, and had left word that we were to lay close, till he returned.

Our excursion over to that old ruin of a palace, we were to learn, had been a bit rash. In fact, before the morning was gone, the woman who had given me the fetish came over to report that black men had been about, with inquiries as to the movements of the two white boys.

Carlos turned up at noon. He had been angling among some of the lesser voodoo devotees. There was no news of any white child being held for sacrifice; but there had been passed word of a big voodoo ceremonial to take place either this night or the next. The place was some ten miles back in the hills.

"Some of the voodoos near here have gone from their home'," he said, "an' some more make ready to go."

The news was disturbing. I had no doubt that a big voodoo ceremonial could mean nothing less than that there was to be the offering of the "goat without horns." And here, too, was the big voodoo doings to follow close upon the arrival of Duran with little Marie Cambon.

And what was to do? Call our friends from the *Pearl*? Manifestly, we could not bring so many whites into the region without attracting attention. Duran would be forewarned, and so our purpose defeated. We two must continue to go it alone, trust to luck and our own devices. And there was our new ally, Carlos Brill.

"We must go and see what's going on," I said to Carlos, "and if it's ten miles, we must start soon."

"Oh, if we go before dark," returned Carlos, "and some one see white boys, they—"

"We have a cure for that," I interrupted. "You'll see, we'll fool them."

Robert and I got our packs together, to which we added some small pieces of clothing that I begged of Carlos. Soon we stood all fixed for a long march.

"And now," said I to Carlos, "you and Melie are to come a short way with us to bid us goodbye, for it is to be understood that we are going back the way we came. But then you are to keep watch on the brush; and if you hear the whistle of a bird you're to come over quietly and meet us."

"Yes, yes," nodded Carlos, comprehending.

And so Carlos and Melie walked with us till we were in the midst of the village; and there we shook hands as we parted, and again waved a goodbye, as we moved out of view, numbers of curious blacks looking on.

When we had gone a mile or more seaward, we turned aside; and from a screen of brush, we watched the path for a quarter of an hour, for possible followers.

"Do you think there were any of the voodoo, there?" questioned Robert at last.

"Perhaps not," I answered, "but they'll soon hear of our going."

We picked a suitable spot in the brush, and set up our dressing room. Forth came the kinky, black wigs, and paints given us by Jules Sevier. We worked on one another, turn about. At the end of twenty minutes I set the wig on Robert's head. The result was satisfactory. His color was a dusky brown, all but black. A few minutes drying, and the stain refused to rub off.

"Bob, you are pretty," I told him. "I'll defy Rufe to know you."

"I'll say the same for you, Wayne," said he. "Even Ray wouldn't know *you*."

A jacket and a jumper, and an old hat, got of Carlos, and a twist and turn to Robert's slouch cover, completed our make-up.

Going back, we skirted the village on the west. We came in time into the brush back of the Brill hut.

A whistled bird-call brought Carlos. When he put aside the bush and stepped into view, that moment his face was a picture—his mind contending between the certainty of our identity and doubt of his eyes.

"Ah," he began, "that is ver' suprise'. How you do it?" And then he must have Melie over to the show.

Carlos had soon got himself ready, and we were off for the hills.

For some miles we kept pretty much in cover as we moved toward the mountains. Carlos knew the way through the forest, where we ofttimes slipped on the moist roots of the great trees, and scrambled amongst the lianas that were everywhere. Two hours had gone when we had our first rest in a clump of cabbage palms.

Towering above us, on a mountain, stood an old abandoned fortress. Carlos said its walls were a hundred feet high and with a thickness of twenty feet. Our way lay to the eastward of that old stronghold.

Our progress now had us puffing, for it was up-up-up. We kept as much as possible in the glades. Pigeons were plentiful, and we spied a predatory hawk, at which Robert and I got our little rifles out of their cases. But Carlos put up his hand in caution.

"To shoot is not safe," said he. "Sound go ver' far, an' we do not want anyone know some ones is here."

And then we gave Carlos another turn of surprise. To see a bird fall, and no sound of the gun,—that was beyond reason. He snapped his finger at his ear to make sure he had not lost his hearing.

We showed him the silencers set on the rifles and tried to explain them, but he shook his head; his physics wasn't up to such juggling with sound.

The shadows were over everything when we stopped beside a brook to rest and make a meal. Carlos found wood that burned with little smoke, and we soon had a bird apiece, broiling. Out of a bag Carlos poured farine. With water he made a paste. Then came macadam—codfish stewed with rice. We topped off with bananas, and water from the stream.

The scene was like to have been the last to my eyes on this earth. A high peak towered some seven miles to the east. We could see the blue sea below, many miles to the north, with the golden-yellow horizon. Great tracts of forest were everywhere between, with bits of glades, and palm groves.

While we looked, the coast line darkened, the valleys blackened; the gloom crept up the slopes; swiftly it enveloped the three of us. Then for several minutes the mountain peaks glowed at the tops as if afire, and then they, too, went out, and it was night. The world was changed. The trees seemed like personalities now, come awake like the owls, with the going out of the light. Tree-ferns below us seemed to whisper with their greater neighbors—mysterious gossip. Night birds piped their solemn dirge, insects tweeked; tree toads shrilled in competition with the bellowing bull-frogs; owls hoarsely laughed, and called their "what-what-what."

A strange oppression crept over me and I yearned for the deck of the *Pearl*.

Suddenly Carlos sat erect—listening. I cocked my ear, but there was nothing but the usual night sounds. A minute passed. Then, ever so faintly I discerned the peculiar low rumble. It was something I had heard before. It rose and fell in waves of sound; and wave upon wave it swelled in volume.

"It's the voodoo drum!" I whispered Robert.

"That's over a mile away," he observed, listening.

"Seex mile!—maybe seven mile!" corrected Carlos.

We collected our belongings and were off in the direction of the sound. When we entered the forest, we no longer heard the sound. But after stumbling among the slimy roots, and bumping our noses on the swinging lianas, for half an hour, we came again out in the open, and again we heard the drumming. Carlos ofttimes avoided the jungles by detours. At the end of an hour the rolling of the drum seemed only a few hundred yards away.

"T'ree more mile, I guess," said Carlos.

On and on we stumbled in the dark. The moon was not due till near morning, and so distinct was the drumming that we did not seem any longer to be approaching the place, but were already arrived.

Then at last the sound seemed more distant.

"Now we ver' close," said Carlos.

Something or other was contradictory.

A quarter of a mile or so through the dense forest, and a bright light showed in front.

Now cautiously we moved forward till we came to the edge of an open space. The place appeared to have been partly cleared by hand, for many tree-stumps presented.

We climbed into the low branches of a great tree. The great fire blazed but a hundred yards from our perch. The drummer sat astride his instrument (a cylinder of wood) the fingers of both hands playing on the skin stretched over the one end. The dancers were very many. Here was a repetition of the things I saw in the company of Jules Sevier.

To the right of the fire there was the raised platform, on which stood the snake-box. Back of all was some form of shelter, out from which in time came a figure cloaked in red, and wearing a red kerchief wound about the head. This was the *papaloi* (voodoo king). This appearance was the signal for a hush, and a halting of the dance. All grouped round. There were the usual requests for favors and the listening at the box for the answers.

Then came the slaughter of the fowls; and the mixing of the rum.

I had begun to breath more freely on my perch. But then Robert touched me on the arm.

"What's that thing on the ground?" he whispered.

I strained my eyes. The figures of the blacks obscured the view. But at last— what I saw froze my blood.

"We must save it," I said. "It's little Marie Cambon."

As I look back on the experience of the hours following, it is as if I were recalling a horrid dream.

"Robert," I whispered, "the rifles!"

We slipped to the ground, seized our little guns, and got back to our places.

The red-robed *papaloi* was fumbling with a rope that hung from a liana. An attendant was kneeling on the ground holding a cup to the lips of the child.

In another moment the child was swinging in the air by the rope, its head just clearing the ground. I heard it whimper in fright. The *papaloi* took up a knife.

"Give it to him in the hand," I said in Robert's ear.

We leveled our guns together. There was no sound of the explosions. The *papaloi* dropped the knife, seized his right hand with his left, and he bent over in pain. I had given my shot to the rope. After my second squeeze of the trigger it hung by a strand; a third lead missile, and the child went gently to the ground.

The voodoo worshipers began to scatter in panic of this strange visitation.

We in the tree slipped to the ground. I thrust my rifle into the hands of Carlos and, intent on making the most of the panic, rushed forward. The *papaloi* saw me coming, and called on the nearest of his followers. But I had up the child before any could interfere, and I sprinted back and thrust it into the arms of Robert.

"Run! both of you!" I cried. And I sought to delay pursuit, hurling piece after piece of dead-wood at the nearest blacks, who were already at the chase, urged on by the wounded *papaloi*.

I meant to run for it, and elude the voodoos in the thick forest, so soon as the laden Robert and Carlos should have a good start. My missiles danced about the shins of the foremost blacks, and they held up.

I was backing toward the edge of the jungle, and in the way of readily making my escape; but some wily black with a club must have taken a thought worth two of that, and got on the wrong side of me. I was just in the thought it was about time to make my break, when I got a crack on the back of my head that put me to sleep.

CHAPTER VII

A DISTRESS CALL GOES TO THE PEARL

I do not know how long I was unconscious, but when I opened my eyes I could see the bright stars, and I made out two black heads of negroes, who bore me in some kind of a litter to which I was bound, wrists and ankles.

I could hear the voices of others ahead, so I knew that there were more in the party. My head felt big, and a dizziness, and a sore spot, reminded me of the whack I'd got. We soon came to a stand, and there sounded a call. A turn of my litter gave me a view of a structure towering near by. Something in the contour was familiar. It was the great palace we were now come to.

I have to make mention of a matter of importance. It was not little Marie Cambon we had saved from the voodoos. This I saw when I grabbed the little one from the ground. It was a young mulatto. So little Marie, then, must still be immured in this old ruin. Perhaps, after all, I should find a way to save her and myself. Some unreasoning blind faith seemed to hold me up, in spite of my desperate situation.

My litter was soon in motion again, and we passed through some kind of portal. A lantern illumined the way, and we went up a broad stairway. In the dim light I made out richly carved pillars; mahogany shone red in the wood work, if I were not dreaming, and marble figures looked down on me.

Again we came to a stand, this time in a great hall, and my litter was let down to the floor. One came out and stood over me. It was the voodoo great-priest—the *papaloi*—as I could see by the red bandanna he still wore on his head, and his hand bound in a blood-stained rag. I noted this black's features were as regular as a white man's; and now there was a sneering smile on them.

"So you think you very wise and can defy the Great Power," he said. He turned and spoke something to an attendant, who stooped and tore open my shirt, while another held the lantern. It was to lay bare my skin where it was unstained and still white.

"Humph!" grunted the *papaloi*, "so I thought. It is one of the white boys."

"You came from Jamaica, in the schooner," he addressed me. "You make plenty good blood for the drink—and plenty good meat for the feast." This last with a malicious grin.

I could perceive that here was one, this voodoo priest, who was in the confidence of Duran. It was doubtless to him Duran delivered the children procured for sacrifice. And so here must be the source of the vast wealth of that white fiend of tinged blood. Something spurred me to defiant speech.

"You can tell Duran, alias Mordaunt," I began, "that I have had my fortune read, and that I would not exchange my fate for his at any price."

He stared for a moment speechless. Then he said something to the two litter bearers, who loosed the ropes that held me to the litter; then they stood me on my feet, and one holding either arm, led me through a doorway, the *papaloi* following, attended by another black with the lantern. It was many steps we went down the bare passage; a turn, and we stood before a door. A heavy bolt was drawn, and the door opened.

"Very soon you die," spoke the *papaloi*, as I was thrust in.

I heard the bolt slide into place with a click, and I stood in darkness. I felt in my pocket for my flash lamp. It was gone. I put my feet forward cautiously, step by step, my hand on the wall; and moved around my dungeon till I came to the door again. I became used to the dark, got my bearings, and paced the damp floor, side to side and end to end. It was four paces one way, eight the other. As I moved about, suddenly I caught in my eye a few stars peeking in on me. There was a slit in the wall high up. By reason of the thickness of the wall the view out was had only when standing directly in line with that narrow porthole.

The cell was barren, there was not even a box for a seat. A half hour was hardly gone, when I heard the click of the bolt again. This time it was food that was pushed in, on a wooden tray. Recalling those stories of the poisoned food given by the voodoos to their victims, I denied myself, even of the drink. In that hot, airless hole, what would I have not given for a draught of pure water!

I got the food off the tray and used it to sit on.

When I thrust the little one into Robert's arms, he and Carlos had run for it, as I directed. They got far enough into the jungle for safe hiding, and then Carlos went back to lead me there. I had already got that whack on the head, and the thing Carlos saw was the crew of blacks securing their prisoner.

It was then Robert decided to call our friends from the *Pearl*. So the two, carrying the little rescued mulatto, turn about, hurried back toward home. When they came to the place where we had cooked our meal, Robert made his signal fire. He made it big, for it was fifteen miles to the *Pearl's* anchorage. The two plaited a big screen of leaves and grasses. Again and again he spelled out in flashes the following:

Come ask for Brill.

To make out any answering signal at so great a distance, was a thing not to be expected, where a mere lantern was to be used. But he knew they would be on the lookout, and could not miss so great a flare.

Daylight had come before the two arrived at the Brill hut. Melie took the little one in charge; and it may here be said that the yellow tot was finally restored to the rejoicing parents.

RAY'S NARRATIVE

When Wayne and Robert had got out of sight, as they started on the trail of that Duran fellow, right away Grant Norris began to fuss.

"I don't think those boys ought to be allowed to go after those cannibals alone," he said. "Suppose those black cusses get wind of them and put up a fight. And they haven't anything but those dinky little rifles!"

"Meaning," I told him, "that they ought to have an old campaigner to protect them, and that old campaigner's name is Grant Norris."

"Oh, go 'long! you red-headed wag, you," he shot back at me.

"'Fess up now," I said. "You're just itching for excitement. But never fear, Wayne will send for you before the fighting begins—he knows you. In the meantime, you know Wayne and Robert well enough; there won't anyone get much the best of them."

When we had rowed back to the *Pearl*, things were got ready for a move to a new anchorage—nearer to the place where we had landed Wayne and Robert. Captain Marat said we must avoid having the lights of the town between us and any signal from Wayne.

Grant Norris was watching the hills back inland while the sun was still holding its fire on the tops of the mountains.

"Say," I asked him, "you don't expect to see fire signals in broad daylight, do you?"

"Daylight!" he sniffed—"It'll be night before you can turn round twice."

And sure enough, while we were talking the sun was off the peaks, and the lower hills were black enough to show a fire.

I hadn't any more than got ready the big lantern with the strong reflector, than Wayne's signal began to flash, eight or ten miles back in the hills. I answered. And then came the message: "Good so far."

"I guess they find out sometheeng," said Captain Marat.

"It's good to know they're already making progress," observed Julian.

"Next," said Norris, "they'll be signalling—'Come on, the trail is hot.'" And he stayed on deck till long after midnight.

The next day dragged for all of us, waiting for night. Nothing was right. Even Rufe's noon meal was no success.

"Say, you-all is jest de cantankerest bunch!" said Rufe. "Dem 'are biscuits is jest de kin' you-all been a braggin' on; an' dat fish, an' de puddin'—W'at's wrong wid dem, ah likes to know?"

But no one had a word on that.

And when the supper went the same way, Rufe put his foot down, said he wouldn't cook another meal till we got the voodoo out of our systems.

"Dat w'at it is, hit's de voodoo w'at's got into you-all's stummicks," he declared. "Dey ain't no use o' my cookin' no more till you is busted wid it."

That hot lazy sun finally dipped down west, and from then on, every candle or firefly on shore had us on the jump. Grant Norris was the worst of the bunch. At ten o'clock he broke loose.

"Those young skunks!" he said. "Won't I give them a piece of my mind! They might give us a word. No sense in keeping mum like this."

At midnight all but Norris gave it up and turned in. He said he wouldn't trust the watch, and anyway there wasn't any sleep in him.

I hadn't any more than got two winks of my first beauty sleep, than something had me by the scruff, and bounced me out of my bunk onto the floor. It was worse than the nightmare.

I was kneading the cobwebs of fairyland out of my eyes, and I heard Norris saying:

"Pile up on deck you sleepy-head! Wayne's talking to you."

I "piled up" on deck; and there, way back in the hills, ever so far away, I saw the flashing of a beacon light. A long flash, a short one, another long, a short. That's C. Three long ones—O. And so on. "Come ask for Brill. Come ask for Brill," the message went.

Norris brought the lamp with the strong reflector, and I flashed back an answer. But they evidently didn't see our smaller light, for they continued with their—"Come, ask for Brill. Come ask for Brill."

Now I can't explain just how, but I knew from the way the flashes were given that it wasn't Wayne, but Robert, who was doing the signalling. Then they were not together up there, for Wayne always did that job.

I told Norris the message, and he began to poke everybody else up. He went banging at Rufe, too, and there was considerable excitement all round.

"Oh, yes, sah, yes, sah, Mistah Norris," said Rufe "dat coffee 'll be a'bilin' in jes' a minute. Glory be to goodness! dis heah voodoo carryin's on is wus dan gittin' religion at a shoutin' Methodis' camp meetin'."

I watched the flashes up in the hills till finally they quit; but there was never a word but just those four: "Come, ask for Brill."

Our packs were already made up; it remained only for Rufe to put the finishing touches to the grub we were going to take. Captain Marat and Grant Norris had their high powered rifles, the hand ax was more than I needed, for my legs were nimble. Julian got out his handsome shot-gun, and a dozen shells Rufe had loaded with buck-shot.

"Jes' two of dem 'ar buck-shot shells in my ol' gun and dat's all I needs," Rufe said. "Dey ain't nobody guine to come nigh dis heah schooner 'less'n I says de word."

We pulled the small boat high on' the beach, near the place where we had parted with Wayne and Robert, and without preliminaries we started off by the road. It was fearfully dark, but the trail was the path of least resistance, so we couldn't get lost. Two hours after the start daylight busted through the trees. In another hour or so we butted into a village. And the first pickaninny we met told us the way to "Brills," on the upper side of the village.

A black man, and a black woman, and a black boy, were at the door of the Brill mansion.

"We're looking for two white boys," announced Norris.

"Dey ain't no white boys 'round heah," said that black boy. And say! that voice had a familiar twang to it.

"Say, Robert," I spit out, "your face goes all right, but you'll have to smear the black better on that voice of yours, if you want to fool this kid."

We were all inside now; and it didn't take Robert long to tell his story.

"And so you are sure they've got Wayne in that old ruin?" said Norris, addressing this black man, Carlos Brill.

"Yes, I think ver' sure," said the man. "I see they go that way with him."

"Well, Captain Marat," began Norris, "I say storm the place at once."

"Yes," assented Captain Marat, "we have to do something."

"But we'll have to go slow," Robert said. "That place must be lousy with those cannibals; and no one knows how many guns they'll have."

Well, Norris was willing to go slow, if he could only go soon. And we were not long getting started.

That black fellow, Carlos Brill, led the way, and that black fellow, Robert Murtry, with him. Julian and I were rear guard. And they gave me Wayne's rifle to carry.

It wasn't long till we got out of the woods into an open spot; and then they showed us what they'd figured out was Wayne's prison. It was way over on the other side of a ravine; and say! it was the queerest looking, half tumble-down old palace!

We went down into the ravine; and on the other side Carlos Brill took us out of the path—afraid of an ambush, or something—and we began to slip and stumble among the roots, and brush, and snaky-looking lianas that hung between the trees. Why the place wasn't full of monkeys I don't know. There wasn't any use of anyone telling us to go slow, this wasn't any fast track.

When we stopped, to let our breaths catch up with us, Carlos told us we hadn't much farther to go. But he wouldn't be able to get us nearer to the palace under shelter of the forest than about four hundred yards.

"Don't let that worry you any," said Norris. "Captain Marat or I, either one, won't ask anything better, if we can draw them out."

"Yes," agreed Captain Marat, "four honderd yard' do ver' well."

I'd seen them both shoot, and I agreed with that. And they had belts and pockets full of ammunition.

Well, we finally got to the place, with that big old half ruin on the opposite side of the clearing. Norris picked a tree, with big branches near the ground. Captain Marat took up a position seventy-five or a hundred yards to the left. Those two big-gun men and Carlos had decided on their plan of campaign, and the rest of us got behind a good screen and awaited developments.

Jean Marat banged away first, sending a ball through an opening in the second story of that old palace. All waited to see some attention paid to it over there. We calculated it ought to start some curiosity at least—that is, if there really was anybody about the shebang. I began to have my doubts; it looked dead as a tomb.

But we didn't have to wait more than about a minute. I saw a black scamp scamper across the open space with a gun in his hand, going from the woods we were in right for that palace. I pointed him out to Norris, who let fly at him with a bullet just as he disappeared round a bush.

Robert said it was most likely a sentry, stationed on that path.

Then Captain Marat's rifle went off again. Robert ran over, and brought back news that Marat had toppled over a black, who was running for the palace from that side.

The next shot fired came from the palace. I saw the smoke up at the second story. Norris banged away—said he saw a black head peep round a piece of stone wall. Two more shots came from the palace, they tore loose a twig or two over our heads.

Then Captain Marat shot twice. It was a minute before the palace artillery opened up again. They must have fired ten shots—they came faster than I could count them. Grant Norris was happy. He up with his rifle, and at his shot I heard a yell over at the palace. Jean Marat got another one, too, Robert came to tell me.

And now Robert got hold of me and dragged me along with him round about through the woods. It was some time before I could hold him up long enough to get it out of him what it was all about. He meant we two should have a little of the kind of sport Marat and Norris were revelling in. There was a patch of trees off to the right—south of the old palace; and it was there we finally won round to. We climbed high in a tree, and got us to where we had a fine view behind that broken wall the blacks were using for a breastworks. There wasn't less than a dozen of those voodoo cannibals there, in plain view of our perch, and we weren't three hundred yards from them.
"Now let's give it to them fast," said Robert, and he began to work the slide handle of his little rifle. I followed suit with Wayne's gun.

There wasn't a sound of our firing, of course, on account of the silencers. So the stings those fellows got on the flank began to puzzle them. There was one black who gave me a good target. I wasn't much of a shot, but after a few pulls on my trigger, I saw that fellow put his hand in a place, and in a way that convinced me that he would be sitting on a sore spot for a day or two anyway. Those blacks quit firing and got to discussing some question or other, and some of them slunk away.

And just about then I heard something familiar, back in the forest. It was the call of the *Whip-poor-will*; and I didn't need anyone to tell me what bird it came from; there was only one particular bird who could be whistling that call in broad daylight.

"There's Wayne!" said Robert. And he almost knocked me off my limb, with his hurry to get to the ground.

And then as we hurried over to the others, we answered Wayne's call; and in just a little, he was among us.

And here's where Wayne takes up the story again.

CHAPTER VIII

THE VOODOO STRONGHOLD

How long I had been dozing the last spell, I don't know, but when my eyes opened, daylight was showing through that little slit high up in the cell wall. It wasn't much light that came in, but it was enough to show me some kind of decorative affair on the otherwise plain walls of the dungeon.

I moved close to the thing; and I set the tray against the wall, below it, and got me up closer. Then I was able to make out it was a kind of shrine, built into the wall. There was a crucifix back in the niche, and kneeling figures at the foot.

Then suddenly I felt a queer sense of creeping in my flesh—a thought, like a revelation, had flashed in my mind. Here was just the sort of thing I had heard that taciturn black fellow, Amos, tell about; a dungeon, in the wall a shrine—Christ on the cross, and figures at the foot! Could this be the very cell and shrine Amos had told of? It seemed too good to be true. And yet there was eloquent argument. For wasn't there that mysterious interest of Amos in Mordaunt, alias Duran, at Kingston? And was it not reasonably certain that Amos had lost his life at the hands of this Duran? And now had we not traced Duran to this very place? Trembling with eagerness and suspense, I sought, and got my hand on, the figure of the Virgin. I shook it gently, ashamed to so manhandle a holy thing. It held fast. I put on greater and greater violence; and finally I felt it give a little. Compunction was all gone now; and at last I lifted out the figure, which was prolonged at the bottom to make a round peg.

My heart thumped with excitement. I pulled on the frame of the shrine. A few tugs and the whole thing swung in like a door, on hinges. And so there was uncovered a black hole behind.

I put my hands on the edge and tried to pull myself up into that hole. It was no go—I hadn't the strength. I tried again and again, but I weakened at every effort.

I went over and looked at that food and drink, tempted to have a few mouthfuls—for strength's sake. But I finally decided against the risk. Instead, I filled my lungs with air—such as there was—and rested.

After five minutes I got my toes on the tray again. And this time I made it. I got through. And I pulled the shrine door shut after me. There was an interstice through which I got my hand, and put that figure-peg in place again. I meant they should not discover the manner of my escape from the cell.

That place I was now in was entirely dark, and the air damp and oppressive. I could touch both walls at once, so narrow was the place.

And now which way to turn? How I wished for my flashlight! I tried it to the left, moving cautiously. I had taken about twenty short paces, when I noted little beams of light coming through the wall. I got my eye to a chink, and made it out that here was another shrine, set in the wall of some room of the palace.

I got a view, too, of some part of that room. A cluster of burning candles stood on a table, which piece of furniture, I could see, was of richly-carved mahogany. And there lay my flashlight in plain view.

A figure moved into the field of my eye. It was the *papaloi*; his wounded hand was still in a bandage. He bustled about, though I could make nothing of his occupation; till finally he set a pomade jar on the table, turned in his clothing at the neck, and began to smear his face. Here was a fastidious black. The process was long and leisurely, and there came a period of wait—to let the oil that shone on his dark skin soak in. And then he took up a cloth and began to wipe.

It was then I got a start, for his face came out from under the rag—white! And it was then I recognized Duran, alias Mordaunt! This voodoo *papaloi*, who put the knife to little innocents, was no other than Duran himself. I was now prepared to believe the stories of the horrifying cruelty, and strange fanaticism—or whatever it may be called—of some of those of mixed blood.

A black attendant came into the room with a vessel of water. Duran washed, while the black busied himself with laying out clothing, as I could see when he moved into my view. These Duran began to don, making himself into more the appearance of a gentleman, a role he had learned to assume. Only now he allowed his features to relax into an expression that was more that of a hardened criminal than of a gentleman. There was little talk, and that was in French; no word of it that I could understand.

I lingered in the hope that the room should be vacated, and I might try if his Calvary—through whose filigree chinks I peeked—should not prove to be another door, and so be the means of my recovering my electric flashlight. It was a thing I wanted, to help me find my way out of that black hole.

The black man went out, finally, soon followed by Duran. I heard the door close. Now was my time! I got my hand through a crevice. I tried one kneeling figure, and then another. It came out, and I swung the gate in. In another moment I was on the floor, though I turned over a chair in the jump. I closed the portal and looked about.

The furnishings were rich, the floors marble. A single window there was, tightly shuttered; a bed, with an end to the wall.

I thrust my flashlight into a pocket of my trousers; I still held the stone peg in my hand.

The candles had been left burning; likely Duran would be back; so it was time I was scrambling out. But my presence was already known, for the door opened, and in sprang a black.

There was no time for anything but defense. The black reached for me. I dodged, and made toward the bed. As I landed on the covers, he had me by the ankle. And then I came down on his woolly pate with my stone peg, using all my force.

The black doubled up on the floor without a sound. I rushed a chair under the secret portal, and in two moments was back in the dark passage, the door with its peg back in place.

I put my eyes to the chink. In a minute Duran appeared. That he was all in a knot—dumfounded at the thing he saw, was plain.

I was curious to know whether I had committed manslaughter, but when Duran opened the door and began to call out to others, I thought it wise to move. I used my light, and went back the way I had come. There showed nothing but bare stone walls; the passage, between four and five feet wide, and not twice so high.

Presently it descended, in steps; at the bottom my light showed a door. I lifted a long, rusty latch, and with repeated strong pulls, swung it open. There was a hole through, ostensibly to permit of reaching the latch with a stick from the outside.

The welcome outdoor air came through a heavy growth of vines. It was perhaps fifteen feet to the ground. I swung the door to after me, and scrambled down by the vines.

Ah, how good that bit of turf felt under my feet! Trees were all about, though just here they were new growth—small. A stream trickled over stones close by. I went down to its edge and drank my fill, and I took the brook for my guide, upward, toward the hills.

I came to a place where I must walk in the water to go round a low cliff. And then I came upon a path, new used, and seeming to come from that great building whose upper walls I could still see peeping through the tree-tops.

I heard voices, and jumped behind a bushy screen. There appeared on the path a half dozen black men, and an old black crone. Two pairs of the men were burdened with litters, and two went before as an advance guard—they were armed with guns. On the litter were bundles, some in gunny sacks, and some tied in blankets. I was sure I saw some movement in the bundle on one litter, as of some living thing there. My heart thumped with the thought that here were some little ones being transported for voodoo slaughter. And my reason told me that little Marie Cambon was of the number.

I followed for some miles, for the most part out of view—but now and then getting glimpses of the blacks ahead. The trail—much used I could see it was—held pretty much to the shores of the stream; at times the way was through the brush, avoiding a bend or some bad going; at times the path lay in the water itself. Grand tree ferns and a great variety of tropic growth made it a wonderfully romantic and beautiful woods path. And yet here it was given over to hell's own purposes.

I went far enough to convince my mind that the blacks were making direct to that castle fortress on the mountain, whose high walls now and anon came into view. I turned short about then, and hurried back. I would go to the Brill cottage for news of Robert and Carlos, and send for my friends on the *Pearl*.

I was still a mile or more from the old ruin where I'd been a prisoner, when I heard shots. I soon cut away from the path, and stumbled through the jungle, in the direction of the sounds of battle. My mind was full with conjecture.

"It must be Jean Marat, and Norris, and the others from the *Pearl*," I said to myself at last. Robert must have signalled them last night, and now they were attacking.

When the sounds of firing told me I was near, I whistled a call. And then I came up with them. And there were Robert, and Ray with my rifle; and Ray had a story of his performance with the gun. "I peppered him at the south end, going northwards," he said, "and it's a hot tack he'll be sitting on every time he 'plunks' down on a stool."

For some reason those at the palace had ceased their firing. Maybe the unscathed blacks had taken their lesson of the things those two crack shots, Marat and Norris, had proven themselves able to do to every black head that showed round the edge of portal or stone wall. And perhaps those mysterious—silent—little missiles sent by Robert and Ray had also had a thing to do with it. Anyway, the old palace opposite, had become as silent as from its appearance it ought to be.

"Now, how did you get away?" demanded Robert.

"Yes, you might have stayed a while longer and let us have the credit of rescuing you," exclaimed Ray.

And so I told my tale. And next I had a word for Carlos. I'd been spoiling for this word from the moment of our reunion.

"Who was Amos?" I asked bluntly.

Carlos jerked himself erect at the word. He was caught with surprise.

"Amos, he is my brother," he said, still staring his wonder.

"I don't know why I never thought to mention it to you," I said, "but Amos was with us from New Orleans to Kingston, Jamaica."

And we gave Carlos the whole story. And when we came to the mention of Amos' death, the poor fellow went all of a heap for a minute. Then he got a grip of himself, and his frame became rigid; and I could see his lips move as he made some silent vow.

Carlos told us how he had been awaiting the coming of his brother, whom he had sent forth to seek help for the recovery of a hidden gold mine, belonging, by right of inheritance, to the Brills.

"My father, he discover that mine somewhar in the hills," said Carlos. "It was when Amos, and I, and Melie ver' small. He tell us how sometime he goin' to show us the place—when we little bigger. He go 'way five—six day, and come back with plenty gold, some piece big as my thumb—Melie got one home. Father go to the city, and bring home plenty fine things, and much to eat. And one day that man Duran come with him. They talk big things—we little, and don't understand. Then they go 'way together in the hills. We wait six day—seven day—more, two week. No use, our father he never come back.

"That Duran then, we find out, have plenty money: he buy fine schooner, wear fine clothes—diamon's, go to France, study, and everything fine he want to have. We—Amos, I, Melie—we say, 'Duran, he kill our father—he steal the gold mine.' And we know what we have to do. We try to watch Duran. We see him with the voodoo. He a *sang mele*.[1] We see him go to the old king's palace. He send warning we to keep away. One time Amos is shot in leg. But we can never find the mine. Duran never go from the palace to the mine. We think he go in the schooner when he go to the mine, so no one can follow. And then, at las' we decide we mus' have help, if we can find some that are honest. And so Amos he go."

And thus we of the *Pearl* came to know that Amos, even despite his untimely death, had led us—or at the least he had set us on the way—to the very place he had meant to pilot us.

Norris suggested that perhaps the mine was worked out long ago. But Carlos declared that a friend he had in the city had seen Duran convert a fresh supply of gold dust and nuggets but a few months ago.

"Well," said Norris, "then we're going to have a try for that gold mine, after all."

"Yes," said Jean Marat, "when we have find little Marie Cambon."

I had renewed my courage with food my friends carried; and now, with Carlos' help I conducted our party to the trail, going to the fortress on the mountain. Carlos had been many times on that trail, he said, and he led us over a number of short-cuts. Robert and I were still in our black paint; and Ray abused us shamefully—in play—at every turn, for presuming to hobnob so freely with our superiors.

Half the hot afternoon was gone when we had climbed to the end of that path. It was at the bottom of a hundred-foot wall. Carlos pointed to where there was to be found a door, sheltered from view by the brush. We did not venture too close, for it was certain the door would be fast, and we planned to try for an entry by a ruse. Carlos knew a call that was much used by these blacks of Duran's, and he was confident he could make it serve our purpose.

So we laid our trap. Norris and Robert crawled cautiously into the bushes up to either side of the door, Robert armed with a strong cord, that Carlos plaited of long grasses. Carlos then sent out his call. It sounded much like the screech of a sea-gull. He repeated it three or four times, and waited. Then again he gave the call. In a minute, now, came an answer from high overhead. Another little space, and that door opened, and a black came forth.

Norris pounced on him, bearing him down, one hand on the black's mouth, to prevent an outcry. Robert soon had the bonds on the fellow's wrists, and the others of us moved forward.

Captain Marat spoke to the black in French. He told him he must answer us truthfully, on pain of torture; and he had Norris give him a twist of the arm for a sample. And so we got it out of the man that Duran was not in the fortress, and that there were three children there, brought this day; one, he admitted was white. There were seven men there, two of them armed.

Then, with a gun at his back, the black was ordered to lead the way.

It was a long climb, by stone steps; then came a long corridor. At last a room, where was a fire and cookery, utilizing a break in the wall, looking on the court, for a fireplace.

The six men, and the voodoo woman, at the cooking, were taken unawares, their two rifles confiscated, and they were lined up against the wall; Norris patting his rifle and winking, to accentuate what Marat was telling them in the French.

The three children sat on the floor in a corner: two of them blacks, about three years of age each—and little Marie Cambon, looking like her portrait, but now big-eyed and dazed with trying to realize the meaning of this new appearance. I divined the prelude to a storm; so I hurried over and took her up in my arms. "Little Marie!" I said. And then burst forth that flood. You have seen children cry. It continued till she was exhausted; and then she sobbed long in her sleep. She wouldn't let me put her down; even while she slept, my attempt to relinquish her little body invariably awakened her. For two hours I must carry her, and we were far from that place before she would let me rest my arms.

The two little pickaninnies were taken on, and we went off the way we had come, leaving the seven blacks to reflect on the words of a lecture Jean Marat delivered them on the evil of their ways, and to consider how they were to account to their lord and master—and *papaloi*—Duran, for the loss of the three "goats without horns."

Night sprung upon us before we reached the Brill cottage. And it was truly a happy throng that gathered there. Melie bustled about preparing a supper, between whiles crooning over the three little ones—white and black.

"Shall I see my papa and mamma?" said little Marie Cambon.

"Yes," Melie assured her. "You shall go to your papa and mamma," and they both giggled, girl-like, for happiness.

And the little pickaninnies echoed: "Maman, maman," and Melie delighted them with creole baby-talk; and they grinned and clapped their hands.

Robert and I had soon got the stain off our skins. Little Marie watched the process, and said I looked "more beautiful" without the black. At supper there was held a council of war. Before we could move about the business of the gold mine, there were two things left to be done: we must take the Brills under our protection, for by enlisting their active help we had got them under the anathema of the voodoos; and we must see to the return of little Marie to the arms of her waiting parents. Some of the effects of the Brills we got over to the care of a friendly neighbor. Norris and Robert were to remain to assist Carlos and Melie with their little wagon to the city. They were also to look out for the two little blacks.

The rest of our party moved seaward over the old trail by which we had come. Little Marie clung to myself; she would have none but the one who had been the first to take her from her captors.

The morning was not yet gone, when we got to the coast. We drew our boat to the water; and then it was—back to the *Pearl* again.

Marat and Julian were at the oars, and our boat swung round and pointed toward the *Pearl*. It was then we perceived a boat coming toward us. And we made it out to be the other small boat from the *Pearl*. Two of the black sailors manned the oars, and a stranger sat in the stern sheets.

The two boats rapidly approached; in another pair of minutes I had identified that new figure.

"It's Monsieur Cambon!" I cried. Little Marie was beside me; I turned her face to the approaching boat.

"See! It's papa!" I told her.

Her little face lighted up, and she seemed to expand with happiness, as she looked.

"Papa! Papa!" she murmured.

The two boats came together, by oars they were held fast; and I passed the child over to the silent, eager father.

"Oh! My little daughter!—Marie!" he said, then. "You are safe! Your mamma will be so happy! So happy!"

Madame Cambon was on the *Pearl*, Monsieur told us. She was worn to a shadow with anguish. The good news must trickle to her gently. It was for that he came to meet us.

A strange thing it seems, that emotions of happiness can be as deadly as the tragic. Monsieur Cambon's boat lingered behind, as ours moved to the *Pearl*. Madame Cambon lay on a hammock set up under the awning. Dark patches were under her eyes. She tried to smile a greeting.

"I am happy that you are here," I began.

I did not rightly hear her murmured reply; and I had no mind for it anyway, whatever it was, for my mind was in a rack—how to proceed?

"You must not give in that way," I protested.

"How can I help?" she said.

"You help us all if you have courage," I said.

"Oh, I have tried," she said. "If only I could have hope."

"If you have courage I promise you hope," I ventured.

She sat up. "Hope! Only give me hope!"

"Yes," I said, with all the assurance of which I was capable, "I give you hope—you have it."

"Oh, I like the way you say that!" And her face took on a new look.

"I even promise you she shall come back to you again," I ventured once more.

Her bosom heaved for some moments; then she got control.

"Please do not give me false hopes," she begged.

"No," I asserted, now more sure of her, "I even promise you shall see her soon."

She looked me in the eyes, to read if I told the whole truth.

"You have come with news!" she cried. "I understand you now. Tell me all—I can bear it—I see; you have prepared me. She is coming. Where is my husband?"

"Yes," I said. "She is coming. She is with her father; they will soon be here."

Her eyes swept the water, but the boat was hidden under the rail. I went to the side, reached down and took up little Marie from her father's hands, and brought her to her mother.

No need to describe that scene. Madame Cambon's now was a quiet, restrained emotion. She shed some tears, but there was no violence. And at last she came to talk of gratitude, and we had to cut off her speech. That task fell to Ray.

"You don't know what you're doing," he said. "You're making us ashamed of all the fun we had. And I want to tell you of the bee I turned loose in one voodoo fellow's bonnet."

And in a minute Ray had her laughing.

Monsieur Cambon told us how Madame's condition made it imperative that they follow us in our search for Marie. He said, "We must go, she insisted, if only to be near."

The Cambons were destined to leave us on the following day, and to carry Melie Brill with them on the steamer to Jamaica. But in the meantime we awaited the coming of that portion of our party left behind up in the foothills.

It was long after dark had come that we heard the call of Robert on the beach opposite. Ray and I hurried the boat to shore, and took on Robert, Norris, Carlos and Melie Brill. And they had a story to tell.

CHAPTER IX

THE STAMPEDE

"You're a long time getting here," I observed, as Norris took up the oars.

"Yes," returned Norris. "And we wouldn't be getting here at all, if those voodoo skunks had had their own way about it."

"Did they give you trouble?" I asked.

"Oh, I guess—yes, some," he said. "But we gave them trouble, eh, Robert?"

Robert acquiesced.

"I reckon they'll some day be telling their voodoo grand-children how a bunch of white devils came to their island and raised particular—"

"Raised particular 'hotel,'" assisted Ray, who saw that Norris was about to stumble on an impolite word.

We climbed aboard the *Pearl* and Rufe fed the four while they gave us their tale.

"We got nearly everything loaded onto Carlos' little wagon, and Carlos was going to hitch up the donkey, when those voodoo skunks showed up," said Norris. "They didn't knock on the door or ring the bell, but stood off like the pack of hyenas they are.

"Carlos talked to them. They said we must give up the kids, or they would burn the shack with us in it. I told Carlos: 'Tell them that if they don't clear out right quick some of them will soon be burning in—in—'"

"Where Beelzebub tends the ovens and the climate is equable," offered Ray, politely.

"I don't know how many voodoo there was in the crowd," continued Norris. "The people from the village came round, too,—I suppose, to see the fun. There were some guns; and those fellows began to get their heads together. I got mad, finally, to see those skunks so cheeky; and I forgot English wasn't their talk, and called out: 'Any of you who don't want to get into the battle better crawl into your holes!'

"There must have been some that got that, for pretty quick there was a scattering, and only about a dozen or so stayed on. They were the ones who'd come on business, I guess.

"Pretty soon Melie said there were some of the blacks sneaking up toward the wagon, out by the barn. I got to the back door with my rifle, and I blowed the high peaked hat off the nearest skunk—sorry now I didn't blow his head off. Those fellows didn't stop to pick up that hat.

"Those cusses in front had begun to move up with their guns ready. But Robert had his little twenty-two ready too; and they hadn't come far when he let the leader have one in his off hind foot. He limped off howling, and the others suddenly recollected other appointments.

"'Now we've got to make our start,' I said."

"While the audience is wondering what'll be the next scene," prompted Ray.

"Something like that," admitted Norris. "So we bundled the black babies up, while Carlos hitched up the mule. And when we started for the barn, I saw Melie sprinkling some seeds about the ground and back stoop. 'What are you planting grass for?' I said. 'You're not coming back.'

"She laughed and said that the voodoo men were barefoot, and the seeds would give them sores that would disable them for weeks. Well, we got started. Carlos drove; Robert went ahead with his rifle, and I followed behind with mine.

"We poked along for about three miles, and no sign of those voodoo cusses. Then Carlos pulled up and waited for me to catch up.

"'Well,' I said, 'do you reckon they've given up the fight?' And Carlos said there was a little steep hill about a mile ahead, that the road passed round; and he was some afraid the enemy might be laying for us there, and would roll rocks down on us. He said we might avoid the place by a roundabout way through the woods, but it would be hard going, and we'd lose time.

"I called Robert and told him our troubles. 'Wait ten minutes,' he said, 'and then drive up to a couple of hundred yards of the place, and stop till I whistle for you to come on.' And then he trotted on ahead. In ten minutes we started. Carlos pulled the donkey to a stop at the right place, and we waited.

"In a minute we heard a howl—then another howl—then a howl every second, for about six howls. Then we heard a stampede in the woods, off to our right.—Better let Bob tell what happened."

"I hurried on ahead till I saw the hill," said Robert. "It was a ridge that ended right at the road, and all covered with the woods. I turned off and climbed to the top of the ridge pretty well back; and I moved toward the road cautiously. Then I saw those black fellows—I guess there was near a dozen— right at the end of the ridge. They had a screen of brush toward the road, but on my side it was all open. They had some big bowlders all ready to push over. I slipped back a little and climbed into a tree. I got a good seat in a crotch, from where the view was good.

"Pretty soon I heard the wagon. And those fellows heard it too. They peeked through the brush, and—"

"And they licked their chops," struck in Ray.

"I had my magazine full," continued Robert, "and I had my peep-sight set. One black's pants were tight with stooping to look—and I gave him the first little bullet."

"Right on the '*spank*,'" said Ray.

"Yes," continued Robert, "I got the idea from Ray. Well that one let out a howl. And then I peppered the next one in the leg, and he howled. Another one got it in the shoulder. They were mightily puzzled—not hearing anything—so they couldn't use their guns. They didn't wait to look round very long, but hiked out, running by right under my tree. Before they got away I hit six or seven—some of them limped as they ran."

"When we heard the stampede," said Grant Norris, "we didn't need Bob's whistle to tell us to come on. There were no voodoo skunks going to hang back for any more, after all that 'whoop-er-up.' We got into town without any more accidents, and—"

"That was mighty fortunate for the voodoos," drawled Ray. "But where's the pickaninnies?"

"Melie here, turned them over to a priest," said Norris. "We lost some time finding him."

Carlos had edged up, and I could see he wanted a word with me. So I led him toward the schooner's bow; and he told me his news, leaning on the rail.

"Duran, he is in the city," he said.

He had touched on the thing that was in my mind; for during Norris's and Robert's recital of their adventures, I was wondering where this white voodoo should be all that while. I was conscious that it was this man—or fiend—that was to continue to be the center and spring of all our interest to the end of the chapter.

"Have you seen him?" I asked.

"No, I have one friend in the city who see him," Carlos said. "He buy new picks, an' he buy pack-straps, for to carry things on thee back, and new rope an' pulleys."

It developed that this friend of Carlos had long been of help to him, in keeping an observant eye on Duran when in his city haunts; and it came out that this friend's home was on the very street on which Robert and I had first encountered Duran.

"Well, Carlos," I said, "if we are to find this gold mine of yours, we'll have to keep an eye on Duran."

"Yes," he nodded. "And he kill' my father, an' my brother." And Carlos smiled a smile with his teeth set, and that gave him a sinister look. In spite of the night I could see so much of his face. It was more lust for vengeance than love of gold that showed there then.

"I can speak for us all, Carlos," I said; "We will see this thing through. And we all want to see this man brought to justice for his crimes."

"Ah, I glad for to hear you say that!" he said. "Maybe we can find for you much gold. I hope that."

I called the others into conference; and we made plans for our next move. We would turn in at once for a good sleep; and before daylight we would go ashore and into the city and pick up Duran's trail. Carlos's friend had promised to keep his eye on Duran's movements, which he had learned to interpret in limited measure.

Before taking to our pallets, on the deck, we bade goodbye to the Cambons, who were to take steamer for home on the morrow. Little Marie made me promise to come to her home some time soon, said she would adopt me for her brother, so that I could have a good mother, too, in the place of the good mother I had lost.

CHAPTER X

ON THE GOLD TRAIL AGAIN

It was Carlos and Rufe, together, who routed us all out long before day; and soon we were set on shore—Captain Marat, Norris, Julian, Ray, Robert and myself. We moved to the eastern edge of the city, and there awaited Carlos, who had hurried off to consult with his friend. We hadn't long to wait. He came with the intelligence that Duran had gone from the city at dusk the evening before. He had doubtless gone to the old ruin, since he had been attended by a man who was wont to wait on him, carrying his burdens, when going inland. When going direct to his ship, his attendants were always two or more sailors.

"Well, then it's for another visit to that old palace, where we had so much fun, eh Wayne?" said Norris.

Carlos led us over an old, seldom used trail; one that ran back of the old ruin.

It was a long, tedious march. And yet the morning was still fresh when we found ourselves at the bottom of the rear wall of the palace, looking up to where that escape door was hidden among the vines. I went up first. With my stick through the hole, I had up the latch, and pushed the door open. Next came Robert.

"Say," spoke up Grant Norris, "is that ladder of yours going to hold two hundred ten pounds?"

"It'll hold three times that," I assured him. And so he came up with ease, in spite of his weight.

Ray, Julian, Carlos, and Marat, soon were standing with us in the dark passage. Flashing my light, I led the way up the stone steps, and along the passage.

We came at last to that little door opening into Duran's room—that door through which I had made my rash entry, and hasty retreat.

There was no light shining through the chinks of the shrine this time. But I put my ear close, and in a little I distinguished the sound of heavy breathing within. Someone slept there. I communicated that piece of intelligence to the others in a low whisper. And we waited for the sleeper to waken.

Near half an hour must have passed and Norris had moved back down the passage, to calm his impatience. It was then we heard a loud knocking on a door of that room. The sleeper was aroused, and then light shone through the crevices.

Captain Marat and Carlos gave ear to the talk of those in the room. Duran, in sleeping garb, and a lame black attendant, were the occupants, as a peek through those chinks showed.

By Marat's report the following was the talk of the two:

"Well," said Duran, "any news of those dogs of Americans having gone?"

"Gani, just come," said the black. "He say French man and woman, and baby, and Brill woman, go way in steamer; schooner stay."

"So! The schooner stay!" thundered Duran. And he cursed and fumed a spell. "The schooner stay! Why do they stay?—It is that Carlos Brill. He has told them something. It is the gold now they want. Why did I not kill him?"

"The men have try," spoke the black. "They cannot—"

"They have try!" thundered Duran. "They try a little, and because he escape one, two bad shots, the fools they say the Zombi protect him. Well, no Zombi protect him when I see him!—They shall not find the gold.—Go, make ready my breakfast."

The black left the room. Duran turned to his toilet, manifesting his ill humor the while with grumbling to himself. The man presently brought in his food, and again retired. The meal finished, Duran sat in deep contemplation for some minutes, staring before him, and intermittently pulling on the lobe of his ear in his characteristic manner.

Finally he stepped to the door, and called. The black man again appeared.

"Tell Gani I go to the *Orion*," he said. The door closed and again Duran fell into soliloquy.

"Yes, I make the gold safe," he said. "That Carlos Brill—I should kill him long ago."

We could hear him in the room, but his activities were, for the most part, out of our range of vision.

Then presently he brought a box to the table. He laid out a money-belt. Then from the box he took bundles of bills, of money; and then came a half dozen fat pouches. That this was gold we had no doubt. The paper money and bags of gold Duran soon had transferred to the money-belt. And this he hung about his waist, with straps over the shoulders. A light jacket concealed the whole. He put away the box again.

His preparations were soon completed, and he went out of the room, having put out the lights.

It was then Marat gave us the account of that which he had heard.

"Well," I said, "if he's going to his schooner, we'll have to get a move on us."

I professed that I wanted to see the place Duran got that box from. And Norris confessed a like curiosity. "And I want to see how this door works," he said. So we two lingered, while the others hurried down the passage, meaning to have an eye on Duran when he should start off toward his ship.

Norris and I crawled through the little door. We first put lights to the candles, and looked to the security of the door. And then came search for a secret recess. After some minutes survey, we found a marble slab of the floor, next the wall, showing dust about the edges. Hung on the wall was a hook of metal. With this we succeeded to pull up an end of the slab.

To take out the stone and thrust our hands into the recess, where it extended under the wall, was the effort of two moments. We pulled forth the box.

It now held only two objects: a small account book, and a gold ring having the form of a serpent. The ring I pocketed. The book held some figures—amounts with many ciphers, and a number of addresses. One in Paris, others in Porto Rico, Jamaica, Cuba—the Cambons' among them. I tore out a leaf and made copies of them.

"That's right, Wayne," said Grant Norris. "They might be of value."

Soon we were out in the passage.

Down in the bed of the stream we found Robert awaiting us.

"He's gone," said Robert. "We were in time to see him and one black man go off through the woods."

Robert led the way; and soon we were on a trail going toward the sea.

We hurried to catch up with the others, and in a little, came upon Julian and Ray, lingering to make sure we'd found the way.

"I suppose you two are now sporting a money-belt apiece," said Ray.

I showed him the serpent ring.

"Ugh!" he grunted. "That voodoo's coat of arms, I guess."

We'd covered about two miles when we got sight of Captain Marat and Carlos. Carlos kept well ahead; and he was never long without a glimpse of Duran and his black, whose progress was slow, because of a burden.

That Duran was on his way to the gold mine, there was little doubt. Carlos assured us that it was always this way he went when he meant to conceal his movements. And on these occasions he would sail away in his schooner in the night. And it was this had made it impossible for Carlos to follow him to the place. That his father had never travelled to the mine by a water route

Carlos was quite sure, though he had been much too young to have much judgment in the matter, or over much curiosity.

Duran's sailors had proven uncorruptible. Voodoo superstition had had much to do with it, doubtless, and they were liberally paid by their master. Carlos knew of only one black who had deserted Duran's service; and he had afterward been found murdered, in the city.

The character of the growth changed as we approached the sea. The greater trees were less plentiful; there were more open spaces; bamboo, tall grasses, came in our way; cocoa palms, royal palms, cabbage palms, looked down upon us as we passed. And then came vistas, giving view of the blue sea. Here the course turned east.

In the comparative sparsity of the growth, there was less need for a path, so now Carlos soon had lost the trail of Duran and his black. He recommended that we remain where we then were, while he was gone forward, to seek for signs of the two.

"Thanks, Carlos," said Ray, throwing himself on the ground, "I never was so hot, and done up."

All were glad of a rest, except perhaps Grant Norris, who was always for going forward. Now, though, the heat must have taken, temporarily, some of the go out of him, for he lay immovable for so much as ten minutes. The mid-day sun was almost directly overhead, and there was scarcely a breath of air stirring.

When an hour had passed, Norris was on nettles again. He had smoked three pipefuls, to calm his nerves. Again and again he made short excursions to the east to anticipate the return of Carlos.

Ray had been observing him. "Say, Norris," he said, "there won't be slow music at your funeral."

Then, finally, Carlos turned up. He beckoned us to follow him. We tramped two more miles, much of it through a heavy bushy growth. And then at last he halted us in a screen of bush, whence we looked out on the waters of a small cove, almost surrounded by palms, whose tall trunks leaned over the white sand beach. Resting in that cove was a schooner—the *Orion*.

"Duran, he go on board," said Carlos.

We could see the figures of black sailors on the deck; and with binoculars distinguished their white master, Duran.

"Well, and now then?" said Norris.

"Yes, what next, Wayne?" said Ray, "Norris and I are ready to bust."

There was only one thing to do. We must have the *Pearl* ready to follow when the *Orion* should sail.

"And when do you think she'll sail?" asked Julian.

"Sometime after dark, more than likely," said Robert.

It was Captain Marat, Robert and Julian, that went for the *Pearl*. They were to bring her to within a few miles of this cove, and pick up the rest of us in a small boat. They had ten miles ahead of them, most of it along the beach, and the going all good, where the sand was hard with moisture.

The hot tropic sun beat down on us in the brush, where we crouched, sweltering, till Carlos found us a less ovenlike lookout, under the palms of a tongue of land to the west of the cove. Our move got us some closer, too, to the object of our interest. And it was but a short run to the opposite side of the point, where we could have an eye on the coming of the *Pearl*.

I took occasion to show Carlos that gold ring I had found in Duran's hiding-place. He showed surprise and some emotion at sight of it.

"That my father's ring," he declared. "He have that ring on his finger that day he went away with Duran—an' never come back. My father he tell us he in the city have that ring made of gold he take from hees mine. He was no voodoo, my father, but I do not know why he have thee ring made like the serpent. He was mostly negro—my mother was Carib."

Carlos refused the ring. He asked that I keep it for him, till he should ask for it. It was when we were all at sea one day, he asked for the ring. I handed it toward him, and he held up a belaying pin, asking me to thrust it on the point. And then with much tapping with a hammer, he blotted out the serpent; and on the broad part, where the head had been, he contrived a cross, using hammer and chisel. This done, he was content to take the ring his father had worn.

"Now thee ring be good luck," he said. And he placed it on his finger.

There was apparently little activity on board the *Orion*, though once or twice we heard the laugh of a sailor wafted in on the light breeze.

The hot, tedious hours dragged along, one after the other, with tropic lassitude; till finally the shadows of the palms had spread over the waters of the cove. And at last, too, Grant Norris came to tell us that the *Pearl* had come to anchor, about three miles away.

It was then activity began on board Duran's schooner: The binoculars showed us sailors throwing off the gaskets. And then—and this to us was a surprise—up went her sails.

"Surely," said Ray, "they can't be going to make a start yet?"

"We'd better hump," began Norris, "or they'll be getting away before we get aboard the *Pearl*."

"Wait," I said, "I don't believe they'll sail before dark."

"Always," offered Carlos, "when they sail from the city it is dark."

"I'm thinking," said Ray, "that what that Duran finds to do in daylight wouldn't make a long sermon."

One thing led to another, and soon we were in the midst of that newly popular discussion of the probable location of the gold mine. "Well," concluded Grant Norris, "it can't be very far, if Carlos's father made the trip overland, there and back, in five or six days."

Carlos re-affirmed his statement. "The first time he is away some weeks, when he come back very happy, and say he have find gold mine, and he show us gold. But he have been away five and six day and come back."

It was then the schooner again took our notice, for the sails began to come down again, and soon they were all snug between gaffs and booms.

"Just shaking the wrinkles out of them," suggested Ray.

The sun was now nearing the horizon. Norris and Ray hurried up the beach, to get themselves aboard the *Pearl*, and have Captain Marat move down, after dark, close to the point on its west. Thus this tongue of land with its tall palms, would still hold a screen between the two schooners.

Night, with the precipitancy peculiar to the tropics, rose up and lay its black cloak over everything. While the stars were out bright, the moon was not due till near daylight. An hour Carlos and I waited, watching that dark spot in the cove that represented the *Orion*. Then Norris and Robert joined us. Our schooner now lay about a mile from shore, they told us. The land breeze soon sprung up, and still there was no movement in the cove.

"Looks like they've settled down there for the night," suggested Robert.

"Don't say that," said Norris.

Then came a faint flash of light over there, and in another minute we heard the squeak of a block.

"The sails are going up!" I said. "Now back to the *Pearl*."

We hurried on among the pillar-like trunks of palms; in a little we were in the small boat, and at last the *Pearl* took us in.

"They're making sail," I told Captain Marat.

He took me into the cabin, and showed me the chart. There was there shown a long shoal, that would necessitate the *Orion* passing us and going some miles west, to round the end of the shoal, and so out to sea, for a run down the coast to the east. "Unless," said Captain Marat, "they have some safe passage through the shoal, say through here." And he pointed to a place opposite the point, where the depth figures indicated such a possible passage.

We got on a jib, and crawled out a bit nearer to the place indicated; and again we let down the anchor.

We had not long to wait this time. A dark object moved into our view. With a distant squeak of a block or two, it turned seaward. We were not many minutes getting under way. We lost sight of the *Orion* before we got way on, and when we were well beyond the shoal, we took our course east at a guess.

We had sailed there an hour, covering some miles, before that dark mass again showed before us. We then almost ran the other schooner down, for she lay hove to, her sails flapping. With quick work Captain Marat likewise brought the *Pearl* about.

During the maneuver I had had opportunity to note that a small boat of the *Orion* had separated itself from that vessel, and was a little way shoreward. But at our coming the boat turned about, and made back to the *Orion* again.

That vessel's sails directly filled once more, its bowsprit pointing down the coast. The *Pearl* was not long in falling into its wake. And then came a flash and report from the *Orion*. Norris rushed into the cabin, brought out his rifle and sent a bullet after that vessel.

"Tit for tat!" he said. "I'll bet that that cooled his enthusiasm."

The enemy did not see fit to continue the exchange.

"Humph—'tit for tat'" mused Ray. "Norris and Duran talk to one another in the old code."

"Oh, and maybe you can tell what we were saying," bantered Norris.

"Sure," said Ray. "That fellow's 'tat' said—'Don't you dare follow me!' and your 'tit' said—'You're another.'"

"You're a mighty wise gazabo," said Norris.

"Of course," said Ray. "And I'm a mind reader, too."

"You, a mind reader!" said Norris. "And do you mean to say you can tell what I'm thinking?"

"Sure," said Ray. "You're thinking—a—you're thinking that I don't know what you're thinking."

And he had to dodge Norris's moccasin.

We were now keeping pretty much in that other schooner's wake. It gave us much satisfaction to find that the *Pearl* had superiority in speed, at least in a moderate breeze.

The *Orion* apparently had on all her sail; we were obliged to shorten sail a bit, to avoid overhauling the other. The waning moon came out of the horizon an hour before daybreak.

It was then we began to draw off a little, for we now had but one purpose— to keep an unwavering eye on the *Orion*. That vessel, it became plain, had come to have its single aim—to shake the *Pearl* from her trail. And now day after day, and night after night, the contest was on. The *Orion* at first put on every effort to outsail us; that was vain. Then she sought to hang us on dangerous shoals; but Captain Marat's charts told him where they lay. The *Orion* tried at night, by sudden changes in her course, to lose us in the dark. But sundown always found us clinging to her apron strings, and a sharp eye on every shift of her.

A week passed thus, and then the island of—well, suffice it to say it was an important island of the West Indies—This island hove in sight. The *Orion* made straight in, the *Pearl* at her heels. The frowning guns of a fort guarded the harbor and city, which lay on the west coast.

At ten of the morning the two schooners came to anchor. The *Pearl* chose a berth less than a hundred fathoms from the other. And it was little thought that these ships would go out of that harbor with rather a different distribution of passengers than that with which they went in.

CHAPTER XI

AT HIDE AND SEEK WITH THE ENEMY

The white buildings of that city, with the green mountain background, and the white beach, overhung with its graceful palms, presented a pleasing picture. I remember I thought what a place this would be to spend a peaceful holiday; to fish, to hunt, to feast on the luscious fruits, and explore those forests of mountain and valley, and the wonders of the caves. If only we had never come up with that fiend, Duran.

When Captain Marat had seen to it that all was snug, and the awning stretched, he turned his eyes toward the *Orion*, who likewise had stowed her cloth under gaskets.

"I did not think that Duran would come in to thees place," he said.

"He tried to shake us off his tail by running fast," said Ray; "and he tried to scrape us off on reefs; and now I guess he's come in here to try to crawl through some hole that'll be too small for us."

"Well, that skunk is here to try some devilment, that's sure," observed Norris.

We kept a sharp eye on the *Orion*. Within the hour we saw a small boat from the city boarding her. In twenty minutes that boat came to the *Pearl*. The port doctor came over the rail. He was a Spaniard, but with a good command of English. He asked the usual questions of Captain Marat.

"Well," he said, when he had his answers, "I am afraid we'll have to hold you in quarantine. I learn there is yellow fever in the port from which you came."

"I believe there is some mistake," said Marat, "we heard of no yellow fever there."

"Pardon me," I interposed, "but did you get your information from the *Orion*?"

"Yes," admitted the doctor, "from Monsieur Duran."

"And is the *Orion* to be quarantined?" I asked.

"No," he said, "the *Orion* has not been in that port for months. The outbreak of yellow fever is less than three weeks old. Duran was hailed by a ship that gave him the news."

"We know," I told him, "that that man Duran was in the port on the day preceding that on which we sailed."

There was a dubious look in the official's face. And now he had come to dividing his attention between myself and a steamer that was just moving in.

He put his binoculars to his eyes. Some moments he looked, and then he turned to us.

"Wait," he said. "There is a steamer from your port. I shall be back presently."

With that he got over the rail and went off in his boat to the steamer.

"Now then," said Norris, when he was gone, "there's that skunk's trick."

"But it's a monkey trick," said Ray. "He ought to know we'd have our story to tell."

"Maybe," suggested Julian, "he thought his wines—and maybe some gold—would give greater weight to his story."

I, too, had got the smell of liquor from the doctor's breath. It was quite probable Duran had been making very friendly with this official.

"Perhaps Duran counted on our going outside the harbor rather than be delayed in quarantine," said Robert.

"Yes, and that would suit him ver' well," said Marat. "He could then try and slip by in thee dark."

The doctor came back, as he had promised. And he spoke us without again coming aboard.

"That was some mistake about the yellow fever," he said. "You will be free to go ashore."

"Well, and what will our voodoo priest try next?" said Grant Norris.

"Next, he'll have us arrested, for disturbing the peace," said Julian.

"His peace of mind," added Ray.

Our discussion became serious now. The more Duran sought to shake us, the more important that we observe his every movement.

That he would be going ashore into the city was reasonably certain. If we were to see what he did there, it might be well to precede him, and lie in wait. Grant Norris, Robert Murtry, and Julian Lamartine, were selected for this expedition. Julian, like Jean Marat, had a fair command of the Spanish, which was the language of this port.

The three were in the small boat, ready to push off, when I recollected the bit of paper in my pocket, on which I had copied the addresses from Duran's book in the old ruin. There was among them an address in this port. I had out the paper, and called out the name to Julian, Paul Marcel was the name.

We saw the boat of our friends go among the wharves. It was not long till—"There he goes now!" cried Ray, and we saw a small boat moving shoreward from the schooner *Orion*.

The moon, approaching its first quarter, set at ten that night, and our three had not returned from the city. The anchor-light on the *Orion* was all we could see of her.

It was near midnight when I heard the dip of oars approaching, and directly Norris, Julian, and Robert climbed over the rail.

"It was a tame party we had," grumbled Norris. "Our friend Duran is back on his schooner."

"But the address was right," said Robert.

"Yes," offered Julian, "Duran spent most of his time at the home of a Monsieur Paul Marcel; and when he came out on the verandah to go, I heard him appoint to come back tomorrow. And they talked of some kind of party for tomorrow night."

Tame as Norris considered their excursion on shore, Robert recounted a feature of that adventure that had not a little to do toward putting Norris in a bad humour. When they saw Duran, accompanied by his two blacks, very evidently making to the boat, our party fell back, not to be seen by Duran at the wharf. But what should happen but that Duran should suddenly step from behind a corner of a shed and laugh derisively in their faces.

It occurred to me that, in view of the circumstance, there might be some talk on the *Orion* that it should profit us to hear a word of. I said as much to Captain Marat; and we two set off forthwith in a small boat, to have a try.

We made a detour, and approached the *Orion* from the far side. There were other boats moving about, making us the less conspicuous, and besides, the inky darkness favored us. So that we came in under the *Orion's* bows unnoted. Voices there were speaking on the deck, and Captain Marat cocked his ear to them, as we held to the stays.

He repeated it all to me afterward, and this is pretty much the way of the talk he heard:

"There will be no risk. Of course, if the big one is there, we will wait till the next night."

"But the noise will—"

"But there need be no noise. It must be—"

"Yes, that won't be so bad, and it will be dark. And now I want you to know, Monsieur, that the men are beginning to fear they will never see the gold you have promised them. This being pursued is a new thing for them. And then, you have always been all powerful, and never had to give over your plans and flee. And we have come so far from—"

"Bah! You must make them to understand again that these infernal Americans have Carlos Brill with them, and they are after my secrets—they want the gold. And I cannot afford to give them the least hint where it lies. We must finally shake them off; then we go back home; I land the regular place, at the foot of Twin Hills. Then no one can follow. And in the week I will have out all the gold that is mined. Then I will give the men more gold than they ever dreamed of having, and they will be free to go and spend. And for two years, maybe three years, I will not go near the mine.

"And no one will ever find it. No, it is safe; that is very sure. Tell them. And you—you know what I have promised you. I make you the most wealthy black, that ever lived, and I will never feel the loss of what I give you. But you must not fail me."

"Oh, monsieur, believe me, I will do my work well."

"If you succeed, you must make no mistake about the place to meet us; we must not leave them behind, here."

"Yes, monsieur; there will be no mistake. I know my work."

The voices became indistinct as the speakers moved away. Then Marat took up the oars again and quietly got our boat away in the dark.

It was then he repeated to me what he had heard.

"Then we came just too late to hear what this thing is they plan," I said.

"Yes," agreed Captain Marat, "but we got one clue to the mine. He say he weel 'land at foot of Twin Hills'—back home. We look on thee chart; that it is near that place where we begin the pursuit."

We were soon aboard the *Pearl*, the chart on the table.

"There!" said Captain Marat. And he put the end of a match on the spot marked, "Twin Hills." It was close to the sea line, less than five miles from the cove in which we discovered the *Orion*.

And then I had a thought.

"That must be where we saw a small boat starting toward shore from the *Orion*," I said.

"Just so," said Marat. "It was Duran, going to land 'The regular place,' to go to his mine."

"Well, now," began Ray, who had followed us into the cabin, "you folks seem to know a heap. Where do you get all your wisdom?"

We got all our party together, and Marat repeated what we had learned.

"So the mine is away back up there where we started from, after all," said Norris. "And here we are a week's sail from the place we're after. If that skunk would only drop some decent clue to the place, I trust Wayne here to find it, and we could leave Mr. 'Monsieur voodoo priest' to sail the globe, if he likes, while we go back and take possession of Carlos's mine."

"But what is the meaning of the other talk," said Julian. "What is this thing they are up to?"

And this is the thing we got news of the following night, as shall be seen.

We were early astir in the morning. Most of us spent the greater part of the day ashore. And we had an eye on Duran's movements, for he, too, put in the day in the city. He was apparently well known among a number of the citizens, for he was often greeted familiarly. And he spent much money that day, for wines, flowers, and dainties for the palate, all of which were carted to the residence of Monsieur Marcel; so it became apparent it was Duran that was giving the party.

Night found Ray and myself among the lookers-on, made up of the poor of the neighborhood. They were allowed to encroach on the lawn, where they stood among the planted bushes and under the palms. And drink and dainties were sent out for the rabble, who gorged themselves at the expense of Duran.

The house was large, with extensive verandas, on which the guests danced to the music of an orchestra. There was a great hum of voices, and much laughter.

Ray and I could see Duran, from time to time, as he played the gay cavalier; and he was apparently very popular with the ladies, with whom he danced and promenaded. His deportment was that of a real gentleman, and his dress was most correct. I thought of that other night, when I had seen this same man in a red robe; in his blackened face, under a turban, the look of a fiend; in his hand a knife ready for a horrid deed. To fathom such a character was beyond my power of reasoning. A learned man has since sought to explain the thing to me, by saying that the little part of black blood in this man was doubtless descended from a cannibal; and those instincts would at times come to the fore. And then, too, he said, much of the white in this man might easily be descended from a "wolf in sheep's clothing," which is not so uncommon a phenomenon in society today.

The mob that was about us was all gone, long before eleven o'clock. But the dancing and gaiety at the house showed no abatement.

We two were in a bit of brush, at a point that gave us a good view of the premises. The moon was long gone, but the house lights made a halo all about.

"Well, I don't see what good we are doing here," said Ray at last. "That Duran will go to his schooner when this thing is over, and we don't care what he does before then."

"He might slip away in some other vessel," I said.

Another hour passed.

And then Duran came out on the verandah, and appeared to be looking directly toward us. I was sure he could not see us, for we crouched in the blackest of shadows.

"There is that white voodoo, again," said Ray. "I wonder if he's going to keep that crowd going till daylight. Folks ought to have some sense of—"

His speech was cut off. And that instant I was enveloped in a cloth, held about me with strong arms; and I felt a pressure on my mouth.

To struggle, I soon found to be useless. Many hands seemed to be holding me, and I was picked off the ground, my bearers pattering along at a rate.

Presently we came to a stop, and I was tumbled into some kind of a wagon, as the creak of the wheels told me. And there was a body jostling me in the wagon-bed—Ray.

CHAPTER XII

IN CAPTIVITY—THE MESSAGE

Here was a mishap entirely unexpected. And it flashed on me that here at last was the explanation of the enigmatic part of the talk Marat heard the night before. That some of us were keeping an eye on him in town, Duran had known; and "the big one" whose absence was desired, was doubtless Norris. And, "there need be no noise," Duran had said. Verily the capture could not have been effected with less.

Where we were to be taken, and what was to be done to us, filled my mind. There was something in the talk last night about a place to meet. And—"We must not leave them behind here," Duran had said. So then the captors were to meet the others at some appointed place, and the captured were not to be left behind. What could that mean other than that we were to be finally taken aboard the schooner *Orion*.

The thing cleared in my mind. Duran counted on the *Pearl* refusing to sail without Ray and myself—that our friends would remain and seek us, even at the risk of losing the trail of Duran. And so the *Orion* would sail away to the mine without fear of discovery. The thought of defeat in the thing we had so much suffered for, caused my heart to sink. I had no real fear that our lives were in danger. Duran had but the one thought now—to save the gold. Now that at last there were those who had penetrated to his lair in the hills, he would not add zest to the pursuit of himself by a needless crime, a crime that would be easily laid to his door.

The wagon went bumping along over the rough road, shaking us thoroughly, while these thoughts were passing in my mind. Hot as was the night, I was almost stifled by this thing over my head, reinforced by the tight binder on my mouth.

We must have traveled at least five miles, I judged, when the wheels ceased to turn. The cloths were taken from our heads. The bonds on our arms and legs remained. There was one black who spoke some English, and he warned us to make no noise.

"We put them on again, if you do," he said.

Once more the wagon moved on. The stars shone overhead, and I could see trees and palms looking down on me, now and then.

"This is a pretty pickle you've pulled me into," Ray said. "My mouth all tied up for more than an hour; and my liver's all scrambled." Ray would make a joke of the rope, if the hangman's noose were round his neck. I've never known a situation so bad as to dampen his spirits. I would have liked to talk with him about our present unhappy situation, and try to devise something by way of bettering it; but there was that black man who spoke English. With him on the seat, and in the wagon box were four other blacks,—as I finally made out—Duran was making sure of our security. I wondered how far it would be to this place on the coast, where we were to be met by the *Orion*.

Day finally came, and we were allowed to sit, thus having our heads more in the air. Ray grumbled about the hardness of the springs—the wagon had none—; and the meat, and bread, and water, that were thrust into his mouth did not make a breakfast to his liking. The morning was not yet half gone, when we came to a stop, at a hut by the roadside. Then came an opportunity that I had not even ventured to hope for—an opportunity to send a message back to our friends.

The black who spoke English came and leaned on the wagon wheel. He had something to say to us. He offered us freedom, on condition that we should prepare a message to be taken back to our friends on the *Pearl*, a writing that should induce them to remain in harbor, and cease to follow the *Orion*.

"You will then let us go back to our friends?" I asked.

"Yes, you go back," he said.

I felt that the fellow lied, for he would not have time to learn the result of the message before meeting with the *Orion*; for that would not appear until the *Orion* had sailed away. And Duran was little likely to permit us to go back and point out to our friends the way the *Orion* had gone. But of course I jumped at the proposal.

"Just plain letter," the black said. "No trick letter," he warned.

A piece of wrapping paper was brought out from the hut, and a pencil to write with.

My arms were freed for the purpose. The black looked on expectantly. How was I to make the most of this opportunity? I had not slept, my mind was confused. I must have time to think. I exaggerated my drowsiness, and my eyes winked and drooped.

"I am too tired now," I told that black. "I must have a little rest, first."

He grunted. "Rest, then write," he said.

The man was himself fatigued, and so, doubtless, eager for a snack of slumber. He went into the hut, leaving one black to guard us.

"Well, I'm going to have a snooze," murmured Ray. "If you need me, ring." And in another minute he was breathing heavily.

I pretended to doze while I sought in my mind to contrive a secret message that should be concealed in this note I was to write our friends on the *Pearl*. First, I must make it very plain to them that they should continue on the trail of the *Orion*, and that we two were to be taken on board that vessel. And then, in order that they might safely stay behind for some hours, when the *Orion* sailed, and thus seem to have given over the chase without actually losing the trail, I must contrive to let them know which way the *Orion* would go to meet us. That it was to the north coast of the island was plain, for the stars had kept me informed as to the general direction we had been moving. But how to conceal all that intelligence in a letter of apparently contrary import?

I had fallen asleep. I awoke with a start, much refreshed. And when I opened my eyes, it was with the feeling that my problem was solved. The thing was now quite clear; it was as if I had dreamed the thing to a conclusion. Years back, we boys, particularly Robert and myself, had worked on various means of secret communication by writing. It was one of those methods that I would now employ. I had the pencil that was brought from the hut, where the English-speaking black still lingered; and beside, I had by habit long carried a bit of indelible pencil in my trousers pocket. Those words I wished to convey to our friends in secret I would write with the indelible pencil; the words I wished to be ignored I would put with the ordinary pencil. I immediately set to work on the message. I have here italicized the words— and the part of a word—that were done with the indelible pencil.

> *Do* not *follow the Orion. We will* not *be on board of her.* We are promised freedom if *you go* not from *the north*west *coast*, where you are, for three days. *Then keep a lookout for us, and we will come to you as soon as we can.*
>
> Wayne Scott.

Now I had not the least doubt that when our friends should come to read this note, they would search for some hidden message. And I was sure that Robert would finally recollect our old practices, and finally put the proper test to it that should bring out the words that I wished to convey to them. I contrived so to use the pencils, that even a sharp eye would not readily detect the fact that two pencils had been employed in the writing. The color in the piece of wrapping paper on which I wrote helped me in this.

I had little doubt that the paper would come under Duran's sharp eye before being delivered to the *Pearl*. But when I surveyed my work, I had little fear that he would discover the trick.

It was still far from noon when the blacks came out of the hut. I gave the note I had written to the one who came for it. He gazed at the writing—I believe pretending to read. He then gave it, well wrapped, to the driver, who was to carry it back to the city.

My hands were again bound to my body, but they loosed the legs of us, and stood us on the ground. When the wagon was gone on the back trail, Ray and I were placed between the four men remaining, and conducted afoot over the rough way to the northward. It was an uneven road we trod; and, tied as our arms were, it was extremely hard to keep balance; so that we would stumble, and bump into one another, at times. Once, when an irregularity caused me to find Ray's shoulder with an unusually hard thump from mine, he said—"Say! Lean on your own flapjacks." Which was by way of ironical pretending he'd had some for his breakfast; and he knew he would have had them of Rufe for the asking, had he been wise, and had not left the *Pearl* to go on shore with me, adventuring. Subtle Ray! And he knew I was fully conscious that he (in his playful way) implied all this.

Cocoa palms were more and more in evidence as we went, so it was plain we were nearing the north coast of the island. And after perhaps two hours laboring over that trail, we turned off to the left, into a narrow path, going through a thicket. Times, crossing open ground, where the hot tropic sun beat down on us unmercifully; times, threading a piece of forest whose shade was most welcome; we at last came to a stop in a grove of palms. For some little while I had seemed to hear a distant sound that was familiar. Now it was become plain; we were near the sea, for the rolling of the surf on the beach was distinct to our ears.

We were denied a sight of the blue expanse, however, for the blacks kept us well within the shelter of the trees, and our legs again were well trussed, and hands freed. They set about preparing a meal; it was some time past the noon hour; and Ray and I were given a portion of the mess, whose chief ingredient was salt codfish. A spring was found, which supplied drink.

Once a wet squall came and gave us a most agreeable, cool wetting, though Ray complained to the blacks of the leaky roof.

The blacks, two and two, turn about, stood guard and slept. We two slept soundly, refreshed by that shower.

Night had come, when I awoke to hear again the rumbling of the surf. Ray still slept, and I refrained from disturbing him. Now and again one of the guards would make an examination of our cords, to see that we were not tampering with them; they had doubtless been well instructed by Duran. Ray finally stirred and sat erect.

"Well," said he, "who blew out the light?" One of the guard crawled close. "Hello, Uncle Tom," said Ray, observing the black. "This is a cheerful crowd. Haven't you got a banjo, or something?"

The fellow grunted in noncomprehension.

"Ugh," continued Ray. "Colored gentlemen where I come from have got some music in them. If Rufe was here he'd show you a double-shuffle that'd make your mouth water."

And thus he continued to babble, until at last he stretched out with a final grumble—"This is a rum crowd. The only way to pass the time is to sleep." And in a minute he was breathing heavily again.

I remained awake for a considerable period. The continued chirping of a cricket, and the bellowing of distant bull-frogs, finally lulled me to sleep.

Day brought us both awake. The two blacks on guard observed us dully.

"See here," began Ray. "Is breakfast ready? I want my breakfast."

The man who had some English chanced to be one of the pair. "You get breakfas' when we ready—not befo'."

"Huh?" grunted Ray, feigning astonishment, and glaring at the black. "I want you to understand I pay my board. I want my money's worth, and if I don't get it, I'll change my hotel."

The fellow had enough comprehension to finally sense Ray's playfulness. He grinned; and forthwith he routed out the two sleeping blacks, and sent them scampering for wood.

And thus had begun the second day of our captivity. We were most carefully watched, the guards—always two—made frequent inspection of the cords; and I should say, they had two guns between them, one a shot-gun, perhaps loaded with buck-shot. So that any thoughts we had of escape found little encouragement. The morning hours dragged, and the heat increased. I had my thoughts much on our friends on board the *Pearl*; wondered when they had got my note, and if they had finally picked out the words I had meant for their understanding; and so, if they had acted on them. During occasional absences on the part of that one black, Ray and I had found opportunity to exchange words on this theme, and I got much encouragement from that cheerful comrade's observations.

"Leave it to Bob," he said, "he's figured it out. He's got his mind so saturated with you, he'll feel out your meaning in anything you put your finger to."

Our captors, one or two at a time, got to absenting themselves with marked regularity. They always went in the direction from which came the music of the surf. We had no difficulty to divine the cause. "It must be getting time for their brother cannibals to show up," said Ray.

And then, at last, two came in, showing some excitement; and there was much jabbering among them. An hour passed. And it was then we were hustled down to the edge of the palms; and the sea opened before us. And there was a schooner, perhaps a mile from the beach, and a small boat coming in. We were thrust forward into the water, and we climbed in. And soon we stood on the deck of the *Orion*, which vessel pointed her bow out to sea. Duran's grinning face confronted us.

"And so," said Duran, "you like very much to sail in my company. I like very much to have you." His smile was derisive.

CHAPTER XIII

JULIAN'S NARRATIVE—THE SECRET MESSAGE

It was dark when we parted with Wayne and Ray, who went to the Marcel place, where Duran was to give a ball. I gathered from the talk I heard that he had often visited the Port, where he loved to display his wealth; and he seemed even to nurse the curiosity people had as to the source of it. I talked with a French tobacconist, who said it was given out that Duran claimed descent from a king.

When we climbed aboard the *Pearl*, Grant Norris had his usual good-natured grumble. "I don't see the sense in losing sleep watching that skunk of a Duran," he said. "If we watch his schooner, that he travels by, he isn't going to slip far to that gold mine without our knowing."

"Yes, if we could be sure," said Captain Marat, "that would be all right. But it may be he give this party to confuse us; and then he sneak away, and go off in some other boat. And then, what I hear las' night when we are by the *Orion*, show he is *up to some theeng*, as you say; and Wayne and Ray they fin' out what it is, maybe."

Most of us on the *Pearl* went to sleep early. Robert alone said he would stay awake till Wayne and Ray should come.

It was long past midnight when Robert came and wakened us. He said he was sure something was wrong. At midnight he had rowed off in the boat, and hovered around the schooner *Orion* to see when Duran should return. He said it was a feeling of uneasiness that prompted him. He had had that uneasiness all evening, though he hadn't liked to talk about it. He said—"Duran went aboard his schooner a little bit ago; and he seemed an awful sight pleased about something. I heard that voice of his laughing while he talked with those black fellows of his."

"I wish you had taken me with you," I told him. "I might have heard what he said."

Robert's fears quickly permeated the rest of us, and soon we were in a small boat, moving toward shore. We passed near the *Orion* in the dark. Duran must have made us out, for we heard his laugh from the rail. It was such a laugh as a villain laughs—with derision in it. Norris almost exploded with rage when he heard. "I'll plug your d——d carcass yet, you low skunk!" he hissed under his breath. Carlos grunted his sympathy with Norris's mood.

We found the other small boat where it was left for the boys. Captain Marat remained with the two boats, while Norris and Robert and I hurried to the Marcel place for traces of Wayne and Ray. Our uneasiness increased with every moment. We got amongst the shrubbery with our lights, for we knew their plan. At last Robert called us to a spot where there were many prints of bare feet, among one or two shoe marks, in the dew-moist sand. Those prints we were able to follow to the edge of a palm grove, where they were lost in a path that was much used. We held to the trail for some way; till finally we came to many branchings, and were compelled to give it up.

"There's no telling which way they went," said Robert. "But those voodoos of Duran's got the boys all right."

It was a disheartening speech.

"If they did," said Norris, "and if they harm them, I'll put a bullet in every d———d carcass; and I'll hang that skunk, Duran, by a hook in his tongue, gold or no gold." And he said more that was not altogether fit to repeat. And he meant it, for he was no mere boaster.

Day was just burst when we came back to Captain Marat.

"Ah," he said, "thad was the theeng, Duran, he talk about las' night. He plan it all, for he feel sure we watch heem at the ball."

"And what will he do to those boys? That's what I want to know," said Norris. And there was fire in his eyes.

"He weel not harm them, I theenk," said Captain Marat, "for he know we suspect him."

"He'll keep them hid," said Robert; "and while we're looking for them, he'll up and run off to the gold mine. That's his game."

"And I, for one," declared Norris, "will stay and hunt for them, gold or no gold."

We rowed back to the *Pearl* for breakfast, and to prepare for the search. It was arranged that I remain on board with Rufe, and if anything should occur, to require the others to return, I was to hoist a red ensign; for back of the town were hills all round, and they would be never far from a vantage-point whence they could have a good view of every vessel in the harbor.

They went, intending to scour the region all about town, beginning the search where we lost that trail beyond the pine grove. They hoped to discover the boys locked in some hut. That they were not over-sanguine was plain. Even Norris must have some notion of the sagacity of Duran.

I used a slit in the awning for my view-port. My binoculars were powerful, and I kept a sharp eye on the *Orion*. Duran I saw using his ship's glasses to observe the *Pearl's* boat going to shore. And some time in each hour I would see him training them on some particular point landward. I speculated much on what might be the object of his interest.

The heat of the afternoon was stifling; the pitch bubbled in the seams of the deck; and the barefoot sailors stepped only on the shadowed places.

It was nearing four o'clock, when I saw Duran go into a boat and start shoreward. Instantly I sent aloft the red ensign.

Twenty minutes must have passed. Cats' paws began to show on the bay, suggesting a squall. I observed a skiff making directly to the *Pearl*. It had but one occupant—a black boy. He came alongside, and held up some paper, folded. I reached down and took it. And the boy was for making off at once. I told him to come aboard, speaking in French. He did not understand, so I tried him in Spanish. No, he said, he was told not to remain. I showed him a handful of silver, at which his expression changed, and he tarried.

"Wait a moment," I said. And I opened the paper. Inside was a small sheet bearing writing, and signed by Wayne. I read hastily.

"Who gave you this?" I asked.

"A black man," he said.

"Was a white man there?" I asked.

"I can't tell," he answered, faltering.

"Not for all this money?" I asked.

"You won't tell on me?" he asked.

"No, I'll not tell," I assured him.

"Yes, a white man gave it to me. He is that rich white man from the schooner."

I gave the boy the money.

Then it was not long till I saw Duran go back to the *Orion*.

Dark clouds had begun to gather and I looked anxiously for the *Pearl's* boat. At last I saw it come into view.

I gave them the writing, telling them the circumstances of its coming. Captain Marat held the paper while all read as follows:

> Do not follow the *Orion*. We will not be on board of her. We are promised freedom if you go not from the northwest coast, where you are, for three days. Then keep a lookout for us, and we will come to you as soon as we can.

Wayne Scott.

The wind was on us, so we hurried down into the cabin. Directly the rain was pattering on the roof.

"So we must give up the gold for the present," spoke Captain Marat. "Ah, thad was it—just like we suspect: Duran plan thees thing to give us the slip."

"Let me see that," said Robert. And he took the paper in his fingers, studying the writing with intentness, and holding it in varying positions.

"It's Wayne's writing, all right, isn't it?" said the wondering Norris.

"Yes," said Robert, "but I know Wayne."

He dug out from the papers on the table a piece of blotting paper; and he called to Rufe to bring him some water. The wondering Rufe jumped for it. Robert wet the blotting paper; then laying Wayne's writing on the table, he pressed the wet blotter on it. When he uncovered the paper we were astounded to see some of the words standing out in purple letters, the purple reading thus:

> Do   follow the *Orion*. We will   be on board of her.
> you go north
>
> coast, Then keep a lookout for us, and we will come to you as soon as we can.
>
> *Wayne Scott.*

"Ah!" said Captain Marat. "Thad look ver' deeferent. They want we shall follow thee *Orion*—and they are to be on board of thee *Orion*. And so that what Duran mean w'en he say—'We must not leave them behind.'"

"And," offered Robert, "he wants us to look out for them. That means that when we get near enough, they'll escape overboard if they get a chance; and they want us to pick them up if they succeed."

"Say," broke in Norris, holding the paper and addressing Robert. "What you kids can't think up isn't in the dictionary, or Shakespeare. That Duran is a sharp one, but let Wayne and Robert, here, alone—we'll beat that skunk yet."

CHAPTER XIV

JULIAN CONTINUES THE NARRATIVE—NORRIS' BIG GUN

There was much discussion now, and the storm having passed, we got up on deck again. It was decided to make it appear to Duran that we meant to remain, waiting for the return of the boys. We got a boat ready, put into it blankets and provisions, and the like, as if for a sojourn on shore. We made certain Duran would be watching our preparations. An hour before night we pushed off, Robert and Rufe, only, remaining aboard with the sailors.

At the wharf we hired a mule and cart, and transferred the cargo; and directly, we were moving to the back of the town, stopping only when we had reached a little wooded eminence. We did not unload, but unhitched the mule and put him to graze.

We had not been long at the place, when Norris went off, saying he had an errand, and would meet us at the boat-landing.

We could see both schooners from the little hill, until darkness came. Then we kept watch for Robert's signal.

"What do you think Norris can be up to?" I said.

"Ah!" returned Marat, "Thad Englishman, he got some buzz in hees bonnet. He ver' good man. He—"

"There thee light!" said Carlos.

I looked, and out of the black harbor, dotted with anchor lights, there appeared a wee flashing, repeated at frequent intervals. We answered with a few flashes from our lantern. Then Robert's signal ceased.

The mule was put to the cart again, and we returned to our boat.

There was Norris, waiting. He sat on the bow of the small boat, twirling his thumbs. While we were transferring our property from the cart to the boat again, I noted a pair of white men seated in a flatboat of some bulk, lying nose on the beach, nearby. When we started for the *Pearl*, Norris made a gesture to the two men who immediately followed with their boat in our wake.

"What have you got there?" I asked of Norris.

"Oh, that's just a couple of dagos doing a job for me," Norris answered.

"The *Orion's* gone," said Robert, as we drew near the *Pearl*.

We threw our outfit aboard. And then Norris unlashed the block from the main gaff and swung it down to the "Dagos," who had come alongside with their boat. They hitched the tackle to a tarpaulin-wrapped article. From its shape, it might be a piece of cordwood. When that had been pulled aboard, the block went down into the boat again, and soon up came a gun carriage. It was that type so much seen in the old fortifications, the supports of wood, with small wheels at the base. Next came about fifty rounds of, perhaps, two-pound balls, and powder in kegs, not forgetting ram-rod and swabber.

The "Dagos" moved quietly away, money in their fists.

"Never heard of a ship on such a chase as ours without some kind of a cannon," explained Norris.

He had seen some old cannon lying useless in an old fortification on shore. He fastened his liking on a brass gun, of not too great size, and 'by hook or by crook,' had made a deal for it—"With the fixin's," as he said. One little wheel of the carriage was broken, but he contrived a temporary prop in its place. He did not rest till he had the brass barrel mounted and lashed up near the bows, and hid under its tarpaulin.

"What are you going to do with that 'barker'?" said Robert.

"First of all," said Norris, "I'm going to polish her up—to decorate the ship. And then, if ever that skunk voodoo gives me an excuse, I'm going to find out what my old training in gunnery has done for me."

The land breeze had been blowing for a long time. Though Captain Marat had his clearing papers all in proper form long ago, we waited till the *Orion* had got near a good three hours start, before we got up our anchor and set the *Pearl's* bow out to sea.

It was past midnight, the moon—in its first quarter—was just setting. In half an hour we went about, and made toward the north. Daylight found us rounding the northwest corner of the island.

"How long do you think it will take us to get sight of that skunk's ship?" asked Norris.

"Ah!" mused Captain Marat, "Maybe one day, maybe two."

"And if the *Orion* is going back home," said Norris, "after she picks up Wayne and Ray, which way will she turn—north and then back, or down around the east end of the island?"

"I theenk," said Marat, "thad she go aroun' thees island. She make faster sail thad way, and Duran weel think we have not so much chance to head him off thad way—if we should happen to come after heem."

That first day, while the *Pearl* plowed steadily eastward, the coast always in view, Norris busied himself with repairs on his gun-carriage. The second day broke with no sight of the *Orion*. And this day Norris gave to polishing his brass cannon; a job that took grit and elbow-grease, for that barrel carried the accumulations of many years of exposure to all weathers.

That afternoon he got out powder and a ball, and charged the gun, and ten minutes before we were to turn on the starboard tack, he set adrift a little raft on which he had rigged a square bit of canvas. And then when we got round on that tack, he called Rufe, who came running with a red hot poker. Norris sighted the gun on that raft, the while shouting orders to the man at the helm. A touch of the red poker, and "Boom!" We saw the splash, perhaps forty feet to the right of the raft, which now floated some three hundred yards distant.

"If that had been the *Orion*," said Norris, "I'd have got her in the bows. That's a good enough shot, I'll say."

It was near nine of the following morning that we sighted the sails of a vessel. There was excitement on the *Pearl*. In two hours we could see a little of the hull. She was a schooner.

"I think thad the *Orion*," said Captain Marat then. The impulsive Norris had declared it that vessel from the first. Finally came an experience I dread to recollect. We had passed the eastern end of the island, and were abreast of some lesser islands. The schooner ahead was on the starboard tack. We held also on the same tack. The other schooner went about on the port tack. We followed suit. In half an hour black clouds suddenly rose out of the southwest. They were preceded by gray clouds that curled like billows.

Captain Marat at once shortened sail—reefed to the uttermost. The schooner ahead went about and made for a small island to the east. The *Pearl* did the same.

The wind struck us. Rapidly it increased in fury. Captain Marat got a loop of rope round the mainmast, whence he called his orders to Norris and two sailors at the wheel. I never had realized that a vessel could skim the sea with such terrific speed. Spray hissed over the deck. The masts bent; the schooner groaned under the strain. The tempest howled in the rigging. Belated birds flew past, shoreward.

Rapidly that island loomed ahead in the semi-night. Marat used his glasses.

"Hard on!" he yelled at last.

We bore down directly on the land, now close aboard. Robert and I braced ourselves for a shock, for we expected the *Pearl* to strike on the shoals.

Another minute and we saw land on both sides of us.

"Luff! Luff!" shouted Captain Marat.

The *Pearl* went about; the sails flapped angrily; the anchor went overboard, and we lay in the lee of a wooded hill. Bits of trees flew over us—some debris lodged in our rigging, as the fury continued overhead.

In ten minutes all our sails were snug.

"God help Wayne and Ray!" said Norris at last.

"They're safe," said Robert, pointing southward.

In the dim light we could make out a vessel lying some hundreds of yards away and in the lee of that same land.

"Thank God!" said Norris. "Then this is an islet that lies across the outside of this harbor."

"Yes," said Captain Marat. "They come in the other side."

The storm presently lost its fury; in a half hour it was gone, and full light came to show us the *Orion* with her foresail in shreds.

And so it is now that Wayne will take up the story again.

CHAPTER XV

AN EXCHANGE OF PRISONS

Ray and I were escorted down the companionway into the cabin of the *Orion*, and were thrust into a room on the port side. A pair of blacks cut away the cords from our arms; and when they went out we heard a bolt pushed home in the door.

"We travel in style," observed Ray, surveying the pair of bunks, one above the other. "Let's see," he continued, "does your ticket call for an upper or a lower?"

A small, round, glazed porthole gave light, and a porcelain wash-bowl with faucets was fixed in the wall.

"And even a bathtub," said Ray, fingering the piece. "It's almost like being back on the *Pearl* again."

We were waited on by the blacks, who brought our food. The day passed uneventfully; though we spent much time at the porthole (which we finally succeeded to open, or we must have stifled) we saw not so much as a sail, nor a glimpse of the land. This last would be explained either on the score that the island lay on the other—the starboard—side, or that the *Orion* had sailed out of view of the land. She might even be on a course to the west, going back home again, now. It was not till the stars were out that this point was settled. It was by those twinklers we learned we were on an eastern course.

The next morning we got a view of the land. It was just after the *Orion* had gone about on the starboard tack. The mountains loomed up but four or five miles away. And while the vessel slowly came up into the wind, I eagerly scanned the horizon for a sail that should seem to be the *Pearl*. But there was no ship of any kind in view. My heart sank. Could it be that after all they had not ferreted out our secret message?

The day following, sometime before noon, we heard sounds of excitement on the vessel. And we heard Duran's voice; "cussing in French," Ray said he was doing.

We got to the porthole.

"They must have got sight of the *Pearl*," I said. Our hopes were high. Even on the starboard tack, we saw nothing but the sea, now fallen almost calm.

A half hour passed; we were again at the porthole.

"There she is!" cried Ray and I together. The *Pearl* was in view.

Soon the wind was on us, as we could hear; and it grew dark. There was much scurrying on the deck overhead. Spray began to come in through our porthole, and we must close it. We could see birds rushing by. Our course was changed; no longer could we see the *Pearl*. The roar of the storm increased every moment.

"It must be a hurricane," said Ray.

At last we saw land close by our porthole. Directly, we were in lee of it, and we heard the anchor go overboard.

"Well, we're in some kind of a harbor," I told Ray.

"But where's the *Pearl*?" returned he.

"I hope she'll make the same harbor," I said.

The storm blew over, and broad daylight came once more. We watched continually at the window of our prison; but while we saw land all about, beaches and palms, and hills beyond, no vessel showed to us. If the *Pearl* were near she must be off our starboard. But we were not left long in doubt.

The bolt clicked, and our door opened. Duran appeared, and four blacks, who set to work to bind our arms again to our sides. We were led up on deck.

There lay the *Pearl*, some hundreds of yards away. My heart jumped at sight of her.

Accompanied by Duran, we were hurried over the side into a boat, which set off immediately toward a beach to the south-east. We could see our friends but imperfectly on the deck of the *Pearl*, where their figures moved about in some hurry.

We were nearing the shore when we saw a boat put off from the *Pearl*. Then a second boat moved out from the *Orion*, filled with blacks, bearing guns. A few minutes, and we were startled by the boom of an explosion, and smoke rose from the *Pearl*.

My heart sank. But then I saw the blacks in the water, and their boat seemed knocked to bits. The smoke dispersed, and I saw the *Pearl* as right as ever.

"They've got a cannon," murmured Ray in my ear. "That is Norris."

The blacks swam toward the *Orion*. Duran gazed, rage in his look; and he swore roundly. He directed the men to a hurried landing. We were hustled out, pushed in among the cocoa palms, thence back into the brush. We came to a stop, and the four blacks, leaving their two guns with Duran, went back. It was doubtless to pull the boat up into concealment; for they soon appeared again, and the march was taken up.

- 85 -

What direction we went I had no means of knowing, but the ground gradually rose, and we came to where the undergrowth was less dense. This proved an agreeable change—if anything in our situation could be called agreeable, for in the briars and brush, Ray's and my arms fast, as they were, we could not protect our faces from the growth, that whacked and scratched us, as we were pushed hurriedly forward.

At last, after some casting about, Duran had the blacks get down on their hands and knees and literally drag the two of us into a most dense thicket, Duran going before, cutting a way. Many yards we went thus, scraping the ground; and we were finally dropped at the foot of a great tree which appeared to stand alone in the midst of the thicket. Here was a small space free of thicket growth; knives removed encroaching pieces of growth. Bags of food, that had been hanging by the necks of the blacks, were transferred to the low-hanging limbs of the trees, and preparations were made for some stay.

Duran crawled out of the place again, doubtless to reconnoiter.

Ray called after him as he started off on hands and knees—"Hey' there! You!" Duran stopped and looked back. "Don't be late back for supper," continued Ray.

Duran cursed him and went, upon which Ray turned with a serious face on one of the blacks, he that spoke English, and said, "Your boss' Sunday School education has been neglected. What do you say we start a mission right here?"

The black grinned. It was not his first experience of Ray's drollery.

We had indeed cause for cheer—knowing that our friends were so near to us. I was now sure that they had fathomed our hidden message. We felt confident, too, that Duran would not attempt again to get us away on board the *Orion*; and that one way or another we would win back to the *Pearl*. Ray and I contrived to talk on these things, by veiling our speech beyond the comprehension of that one black listener.

"And where do you think they got their dog?" said Ray, meaning, of course, the barker—cannon.

"Back in that town, of course," I returned. "I've no doubt if we'd have gone sight-seeing, we'd found many old dogs of that species on the tumble-down ramparts."

"Just like Norris," said Ray. "And I suppose the 'skunk's' new game of 'pussy wants a corner' is like the old one."

"Yes," I said. "When they're off hunting for this new corner, he's got Ray and Wayne in, the 'skunk' means to make after that hole of his without company."

And so on we continued.

The black man listened to our talk, eyes large with noncomprehension. He, of course, could not know that "skunk" was Norris' pet name for Duran.

That our friends would immediately be searching the island for us, we had not the least doubt. That they had seen us in the boat making shoreward, and had put off in a boat, to intercept the blacks and rescue us, was a thing plain enough. We understood well that that cannon-shot—that had found its mark with such telling effect—was sent to destroy the boat full of blacks that had left the *Orion* to reinforce the blacks in our boat.

That our friends would have great difficulty to find us amongst all this jungle growth was certain. But now what would Duran contrive, to accomplish his purpose? He was intelligent enough to know that however securely he might truss and gag us, there was no assurance that we might not succeed to worm out of our bonds and get to the *Pearl*, before the *Orion* should be far enough away to insure against our catching up with him again. Would he leave some of his blacks to guard us? None would agree to this; for it would mean nothing less than finally to fall into the hands of our party. Who among them would have the stomach for that—particularly in view of that gold that lay at the other end of the rainbow?

There was no fire made for supper, which was eaten cold. Ray and I had our arms freed by the blacks, who put the cords on our legs. It was a great relief to have the use of our hands again, for we had become infested by "chiggers"—wee red insects that burrowed into our skins, causing severe itching and pain. Therefore it was little sleep we got when night came. The blacks were not free of the pests, and so we had four waking guards; and two guns between them to discourage ideas we had of escape.

The moon was well down behind the trees when Duran came crawling back. He had a strange white man with him. I got no proper look at the man in the dark, but his voice and manner put no encouragement in my heart. That he was some sort of scoundrel was not hard to perceive.

"Here they are," spoke Duran, in a low tone.

"Well," returned the man, "shake yourself, and let's get out o' this."

In two minutes we were being dragged out of the thicket again. Silently, and with some hurry, the party stumbled through the woods. When I got a view of the stars, I perceived that we were making in an easterly direction. In less than an hour a halt was made. We were still in the forest, but I could hear the surf not far off, and so knew we were close to water.

There was a tent under the trees, and four other white men came forward. The blacks squatted on the ground, Ray and I between them. Duran was in colloquy with one of the whites.

"There's no use wastin' yer breath on that, I'm tellin' ye," said the man. "We don't sail away from here. We got business here that's pressin'. Five thousan' ain't temptin' us, with others on the island."

"Yes, but I give five t'ousand more if you keep them one week," said Duran. "And—"

"Now looky here," interrupted the other. "It's no use. Besides we got as purty a little place to hide them in, the devil himself couldn't find them. We don't sail away with them, that's sure as shootin'. It's just a thousand apiece down, we hold them a week, and if you succeed, it's a thousand apiece more, when you come back in a month, that's all there is to it. Now mush along after the spondulicks afore it's daylight an' too late, or maybe their friends has got some gold, and—"

"No—No!" said Duran. "They can never have what I have. When I come back I breeng ten thousand—you see!"

Duran and the four blacks were soon gone, and Ray and I had new keepers. One of the five white men remained by us, while the other four moved off out of ear-shot for some sort of discussion. Ray sought to talk with our guard, but he would have none of it.

"Shut your palaver!" he ordered. And he made a threatening gesture.

Within two hours Duran appeared. Then came the counting of money, in bills and gold, in the light of the lantern. Each white man took his own share, and smacked his lips over it.

"You keep them one week," said Duran, then. "I come back in one month, and I give you ten thousand, maybe more if I succeed well."

And he was off again in the dark forest.

CHAPTER XVI

THE ESCAPE

"That was good business," said the leader of the five.

"And bad policy," broke in Ray.

"Shut your yap!" said the man. "And who was askin' your opines?"

"Oh, I've got a big heart for the miserable and ignorant," returned Ray.

"And a long tongue for a kid, I'm thinkin'," said the man.

"It'll be short when I get to talking to some purpose," snapped Ray.

"It's time we're shovin' them in the hole," said the leader now. "Darby, it'll be your watch first," he continued as they led us away.

In ten minutes we were at the foot of a hill, stumbling over roots, and stooping to avoid the branches.

"Now bend your backs an' come on," ordered the man in front.

We pushed through a tangle of growth, and next, stood in the cool of a cave, as we saw by the light of the lantern. It was a room fifty or sixty feet across.

"Looks like there's been an earthquake in here," observed Ray.

The dirt of the floor, for the greater part, was in irregular mounds. It was evidently done with spade and pick, for nothing else would account for the condition it was in.

"They're hunting for treasure," I said in Ray's ear.

We sat crouched against the cool of one of the heaps.

The men had squatted close to the entrance. A bottle was produced.

"Here's two fingers to the success o' this new deal," said the leader, turning the bottle bottom up in the midst of his beard.

The flask went round to the others. One said—"Here's hopin' he'll come back with the ten thousand." And another—"Here's wishin' him in h—l if he don't," as he drank.

"Well the kids' party ain't after our game, that's a comfort," said one, lighting his pipe.

"Why not turn the kids loose, an' so we'll get rid o' the whole mob o' them?"

"Why not? you says; an' you claim to have brains in that thing on your shoulders! Now didn't our man with the money say as how his success depended on keepin' the kids' party here a week, an' ain't our ten thousand dependin' on his success?"

"Well, he'll never come back with no ten thousand, success or no success."

"Maybe no, but I'm willin' to take a chance on it, since the chance is so cheap."

They soon fell into discussion of other topics.

"Granddaddy Par always said it was buried in three places. Now because some others have been before us in this cave, it's no sign they have been before us in the other places. If I hadn't been such a little kid when he showed me that map, and said as how he'd take me with him some day an' go after the stuff—it was always 'some day,' and the rheumatiz never left him till he died. As I was sayin', if I hadn't been such a little kid, I'd made a copy o' the map."

"It's queer you can't remember nothin' on the map."

"I see it in my dreams, times; but when I wakes it's all gone. But I think we're on the right track. That old harpoon grown tight in that crotch o' the tree, pointin' over to the two trees, blazed, wasn't for nothin'."

"How do ye know them's blazes on the trees?"

"It's plain ye ain't no woodsman. They ain't nothin' can cause such marks 'cept blazin'. An' the best thing about it—there ain't been no diggin' anywhere in that place."

And so they continued till the bottle was finished, and all had dozed off except the man they called Darby, who came over and had a good look at our bonds.

Ray and I were wakened by voices. The treasure-hunters were all stirring, preparing to go off to their day's digging. One they called Stephen Conry remained to be our guard. He brought us food when the others had gone.

"Now, ye'll not monkey with the ropes," said our guard, examining the knots on our limbs, after having given our hands freedom. "I'm quick on the trigger when I'm mad. So no gum games on Conry. Heed that!"

"Oh! I wouldn't part with these ropes for anything," said Ray. "I'm getting so used to them I couldn't sleep without them. I'd be afraid someone would kidnap me if I didn't have them."

The man stared, lacking humor.

"You'd be none the worse off, if you turned us loose," I told the man. "And you'll be no better off if you keep us. That man will never come back. He isn't the kind—"

"We ain't goin' to discuss that," returned the man. "We'll turn you two loose, 'none the worse off,' when the time's up, not afore." And he went back to the entrance of the cave, leaving the lighted lantern on a box.

My mind was taken with painful reveries. Our party was now facing failure again. Here had Duran got the two of us hidden in a place, our new guards declared, would never be found out by our friends. Never is a long time, you'll say. But suppose our party was to delay two or three days in the search for us? Would not Duran then be off beyond possibility of following, and so gain to the mine without fear of detection? That he had much reason to fear our pursuit there had been ample evidence. And now he had paid five thousand dollars to these men to hold us—and thus indirectly to hold all our party—for a week, that he might safely hie away to finish enriching himself from the mine of the Brills.

These reflections made me squirm with impatience. Some way must be found to accomplish escape before night, for then Duran would surely be off, and all of us undone. Our guard, I saw, kept a sharp eye out, so we durst not even look at our bonds.

A little before noon, John Mullins, the leader of the treasure-hunters, came crawling into the cave, chuckling over a bit of news.

"And what do you think, Steve? The kids' friends have been 'round, askin' if we'd seen anything of them. There was three on 'em; a big fellow with a rifle and two kids. He said it was two boys they was lookin' for. I says I ain't never seen no boys on this island 'cept them he had with him. An' then he wants to know if we'd seen some black cannibals, an' a white cannibal amongst 'em. Think o' that, Steve, cannibals!

"'Lor' bless you!' I says, 'there ain't no cannibals in this part o' the world!'

"'Well,' says he, 'you can take it from me as how there's no less'n a dozen cannibals on this here island now, an' a white skunk is their leader.' Now what do you think o' that, Steve Conry?"

"I—I don't rightly make it out," said Steve, ruminating—scratching his head. "They must o' had their bellies full when they left the kids with us to keep. Now do you suppose," went on Steve with a new thought, "as how maybe they mean to come back at the end o' the week we was to keep the kids, an' that then they're expectin' to have their appetites again, an' eat the kids—an' then eat us too, an' get back the five thousan' to boot?"

I nudged Ray at this, and got a poke in return.

"Ha! That's all bosh," laughed the other. "They ain't no more cannibals than you an' me. The feller was just tryin' to scare us—maybe thought he'd get us to help them against the black crowd—whatever the game is, but I let him see John Mullins wasn't born yesterday, and not frightened o' bogey stories. So when he saw it was no use he just moved on. Well, Steve, you go an' get your grub, an' bring a snack for the kids. We got to keep 'em fed up for the cannibals." And he laughed at his joke.

Steve disappeared through the hole, and Mullins turned to Ray and myself.

"I reckon your friends 'd pay a nice little wad to get ye back," he ventured.

"I reckon they wouldn't," I promptly told him. I began to fear he might try them, and perhaps find Julian too willing to offer a reward for us. I had another idea than that.

"Oh, you don't think they would, hey?" said Mullins, a bit taken aback by my answer. "I thought," he said, "they was kind o' keen to get ye."

The thought of that piece of indelible pencil in my pocket rose in my mind again. "Well, they might if I was to write them a note telling them to."

"Oh," said Mullins, "if you was to write them a note." He ruminated. "Now that would be tellin' them we knew where you was. Well, we'll think about it a day or two."

A day or two, I thought, wouldn't suit our book.

Steve had soon returned, and Mullins went out. Our guard came to see to our bonds; and he twisted his head in a way that told me he had something on his mind.

"These here niggers," he began, "they ain't no cannibals, I reckon?"

"Well, they sure are," said Ray. "I reckon we ought to know."

The man looked to me, as if for my verification.

"Yes, they're cannibals," I told him. And then went on to relate to him something of the doings that night in the forest, recounting how I'd seen Duran with the knife at the throat of the child, and the kettle for the boiling of the human meat. And I was careful to tell him about the grown man who had been buried alive, and in the night disinterred by the voodoos who had torn out his heart and lungs to be devoured. I assured him I had looked on the wife of the man, while she told the story, which had been verified by others. My story, being fact, rang true, and I could see the man was nine parts convinced, and not a little frightened.

A number of things had come under my observation. Our guard kept a knife on a little ledge by the entrance to the cave, which knife he used to cut tobacco for his pipe. And it was the practice to tie our hands tight with thongs whenever the guard wished to leave the cave for a minute or two. While the man, Steve—he was the weakest of the five—smoked his pipe near the entrance and ruminated over the story I'd told him, I whispered to Ray, giving him a plan I had for escape. Our present guard was to remain on till the next morning, when he would be relieved by one called Joseph Glasby.

Once, when Steve Conry came to set the thongs on our wrists preparatory to a turn outside, Ray showed a pair of sore wrists—he had contrived the marks—and begged that he would not pull the strings so tight as to crucify him that way. The man was impressed, and the thongs were set a bit looser.

When the guard was gone, Ray tugged for a moment, and—"It's easy," he said, and he held up his hand. His hands were thin, a little easing of the knot, and he slipped them out of the thongs. But we heard the guard coming, and he slipped his hands back into his bonds again.

"They're a long time away," grumbled Conry. "I'm gettin' tired o' this."

"Where are they gone?" said Ray.

"They've gone to have a look at the ships—your friends' an' the other one," he said. "There's too much o' this puttin' things on—"

His grumbling was cut short. There occurred some kind of concussion, that shook the earth. Particles fell from the roof of the cave to the floor.

"An earthquake!" shouted Ray.

Conry jumped erect. And the next moment he was scrambling out through the hole.

"Now, Ray!" I said.

Ray had his hands out. He rolled to the entrance, got up to the knife. In a half minute both of us were free of our bonds. I grasped a box of matches, then blew out the lantern light.

Conry came crawling back into the cave.

"Humph! What's come o' the light," grunted Conry.

When he went groping for the lantern, Ray and I scrambled out. We were astonished to find it was night, when we came into the open. We hurried through the forest, not caring what the direction, till we should be safely away from the region.

We made what speed we could for a considerable time amongst the undergrowth; and when at last we came to an open space, we heard the surf close by. And we were a good deal taken aback to see a schooner lying at anchor, some way off from the beach, in the small harbor. The bright moonlight showed her outlines plain to us, and she was neither the *Pearl* nor the *Orion*. We had traveled in a circle apparently; and there came the shouting voice of Stephen Conry, nearby, calling his comrades.

"We're back almost where we started from," said Ray.

"Yes," I said. "We'll have to go by the moon, now, or we'll not get anywhere."

We plunged again into the forest, and were careful to keep the moon on our left; this insured our holding our course in a westerly direction. We kept, too, as much as possible to the higher ground, for the going was easier, there being less undergrowth to tangle our feet.

We hadn't been twenty minutes struggling on, when we were startled by a voice just before us. I seized Ray by the arm and dragged him with me into a thick bush.

"It's just like I've been a tellin' ye. The kids' friends tried to sink the other schooner," said the voice of Mullins.

"An' I've been axin' ye," spoke another voice, "for why would they be suddenly—now—be wantin' to sink them. Why didn't they try it afore, if—"

The voices were lost in the forest, as the men went back the way Ray and I had come. We took up our march again, and a half hour had not gone when we arrived at the western end of the island, and stood under the cocoanut palms, looking on the two schooners, the *Pearl* and the *Orion*. A little breeze rippled the waters of the bay. No lights showed on either vessel.

"Doesn't she look good?" said Ray.

"Yes," I assented. "I wish we were aboard."

I led the way up the beach to the north a piece. We wove a bit of matting of palm fans, for a screen; and then soon had collected some dry wood for a signal-fire. We selected our fireplace at the edge of the palms, and so disposed the screen that the fire would be visible to the *Pearl* but not to the *Orion*.

A match was struck; we had a blaze. Using my shirt, I let out flash after flash for the benefit of those on the *Pearl*; and we watched for an answer. For a considerable time we fed the fire, signalled, and watched. But no answering flash came. "Looks like they're dead," grumbled Ray.

"That Mullins didn't talk like it," I returned. "Well, they'll look this way yet!" And I continued to signal.

Then suddenly we heard voices down the beach. Fortunately it was on the screened side of the fire.

"Quick, Ray!" I said. And we buried the fire in sand. We grasped the screen and fled into the brush.

"It's Mullins and his crowd again," I said.

"They've come looking for us," observed Ray.

We went a little way to the north in the forest, and came again to the beach.

"There's a boat from the *Pearl*!" said Ray.

The boat was moving fast toward the beach.

"They're already too far in to signal them," I said. "Let's swim down and crawl to the boat while they're talking with Mullins and his gang."

We entered the water. The little waves helped to keep our heads invisible. We kept out from the beach till we were in line with the boat and the group on shore. It was then we moved directly to the boat, and got our heads close under the gunwale. I then rose close to a thole and peeped over. The moon was fairly bright.

I could see Robert and Julian between the group and the boat. I gave a low whistle intended to carry only so far as to the boys. Twice I repeated it. Then Robert started. Once more I whistled low. Robert now joined Julian, and the two came into the boat.

They made of themselves a screen for us, while Ray and I climbed in. And we lay ourselves down under the thwarts.

CHAPTER XVII

JULIAN'S STORY AGAIN—THE SEARCH FOR THE LOST COMRADES

The storm had put things on the *Pearl* topsy-turvy. Norris' first care was for his cannon, of which he was happy to find the lashings had held. He threw off the tarpaulin.

"Ah!" he said, "she's O. K. Just a little—"

He was cut short by Robert.

"There goes a boat!" cried Robert. "And there's Wayne and Ray in it!"

"The h—l!" said the staring Norris, and he ran to where Captain Marat and two sailors were unlashing one of our boats. In a pair of minutes we had it in the water.

"Robert, Julian, Carlos," spoke Captain Marat. "We go."

Captain Marat and Carlos each took up a rifle, and the next minute we were pulling for shore. We had not covered half the distance to the beach, when we were attracted to another boat moving from the *Orion*, this one full of black men. Then Norris' cannon boomed. That boat full of black men took the shot in the middle and ceased to be a boat. I saw men swimming toward the *Orion*. Some must have been killed, though I could not tell for the debris.

"Norris got them!" Robert said, exulting.

Captain Marat's eyes danced. "Thad Englishman one ver' good man," he said.

We hurriedly pulled to the beach and sprang out. We ran down the beach a way, then pushed through the cocoanut palms and into the forest, to head off those with Wayne and Ray. But we were too late, and the forest too thick, we could not see them. We searched for hours; and then it began to grow dark, so we went back to the *Pearl*.

"When they got in the jungle you had no chance," said Norris, when we told of our failure. "I'll have a try in the morning," he added.

Rufe had supper on the table. While we ate, we talked over what was to be done.

"It ver' plain what Duran he want to do," said Captain Marat. "He want to hide thee boys again, an' w'en we look for them, then he sail away."

"Well it's up to us," said Norris, "to see that he doesn't sail away till we find them. Now, and I'll bet he don't!"

We divided the night into two watches; nine to twelve, and twelve to three. Norris, Robert, and I were to take the first watch, Captain Marat and Carlos that from twelve to three. We were to go in the small boat to the islet, and move along the beach to some place near the *Orion*, and observe any activity that might be going on there.

During that first watch all was quiet on the *Orion*. There was little movement on her deck, which was plainly visible in the bright moonlight. There were one or two wounded, as we could see by the conduct of those waiting on them.

It was during Captain Marat's watch that Duran returned aboard in the other boat. It was plain, Captain Marat said, that Wayne and Ray were not in the boat with him.

Day had just dawned when Norris and Robert and I climbed down into the boat to go ashore in search of the boys.

"Now, Captain Marat," said Norris, as we cast loose, "the first signs that skunk shows of clearing out, give him that shot alongside. I'll hear it an'll be back in a jiffy. And we'll soon have him out of his notion."

"All righ'," said Captain Marat. "I do like you wish."

We pulled our boat high on the beach and cut brush and covered it, to hide it and protect it from the hot sun. We searched all over the south half of the island—it was three or four miles long. We saw no signs of our two missing friends.

Near noon, we came to the eastern end of the island, where were two hills. And there we were surprised to see a schooner in a small bay. A tent was among the trees close to the beach.

"We'll have to see what's here," said Grant Norris. And he walked up and lifted the flap of the tent. "No one home, it seems," he added.

We had a good look at the schooner. *Susanna* showed on her bows.

"I won't be satisfied till we've had a look at the Susannians," said Norris. "We'll take a look round for them."

"Here's a new trail, going up this way," said Robert, moving toward the north.

We'd gone above half a mile, a good deal of it in forest not so thick in underbrush, when we heard voices. Then we came upon four rough-looking, bearded men, digging. They saw us, and one of them came forward.

"Good morning," said Norris. "We're looking for a couple of boys that are on this island—wonder if you've seen anything of them."

"Boys," said the man, "I ain't ever seen no boys on this island 'cept them two you got with ye."

"Well," said Norris, "maybe you've seen some black cannibals with a white cannibal among them?"

"Lor' bless you!" returned the man, "there ain't no cannibals in these parts."

"Well," said Norris, "you can take it from me, there's no less than a dozen cannibals on this here island right now, and a white skunk is their leader."

The man had no reply. He looked a little nonplused.

"Well, boys," said Norris, "I guess we'll hike along."

And we moved off, leaving the man staring after us.

It was nearing noon, so we moved directly west. We had promised to be back at mid-day.

"I don't like the looks of those men," said Robert. "And that fellow we talked with—I think he pretended to be surprised when you told him about the black men."

"They don't any of them shine with honesty, that's certain," said Norris. "We'll have to have another look at their place, and their boat."

He had some thought he didn't express.

"What do you suppose they're digging for?" I asked.

"I guess they've got a hunch there's treasure buried on this island," answered Norris. "I wouldn't wonder if this place has been dug over twenty times."

We approached a region of low, wet ground. The smell of the place was sickening. It gave me a feeling of giddiness, a nausea, and depression of spirits. Robert afterward confessed the same thing. He said it made him feel something like death and corruption was rising and surrounding him.

At last we got to our boat, and rowed aboard the *Pearl*. Captain Marat reported that Duran had remained on board the *Orion* all morning, and that the blacks had been busy putting on a new foresail.

Captain Marat and Carlos took their turn on shore, after the noon meal, to search over the north half of the island. Norris, Robert, and myself were to keep watch over the movements of Duran and his black crew.

"What do you think, boys?" said Norris, when we had seen Marat and Carlos disappear among the palms on shore. "Do you think Wayne and Ray might be on that ship of those treasure-hunters?"

"Not very likely," said Robert. "Duran has found a better hiding place. The boat is too public. But I shouldn't wonder if he hasn't some deal with those men."

"Just what I've been thinking," agreed Norris. "But if they're not found by dark we'll have to look out; the *Orion* will sure be trying for a getaway tonight, and we've got to prevent that. I don't think he'll try it in daylight, for he isn't so sure what we might do. But we'll have to know what he's up to."

So we three prepared to embark in the small boat. It was deep water close under the sheltering isle, so both schooners lay fairly close in to the narrow beach of it. We were soon over, and up among the brush of the hill. We found a good lookout, from which we could peer down on the deck of the *Orion*, where the blacks lounged lazily.

"Everything's ready for sailing," said Norris. "And there's that white cuss using his glasses to see what he can see on shore."

It was a tedious afternoon, hot, not a breath stirring. We were glad when the sun set and we saw Captain Marat and Carlos returning. We hurried back to the *Pearl* to meet them.

They were alone. Their faces were gloomy with failure. Not a sign of any kind had they found to encourage them. Rufe was so disappointed, tears were in his eyes.

"I jes' had a kind o' notion," he said, "you-all would a' had dem boys back wid ye dis time. I jes' been fixin' de bes' kin' o' bread puddin', de kin' dem boys was so crazy about. Dey ain't had a decen' meal for ebber so long!"

When we were at supper, and Rufe had poured a second cup of coffee all round; I heard him mumbling to himself, as he went to the galley, "I jes' goin' to save dat puddin' anyway. I ain't goin' to give up—no sah, I ain't goin' to give up." And the pudding was not forthcoming; and no one inquired for it.

Captain Marat and Carlos went to watch the *Orion* this time. The moon was very bright; the cocoanut palms stood out distinct on that shore to the east. Somewhere behind them lay our two friends, Wayne and Ray, and I wondered how they were faring. A light breeze sprang up after nine o'clock, and the ripples danced on the waters of the bay. It was then we saw Captain Marat and Carlos coming in the boat.

"They make ready to sail," said Captain Marat, before he scrambled over the rail.

"High there! Rufe!" called Norris. "Heat that poker." And he went to his gun and threw off the tarpaulin, and with help rolled the carriage round, and trained the gun.

Presently we heard the squeal of a block coming from the *Orion*.

"That means a sail going up," said Robert.

"Now, the poker!" cried Norris.

Rufe came running forward with the glowing iron.

There came a flash and a "Boom!"—and a splash over near the *Orion*. Then we heard the rattle of the block as the sail was allowed to drop.

"They took the hint," said Norris. "That fellow is not so dull."

Marat and Carlos were soon again off to the isle to watch; and Norris rammed home another charge in the brass cannon; and Rufe kept a little fire going in the galley stove. We waited long for another attempt to sail on the part of the *Orion*, but no such news came from the watchers.

At last came an alarm from Rufe. "Dar!" he cried. "You-all—look dar!"

Instinctively we looked toward the *Orion*. Then we turned to Rufe who pointed shoreward. There, under the palms we saw a beacon flashing—flash followed flash.

"It's Wayne and Ray!" cried Robert.

We produced a lantern and signalled back. But the shore signals had suddenly ceased.

"To the boat!" cried Norris.

Directly, the three of us were moving shoreward, Norris and Robert pulling with all their might.

When we touched shore, we saw four men coming from down the beach.

"It wasn't them," said Robert. "The light was up here."

The four were the treasure-hunters.

"It's a fine night," said Norris, moving to meet the men.

"Tolerable," returned the leader.

"But it's awful dry," said Norris. "We've been trying to make it rain. Hear the shot?"

Robert and I fell back, gazing into the shadows under the palms, hoping for signs of Wayne and Ray. Presently I heard a low whistle, just as Robert plucked me by the sleeve and pulled me to the boat.

There were the two boys in the water. We covered them while they climbed in and crawled under the seats.

And so Robert and I moved back to the group. Just to make talk, Norris was quizzing the men about the game on the island; but we contrived, by signs, to convey to Norris that we had news.

"Well, boys," said Norris at last, "let's have another little row before we turn in."

It was a jolly crowd rowed back to the *Pearl*.

"Say, Ray," said Norris. "What did you want to run off and hide yourself that way for?"

"Want to," sniffed Ray. "Oh, just to see how good a hunter you were—wonderful how easy you found us!"

"Well, let's try it again," said Norris, "and I'll bet you my new gun—"

"Thanks," said Ray. "Turn about's fair play, I'm going to stay in base and keep Rufe company."

And here again Wayne takes up the tale.

CHAPTER XVIII

OUR BOAT IS SCUTTLED

When Ray and I set our feet on the deck of the *Pearl* again, I felt a thrill go all through me. I felt like hugging the mainmast. Captain Marat and Carlos were there, and Rufe. Rufe fairly blubbered with happiness.

"Oh, Lordy!" he said, "somebody clap foh me, I jes' got to dance."

And we clapped our hands and patted our thighs in time for him, and he began his "double-shuffle." Carlos caught the infection and jumped into the ring, and there the two black men footed it hot on the deck for five minutes. "Hoo-o-we," yelled Rufe at last, and ran for the galley.

In a little a sumptuous meal was on the table for Ray and me; and while we ate, waited on by the others, we told our story.

"Five thousand dollars!" said Norris. "Duran spending five thousand on the chance of getting us off his trail. That must be some gold mine, that of yours, Carlos."

"Yes, I think," agreed Carlos.

At last came a whole big bread pudding. "I jes' know you was a'comin', an' I saved it," said Rufe.

Ray turned over his stool, as he jumped to give the black a hug. "Oh, if I'd only known that was coming." And he put his hand on his stomach.

When we two had stuffed ourselves the limit, Ray lingered at the table, looking very sober, his chin in his hand, his eyes on the big remaining portion of the pudding. Rufe sidled up.

"What it is make you so sad?" he said.

"Say, Rufe," said Ray, "isn't it the chicken that has two stomachs?"

"I reckon dat's right," said Rufe.

"Well, I guess I'm half a chicken," said Ray.

"Why," said Rufe, "has you got two stummicks?"

"No," returned Ray, a wail in his tone, "but I've got two appetites."

And Rufe rolled on the deck.

"Well, now," said Norris at last, "that voodoo skunk can sail when he gets ready, the sooner the better."

"Yes," agreed Captain Marat. "Now we ready for heem. He ver' clever if he fool us some more, now."

Norris volunteered to take the watch till two o'clock; then Robert offered to follow him. All others turned in.

I awoke, hearing Robert in talk with Captain Marat. "It looks to me like the *Orion's* moving, slowly—no sails up," Robert was saying. In a little while the two climbed into a small boat. The moon had gone down, and it was quite dark. The night breeze was still blowing gently. I again dozed off, too tired to note what was going forward.

I do not know how long I slept this time, but when I opened my eyes next, it was to hear blocks creaking; and jib and mainsail were already set, and the foresail was going up. Marat and Robert had gone to the isle, and hurried over opposite the *Orion's* berth, to find that that schooner's crew had been warping the vessel out toward the south passage. The two waited till the *Orion* had made sufficient progress to set her sails and attain headway, then they had hurried back to set the *Pearl* in pursuit again.

The tail end of a squall came to give us a boost. The *Orion* got a greater portion of it.

Ray did not waken till we were well out in the open sea.

"What!" said he, looking abroad. "Has the island sunk?"

In half an hour the sun burst out of the sea, showing that island astern. The *Orion* was perhaps three miles away, heading a little south of west. It was not till eleven that morning that we got a wind to give us good headway.

Day after day, now again, we kept the schooner, *Orion*, company. She seemed to make no effort to elude us. The nights were bright moonlight, making us an easy task. Then at last we sighted the towering, ragged mountains of the great island of the voodoos. We were to the south of the island this time.

"Looks like that skunk is going the long way round," said Norris.

"Hopes to shake us off somewhere on the south coast, maybe," I suggested.

"Thad is ver' evident," said Captain Marat. "He could save ver' much time to go back by the north coast."

"He'll be up to some new 'gum-game'," said Norris.

And so it proved, as we came to know.

We weathered a number of severe squalls, and sizzled during some calm days. We followed the *Orion* around a point of the island, and into a harbor of that south coast.

We were somewhat disturbed by that movement of Duran's, feeling that it meant some new trouble to meet. We picked a berth for the *Pearl* rather close to the *Orion's*, for we must have a close eye on Duran.

"Perhaps he's going overland," suggested Julian.

"If he does, we'll go overland too," I offered.

"I believe he too lazy," said Carlos. "No railroad—big mountain."

"Well," said Norris, "we'll keep a sharp lookout, and see."

It was past noon when we cast anchor in that harbor. The officials of the place came and went. Duran did not go ashore, though he sent some blacks. Carlos we sent with two sailors, after some needed provisions and water.

The hot tropic sun beat down on us unmercifully; there was scarce a breath of air coming into that place. I sauntered up to Grant Norris, where he leaned, dripping sweat on his tarpaulin-covered cannon, looking over toward the *Orion*.

"To think," he said, "that it depends on that skunk how long we're to lie in this blazing hole. I can almost see him sneering over there."

"Never mind, Mr. Norris," I told him. "Maybe when our turn comes we can pay him back."

"And, oh! Let me at him!" said Norris, "when that time comes."

Then the end of the day came; darkness fell. It turned almost chill, and we turned in below. The moon was due to rise some time after nine, so that there would be but a short time of darkness; and then would come moonlight, making the watch on Duran's movements easy. It was Julian took the first watch, eight to ten. When he called Norris, at four bells—or ten o'clock—the land breeze had already risen. I awoke at the change of watch, for I had come to be a light sleeper, and I heard the little waves rippling along the schooner's hull. I saw, too, that it was bright moonlight; the moon was just past the full.

It was not yet midnight, when I was aroused by a clamor in the cabin. Norris had come in.

"Out with you! Every mother's son of you," he said. "We're sinking."

There was much consternation as we all turned out, jerking on bits of clothing.

We followed Captain Marat into the hold. As we neared the bows, we heard the splash of the water. Marat sent two sailors to the pumps. The rest of us set to work to shift the stores to places out of reach of the incoming water.

To find the leak would require considerable time. Marat soon determined that the water was not coming in so fast but that the pump would be able to hold its own against it.

"We must put thee schooner on the beach," said Captain Marat.

Both boats were manned, and tow-lines put aboard them. The tide was ebbing, so we had great labor to move the schooner toward the mouth of the little river, where Captain Marat looked for a favorable place to lay the bow of the *Pearl*. When we were in the boats and beginning to bend our backs to the labor, we heard the voice of Duran on the *Orion* in a loud, hearty laugh.

"Laugh, you filthy skunk," said Norris, who sat next to me, "I'll never rest till you're paid for all your foul doings."

It was not many minutes till we saw the sails of the *Orion* go up, and the land breeze and ebbing tide, together, carried that schooner off into the open sea, at last beyond our vigilance. I felt a sinking within me at the realization. But I had already had thoughts of what should be done in case we were by some chance to lose sight of Duran.

We had been tugging at our oars for little above half an hour, making very poor progress, when the tide came to the turn. And then we had it with us, and it was not long till we were moving in at a rate almost to make us cheerful again.

It was a black sailor who had discovered the fact of the leak in the *Pearl*. He had heard an unusual sound. It was the trickling water more or less confused with the rippling of the waves against the hull. He had gone to Norris with the news. And Norris had given his ear to the thing only for a moment, before sounding the alarm.

At last we came to the piece of beach aimed for. We took the anchor in a small boat well in to shore, so that as the tide rose the bow of the schooner was pulled more and more on the sand. It would be well toward noon of the new day, before the tide will have reached its height, and so begin to recede, and leave the *Pearl* showing gradually more and more of her hull above water.

We found time to discuss the situation and the probable means employed for our undoing; for no one of us was in any doubt that it was Duran who had done this thing.

"He send one black weeth the augur, or brace and bit, an' drill holes in thee hull," said Captain Marat. And he pointed to a loop of rope still hanging on a starboard bowsprit stay. It was by that rope that the worker had swung himself, while he bored holes into the hull below water-line.

"And to think he sneaked up on me in broad moonlight and did that thing!" said Grant Norris.

"Well, you see," I offered, "the swimmer approached on the opposite side from the *Orion*; and the waves helped hide his head. We none of us dreamed of his trying anything like that."

"We should have done even more than ever dream it," wailed Norris. "And now he'll have at least twenty-four hours the start of us, the best we can do."

CHAPTER XIX

WE STEAL A MARCH ON THE ENEMY

"What I'd like to know," said Robert, "are we going to let that—that—"

"Kidnapper-voodoo priest—cannibal—son-of-a-polecat," prompted Ray.

"What I'd like to know," continued Robert, "are we going to let him beat us after all?"

"Not if I have to go after him single-handed," declared Grant Norris.

"But he's making direct for that gold mine," said Robert.

"There's only one thing to do," Julian offered. "Some of us will have to go overland."

"Yes, that ees it," said Carlos. "We beat him there!"

"What!" said Ray. "Jump over those mountains!" He looked up to those peaks towering many thousands of feet; the morning sun had just set his glow on them.

"Yes," I said. "There are roads over the passes, and the distance can't be over two hundred miles."

"Id is thee only chance," said Captain Marat, "I get thee chart."

The chart was spread on the table.

"Id take anyway five day for the *Orion* to sail round to thee places," said Captain Marat, making measurements, "if she have most favorable wind."

"It won't take over four days to make it overland," I offered, "if we make only thirty miles a day with horses."

"Just so," agreed Captain Marat, verifying my measurements.

"What is more," Robert added, "we know pretty accurately where Duran will land to go to the gold mine."

We all of us caught afire with the prospect, Carlos not the least, for the sailing away of Duran had set a melancholy on his face.

"Hurray!" cried Norris, "we'll beat that skunk yet."

Preparations went immediately forward. Norris, Julian, and Carlos hurried over to the town, to secure horses and a guide. Robert and I set to work on our packs, for it was we two that were to make the overland journey, accompanied by Carlos.

It wanted an hour of noon when the three came back, having been eminently successful. They had found horses in plenty, and no lack of guides.

"Now looky heah," began Rufe, when Robert, Carlos, and I had taken our seats in the small boat. "Don' you-all let dat white voodoo debbil git his han's on you no moh. Keep yo' eyes peeled foh him; he's jes' dat sneaking."

The tide was ebbing when we left the *Pearl*, though it would be some time before the leak in her hull would be uncovered. The horses and guide were waiting at the edge of town. The saddles were on, and the black fellow—our guide—was looking to the cinches. To make fast our packs to the saddles was the work of but a few minutes. The guide had already distributed the needed provisions to the various ponies. Captain Marat, Norris, Ray, and Julian stood in a row when we had mounted.

"Now remember," we told them. "We'll leave a note in the cleft end of a stake—on the top of the first hill, or at the bottom. And we'll blaze trees or bushes, or whatever there is to show the way to it."

"Trust us," said Norris. "We'll find it."

"And say!" broke in Ray. "If there should be any battles on the docket, just hold up operations till Norris gets there with his brass barker and Rufe's red hot poker."

The trees of the forest, into which our road plunged, soon cut off our view of our friends. I felt a little sinking of the heart at this new separation, for there was still much room for mishap before our coming together again. Our guide (Jan was his name) and Carlos rode before; Robert and I carried our little rifles slung at our backs. The ponies were evidently trained to the saddle, and moved at a gait that was something between a walk and a trot, so that our progress was agreeably rapid.

We traversed first the bamboo; then palms, oaks, and mahogany sheltered our way for long stretches. When we came to the foothills, occasionally an open vista gave us view of waving golden-yellow cane fields. The streams were overhung with the wonderful feathery tree-ferns. Oranges, bananas, limes, mangoes, grew in abundance, though only berries were ripe at this season. Our road took us at times into the twilight of the heavier forests, among lofty trunks, from which hung, in festoons and tangles, the rope-like lianas. It was as if innumerable ships had been crammed together in some great storm, their rigging intertwined, and in time all overgrown with green parasites and slimy mosses.

All this display of nature that showed to us on our way, and much more than I have mentioned, I noted; and had my mind been untroubled by serious business, I would have found much delight in this journey into a tropic interior. But we were under the necessity of pressing forward, always with the fear that Duran might come before us to that certain spot of the northern coast, and so elude us and arrive at the hidden mine secure from discovery.

By night we had mounted high among the hills. It was when we saw the azure of the sea and the coast lines begin to darken, and the hills below us fall into shadow, that we dismounted and removed the saddles from our ponies. A quick meal, and soon we were under our mosquito-bars, sleeping.

We were again on the move before the sun had thrown his rays on the highest peaks. And this day it was up and down, and a winding about among the mountains. The day following was but a repetition, except that before night our guide told us that we had passed the greatest of the mountains and were on the downward slope toward the northern coast of the island. But we got no view of the sea till the third day, and then the road rounded a spur of mountain, and there opened to our vision that great blue expanse of sea and the irregular coast line below us.

"We're sure to make it in time now," observed Robert.

"Yes," I said. "The *Orion* cannot get there before us now."

And then, as our ponies continued to plod onward behind those of our guide and Carlos, we made some discussion of our plan of action. It was decided to discharge our guide some way short of our destination, and start him back before he should find opportunity to tell anyone there of having led a pair of white boys across the island and into the region of the voodoos. News of our exploits in those hills had doubtless been spread among all of the voodoo faith; and so if the fact of our return were noised about, we would doubtless have the pack at our heels, and all our plans gone topsy-turvy again.

By noon we were come to a place in the hills fifteen miles from Carlos' old home. It was a region well known to Carlos, as he professed.

"Here very good place to stop," said Carlos. "I go for the provision while you rest here."

We pulled the saddles from the ponies, and Carlos set off alone through the forest. And when he came back, after less than half an hour, he had food to replenish the stock of the guide, who after an hour's rest expressed himself as happy to be on the way back to his home on the south coast of the island. When the guide was gone, Robert and I set to work to stain our faces and hands, and don again those curly wigs. White faces were too rare and unpopular in this region to escape comment and more or less unpleasant attention.

So when we again took up the march we all went afoot; and in three hours we had arrived at the little cove where we had seen Duran's schooner, *Orion*, just before her sailing away with the *Pearl* in chase. We were now ten miles from the city, toward which we turned our steps, keeping under shelter of the palms that skirted the beach.

When we were come within four miles of the city we halted. It was near to the huts where we had made that landing—to go to the interior, trailing Duran to the old palace ruin. It was our plan to send Carlos into the city for articles of food and a rowboat of some kind. When we had come so far, the sun was less than two hours high; so Carlos had but an hour's rest before setting off on his mission.

When at last Carlos had gone, Robert and I settled down amongst the cocoanut palms just above the beach. We watched land crabs and turtles crawling up on the sand; anon we would look into one another's black faces.

"When do you think the *Orion* will get here?" said Robert.

"Tomorrow, if the winds are favorable," I answered; "or a day or two after, if they're not. Duran will come as fast as he can, of course."

"Of course," agreed Robert. "But I can't make my mind give in to the idea that he will land at that place on the beach that you and Captain Marat marked. There can't be any gold mine about that place. Except those two hills, the map shows nothing but sand and palms, and marshes, and bushes."

I brought out of my pocket a folded paper on which I had copied from Marat's chart this portion of the coast. I put my fingers on the Twin Hills, near the foot of which we expected Duran would land; for it will be remembered Marat had heard him say as much, that night when Marat and I, in our own boat, had crept up to the *Orion* in the dark. To the west of the hills was a shallow bay of which the little cove mentioned was a part. To the east and south of the hills lay a greater bay, (not to mention its proper name, we will call it Crow Bay, for it is much the shape of a crow's foot). The neck of land between the two bays was all low, marshy and impenetrable thickets.

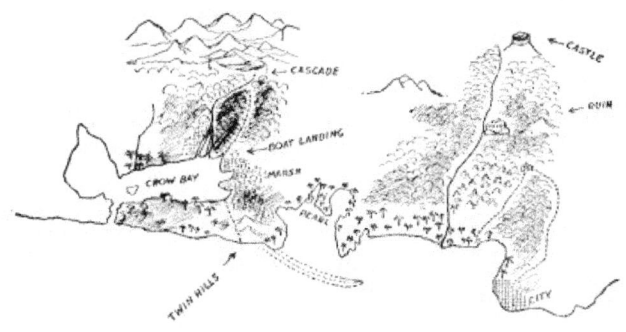

"Now," I said, "I agree with you that this seems not a proper place—at these hills—to make a start for anything like a gold mine. But is not that the very reason that Duran makes his landing here? Isn't it, for some reason or other, the most favorable for covering up his trail? And then, too, landing out there on the open beach, he can easily see whether anyone is following him."

"Yes," said Robert, "that must be it. He's just that shrewd. And then, when he sees his crew row back to the *Orion* and sail away, he knows none of his blacks are following him."

Darkness had soon spread over everything. And it must have been ten o'clock, when we heard Carlos' whistle. And then at our answer a boat's prow touched the sand of the beach. We had our packs and guns aboard in a minute, and Robert and I, each pulling an oar, we moved, paralleling the beach, to the east. The boat was as light as a canoe, almost, and our progress was rapid.

"I find my friend," said Carlos, telling of his visit to the city. "An' he wonder where I been so long. He say Duran have not come back. But he hear much talk among voodoo about devil-guns—shoot, make no noise. My friend help me find this boat. He buy it for me—eight dollar. The man glad to sell for much money."

In an hour the moon—now in the last quarter—came out of the sea in front of us. We rowed round the point, into the bay. We passed the narrow entrance to the little cove, and made for the east side of the bay, where a bight of the bay pushed in to within a mile and a half of the back of the Twin Hills, as our bit of chart showed us.

We carried our boat above the beach into the bushes, and so made our camp, at midnight.

When the sun rose we were abroad, and soon we had picked our way over to the Twin Hills. They lay some way apart, towered perhaps a hundred feet, and were grown over with brush. We climbed to the top of that nearest the beach. That vantage point gave us a splendid view of the beach and sea.

All that day some of us remained there on the lookout. The *Orion* did not come. We all three made our beds there that night. Before morning a squall sent us scampering back to our boat, and we escaped a drenching by turning the little vessel bottom up and creeping under.

Another day passed on the hill-top, and no *Orion* came.

"I wonder if he's fooled us again," said Robert.

"I don't think it," I answered.

"I think he come," encouraged Carlos.

I was sleeping soundly when an insistent hand on my shoulder brought me suddenly awake. It was Robert, whose watch was eleven to one.

"They're here," he said. "I heard a block rattle."

Carlos was now up. We could barely make out a dark mass well out from the beach; the night was very dark in spite of the brilliancy of the stars. We scrambled down the hill, and in a few minutes were in the bushes that fringed the beach.

Not many minutes more passed till we heard oars knocking in the tholes. And then a small boat touched the sand, and a figure stepped out.

CHAPTER XX

THE MYSTERIOUS TRAIL

That figure stood there many minutes, almost immobile, like a tree-stump. Then, when I saw that black mass of ship out on the sea begin to move, the figure stooped, took some bulky thing from the ground and started off inland.

We followed cautiously—ah, how cautiously! It was a ticklish period of our business. The rustling in the brush ahead, now and then, told us how he went.

Near two miles that figure led us thus. And then came a halt on the shore of Crow Bay. We could hear him in the water, into which he waded. And we crawled close, and made out he was tugging at something on the bottom.

In a little, he had dragged a canoe onto the shore, and with some labor he turned out the water. I could hear him mumbling to himself, and chuckling, as it seemed, while he took up his burden and set it in the canoe. That sound of his voice with its unpleasing quality settled his identity for me. It was Duran.

He sat himself in the little boat, and pushing with a paddle, moved off from shore.

"We've got to follow close," I whispered to my comrades. "Robert, you better stay, and Carlos and I will try swimming for it. If I send for you, leave a note on the top of the hill."

I removed my shoes while I talked, and Carlos and I waded in. The water was shallow, and we pushed along with some rapidity, digging our toes into the sandy bottom. We came, in time, to deeper water, and swam a short way, then touched bottom again. And presently we came up on a piece of beach and sprinted round a tongue of land. This brought our quarry within view again. So, though we lost sight of him when again we were obliged to enter the water and cross another broad bayou, a second and longer run on the beach, round a broader tongue of land, gave us his view once more.

One more swim for it, and we came up in time to see Duran paddling into an inlet, or bayou, in the south shore of Crow Bay. By this time the moon had risen. But its light served only to show us the extent of the marshy place we were in, among the tall reeds. Progress was impossible, except by way of the shallow water of the inlet, for there was no beach here.

Wading, we continued on the trail, though the canoe was beyond our view. We had gone thus, in the bayou, some little way, when we noted, in the dim moonlight, the place where the canoe had been dragged in among the reeds.

And close by was the beginning of a path, and the ground was solid; and heavy, bushy growth replaced the grasses.

We now ran forward, hoping to sight Duran before he should come to some turning and be lost to us. We went thus, miles it seemed, and the path took us, in time, out of the open and into the forest. Here the feel of our bare feet on the path was our only guide. The forest ended, and we came out into a glade; still there was no sign of him we followed. Carlos stooped to the ground, pushing aside the grasses that lined the trail. With eyes and fingers employed together he sought for marks.

"Yes," he said at last, "he go here."

And so we pushed on, the trail soon taking us into another piece of forest growth. But our path came to an abrupt end at the bank of a stream. And here some rays of moonlight, coming in through interstices of the green canopy, showed fresh marks of some one having gone into the water. We hesitated but a few moments, and stepped into that cool stream, following up its course a hundred yards.

It was then we came, of necessity, to a final stand. Before us towered, for hundreds of feet, sheer cliffs of rock. The stream came pouring out of a hole at the foot. The waters, where they made their exit from the earth, were divided by a large rock. That part on the left rolled out in a smooth flood. On the right of the rock the water came over a ledge, to tumble down in a thin cascade of three feet in height.

The light of the moon came more and more into that space among the trees; and we examined the banks for marks of the way Duran had gone. Within two hours day broke; and, retracing our steps, we went back to where that trail entered the stream, and we carefully searched both banks all up and down for traces. But nowhere was there a mark of any kind to show where he we sought had left the water.

"Well," I said at last to Carlos, "he might soon be coming back this way; so we'll have to watch. If I stay here do you think that you and Robert can carry our boat across the neck of land into Crow Bay?"

"Yes," said Carlos, "that not so very hard. The boat light."

"Well, then," I said, "suppose you go back, and you and Robert get the boat into the bay, and hide it in the reeds somewhere near where Duran hid his canoe. But tell Robert to leave a note on the top of the hill, telling our friends on the *Pearl* to wait there to hear from us."

"Yes," returned Carlos, "I do that."

But I got an hour's sleep before Carlos was started on the back trail, and then settled down in a nest of brush on the stream's bank, to watch for the possible return of Duran.

Over my head, and almost meeting the trees of the opposite bank of the stream, were the tree-tops, through which the rays of the morning sun were now creeping. The lianas hung all about; birds glided from limb to limb. And there, on my right, was that high wall of cliffs, and the water gushing out of the rocks. The splashing of the little cascade on the rocks overwhelmed other sounds, of insects and birds.

I thought long on the curious disappearance of Duran, leaving no trace to point the way he had gone. I looked at that rock wall and wondered if perhaps he could have had a rope ladder hanging there, up which he had gone, pulling it after him. I had read of such things. But the cliff was too high, and there was no landing-place on that sheer wall that would have given foothold even to a mountain goat. It was very certain that he could not have climbed from the water out on the bank anywhere above that spot where his path went into the stream, without leaving unmistakable marks on the ground. So that the only surmise left me was that he had waded down the stream, and climbed out on the opposite bank. When Carlos and Robert should come we would see. But it was chagrining to have followed Duran so far, and then to have lost him just when we had reason to believe we were coming near to the hidden mine.

CHAPTER XXI

WE SEEK IN VAIN FOR A LOST TRAIL AND DISCOVER A LONE MONKEY

The sun's rays were coming down almost perpendicularly through the interstices in that green canopy over my head, when Robert and Carlos appeared, wading in the stream.

"Did you get the boat over?" I asked.

"Yes," said Robert, "and it's hid in the high grass not far from that canoe."

"And you left a note on the top of the hill?"

"Yes," he answered. "I told them to wait for us."

I explained the situation to Robert, showing him where we had lost the trail of Duran. And while we made a meal on food brought by the two, we discussed our situation and determined our movements.

"Well, then, Bob," I concluded, "if you'll stay here and watch, Carlos and I will have a look down stream, and then, maybe, along the cliff."

We two had soon got to the other bank, and in a few minutes had passed a point opposite the spot where the path entered the water. We kept to the water as we scrutinized the soft dirt banks. The brook soon widened, and it became more shallow, till finally—some mile or more toward the bay—it emerged from the forest and spread out to diffuse itself into a number of bayous, taking slow movement among the grasses and reeds.

Nowhere along that course were there any signs of anyone having climbed out over the banks. So now Carlos and I retraced our steps, and picked our way through the forest till we came to the foot of those high cliffs. For above two miles we searched for a break in that great wall, and the forest continuing all that way. Then we went back to where Robert kept watch by the stream. We stopped to report our failure, and again set off, this time skirting the cliffs to the west.

We must have covered three miles this way, when the cliffs melted into more sloping ground, till finally we came to where it should be possible to climb to the heights. But nowhere did we see any path, or any mark to show that others had trod the region before us. The afternoon now was nearly gone, and I turned to Carlos.

"Well, Carlos," I said, "the only thing left for us is to camp back there where we lost Duran's trail and wait for the *Pearl*."

"Yes," returned Carlos. "Duran he sure to come back sometime—maybe one week—maybe little more."

Night was nearly on us when we had joined Robert again.

"Isn't it about time for the *Pearl*?" asked Robert.

"The moon will be up about half-past-two," I answered. "Then two of us might go and have a lookout for her."

Taking two-hour watches turn about, we slept till morning. Then Robert and I started, leaving Carlos to keep the watch for Duran. Crossing the west end of Crow Bay, we made landing at the end of the trail that led from the sea side, and by half-past-four of the morning came to Twin Hills.

On the peak of that hill which stood nearest the beach, we came upon a figure stretched on the ground, sleeping peacefully. It was Ray Reid. It was good to see the dear lad.

I shook him gently.

"Don't, Wayne," he said. "You'll shake the gas out of the balloon. We've got to make the other side of the mountain—that's where the gold mine is."

He was either dreaming or pretending. I lifted him by the shoulders. "Ray! We're here," I said.

"Not yet," he returned. "It's not—" And then he opened his eyes.

"What the Sam—" he began. And he gazed on Robert and myself, wonderingly.

"Say!" he continued. "You spoiled the most scrumptious dream I ever had. I was sailing through the clouds—that soft and nice—on the way to the gold mine. But I suppose you kids have got your pockets full of gold; let's see the color of it; what have you done with Duran and the rest of those voodoos? Do you know I came up on top of this hill so's to get a good running start if that polecat (as Norris calls him) got after me; well, what have you been up to—why don't you say something?"

"Say something!" I mocked. I guess my smile nettled him.

"Say," he began again, "if I talked as much as you don't, Wayne, my tongue would soon grow callouses on it. But back to business," he continued. "What have you done with that Duran? I haven't seen him for a coon's age. I've got so I'm not happy if I don't see him around."

"Take us to the *Pearl*," I answered, "and I'll tell you all there is to tell."

We descended the hill, and Ray led us to that bay, a mile and a half west, even past the spot where Robert, Carlos, and I had first pulled up our little boat.

A half mile more, and we came upon the *Pearl*, looking pretty in the moonlight, resting just within a deep water inlet, and hidden behind the tall cocoanut palms. A low whistle brought the small boat to shore for us.

It was again a happy reunion, and there came the exchange of tales. That of the *Pearl's* adventures was simple; they had mended those augur-bored leaks with little difficulty. But they were delayed thirty-odd hours, waiting for a spring tide, enough to float them off. The voyage round the upper end of the island had been without unusual happenings. Captain Marat had seen fit to pass the city after dark; and his chart had guided him to the present berth of the *Pearl*, the markings on the map showing water a plenty; and it seemed a likely hiding place, one Duran and his voodoos were not apt to visit, if Carlos' account of their usual practice had any value.

"I mightily would like to have a look at that place where you lost that skunk's trail," observed Norris. "That gold mine can't be very far away from there, and we'll find it whether or no."

"And where did they go with the *Orion*, do you think?" asked Julian.

"They sail her on down thee coast, to draw us away from here, w'en we come," said Captain Marat.

"It's a wonder they didn't go into Crow Bay," said Norris. "It's a fine hiding place, according to the chart."

"And yet Duran might have considered it too near the place he's wanting to hide from us," I offered.

"Well, now, when are we going to get up there where Carlos is?" said Norris, impatient to be doing.

"Say, Wayne," said Ray. "Norris has pretty nigh worn out the deck, tramping up and down; and over there on shore his clod-hoppers have flattened out all the grass for a mile around. For heaven's sake sick him after that 'polecat' before he starts an earthquake."

Julian volunteered to remain behind with Rufe and the sailors to guard the schooner. Captain Marat, Norris, Ray, Robert, and myself, set off to rejoin Carlos. The little boat was well laden with the five of us in her, but it was quiet water we moved on.

It was broad day, which suited us illy, since we did not wish to be seen in the region by anyone who might get the news to Duran. But in the crossing of Crow Bay, only Robert and I showed our faces above the gunwale; and the visible portions of our skins, it will be remembered, were stained black.

We concealed the rowboat again among the reeds, not far from where lay that canoe of Duran's, and it was not long till we had joined Carlos.

"Duran—no one—come," reported Carlos.

"Well, it's up to us to find out where he's gone," said Grant Norris.

"Well, here's the chance you've been steaming for," said Ray. "Here's the end of the trail, where it goes into the water; only I'll bet he took to a balloon right here. You know, too, I dreamed of a balloon last night, and if Wayne hadn't waked me just when he did, I'd be at that gold mine right now."

"Yes," returned Norris, "and you'd have to go to sleep to dream yourself back again."

"Well," shot back Ray, "why not? Maybe the gold mine is all a dream, after all."

"Ah, no," declared Carlos, "it no dream. I see the gold—my father show me."

We made up three parties for the search. Norris and Carlos went east; Captain Jean Marat and I west; Robert and Ray remained to watch by the stream.

Captain Marat and I picked our way through the forest to the west for the three miles, to the place where the sloping ground permitted an ascent to the heights backing the cliffs.

The climb was a stiff one, and there was no path or way cleared of the brush, and so were our difficulties increased. When we had gained a sufficient height we moved toward the east, intending to explore the region that looked down on the stream where were Robert and Ray. But we encountered cliffs again, above those other cliffs, that kept us off some miles to the back of that region we hoped to penetrate.

After a short stop at noon, for a bite of food out of our pockets, we continued moving eastward through the cedars that ornamented this new line of cliffs, towering so many hundreds of feet above those lying between us and Crow Bay. Now and then we got unobstructed views of that region below, all forest-clad, and there seemed to be pits and basins there; but nowhere a slope permitting a descent. We got a view of the little bay where the *Pearl* lay, but the distance (some seven or eight miles) was too great to permit us to distinguish the masts among the palms, even with the glasses that Captain Marat carried.

The afternoon was not far gone when we met Grant Norris and Carlos, who, by their report, had encountered practically the same conditions as we. Except only that they had come upon a brook that disappeared into the hillside, a thing that Carlos declared was common enough in these mountains. But the direction of the stream was such as to suggest that it was the same rivulet that made its exit from the rocks right where Ray and Robert kept watch. Norris and Carlos had ascended this mountain brook above a mile, on the chance that it might bring them to some trail to the haunt of Duran. But they had met with no signs, and had at last taken to the heights.

"Now, I'll tell you, fellows," observed Norris, "I propose to follow up that creek some miles farther, tomorrow. I've been in more than one gold country, and that creek looks darned likely to me. I dug down at the edge with my hand, in a couple of places, and found black sand. If there isn't gold somewhere up that stream I miss my guess."

"Well, the sun soon be getting low," said Captain Marat. "It is time we go back."

The way Norris and Carlos had come was considered the shorter way back, so we took up the march, moving eastward. I was ahead with Carlos, and we hadn't taken many steps on our way, when I was startled by the sight of some furry object scampering up a cedar just below. Norris saw it too, and raised his rifle. It was then I got another view of the being, and reached out to stop Norris whose finger was on the trigger.

"Wait!" I cried. "It's a monkey."

Carlos, too, was surprised at the spectacle. He declared that he had never heard of monkeys inhabiting the island.

"It must be tame monkey," he said.

The animal swung from a branch of the tree to that of the next, and soon disappeared over the edge of the cliff.

"Well then," declared Norris, "if he's tame, he's either got loose in town and wandered a long way off, or there are other people beside ourselves about here."

No one had anything to add to Norris' observations, and we continued our return journey, little thinking that we were destined to see that monkey again.

We presently came to where descent was possible; and when the brook finally came in our way, I found much interest in the spot where the waters flowed into the hole in the rocks.

"It seems a queer freak," I told Norris, "that it should make its way through the hill like that."

"It isn't the first time I have seen nature doing such stunts," he returned. "I guess volcanic action has had most to do with it."

CHAPTER XXII

THE ISLE IN CROW BAY

We had barely got ourselves back to where Ray and Robert lay awaiting us, when night came. They had everything ready for the cooking of a meal, so that our bearish appetites had not long to suffer.

Our non-success did not sit heavily on us, and it was with some cheer we gathered round the fire, that was made in the midst of the underbrush, far enough from the stream to be invisible from any part of Duran's trail. Robert remained over there alone on watch.

"Now, I'll tell you," said Ray, addressing Grant Norris, "if you're going to find that gold mine, you'll just have to rig up a balloon, and fly all over these mountains—like I did in my dream."

"Well," returned Norris, plucking the bones from his fish, "I'm thinking there'll be no lack of gas for it while you're awake. When you're not awake—well, you'll dream enough hot air to—"

"Just what I was going to say," broke in Ray. "It delights me to see you've come round to my dream idea. You're awake at last. Not that you're to blame for having golden dreams; even I, in my younger days—"

"Not on your life!" interrupted Norris, "I—"

"Even Wayne, here, has dreams," continued Ray. "He follows that nightmare, Duran, and suddenly he vanishes into nothing—all dreams."

"Not on your life!" declared Norris, taking Ray half in earnest. "There's gold somewhere in that creek we were on today, and I'll show you before we get through with it."

"Maybe Duran has already cleaned it out," I suggested.

"Don't you believe it!" said the optimistic Norris. "He hasn't got away with it at any rate, or what is he doing back here?"

We crawled under our mosquito bars early, leaving Ray on watch by the stream. I fell asleep to the music of the little cascade, whose continual plash kept from my ears the harassing song of the mosquitoes, who with voodoo thirst sought flaws in my citadel.

I was awakened at last by an insistent hand on my shoulder and Robert's voice in my ear.

"I think Duran or somebody just went by," he said.

He had detected a sound of plashing in the water, like someone wading, though he heard it imperfectly, confused as as it was with the noise of the little waterfall. He had peered hard into that inky darkness, and it seemed to him that a shape crept along the bank of the creek.

We aroused the others, who began at once to gather our traps together, while Robert and I, with utmost caution, sought the path, and with more or less difficulty followed its course toward the bay.

It was about two o'clock when we started, and when we came to the inlet, there showed in the east signs of the moon coming, topping the horizon. That was half-past-three; so that we were an hour and a half covering those three or four miles.

I crept to the spot where we had seen Duran's canoe concealed in the tall grass.

"It's gone!" I told Robert. "Let's hurry the others."

A few hundred yards back Robert came upon them. And now not a minute was lost in setting our little boat in the water. The moon lay a timid light on the bay by the time we had come out of the inlet.

"There!" cried Robert, pointing to the east.

Barely a half mile away we made out an object on the water.

"He's going down the bay," I observed, "not across to the Twin Hills."

"Well, let's keep him in sight," said Norris, "now that we've got our peepers on him at last."

"He'll see us if we go too fast," cautioned Robert.

A camouflage for our boat was suggested. So we hurried to the shore, and six pairs of hands quickly harvested an abundance of reeds and grasses. With this we wove a screen, as for duck-stalking. And with the shore for a background, it would have taken a sharper eye than a human's to distinguish us. Fortunately, the moon, being but a thin, fading crescent, gave a rather imperfect light.

Now we moved at a swift pace down the shore, Norris and Marat at the oars. And so we gained on Duran, who was out nearer the middle of the bay, little thinking that his plans were *gaun agley*, with his enemies hanging on his tail in spite of all his devices.

Nearly every eye was on that canoe and its paddler, and barely a word spoken till we had navigated almost a mile of the bay.

"Now where is that skunk making for, I wonder?" said Norris, resting on his oar and peering through the screen.

"He go to the island, there, I theenk," offered Jean Marat.

"Yes," added Carlos. "He go right for thee island."

I had noted the island when we were on the cliffs. It was triangular, and on Marat's chart it measured a half mile in its greatest dimension.

"What's on it?" queried Norris, again resuming his rowing.

Carlos said he had been there many years ago, and then there were palms and brush, and in the midst, a hut and garden.

"There! He's going to land," spoke Robert.

Captain Marat trained his glasses on the island, now barely more than a half mile away.

"Yes," he said, "he land. He is on thee shore now, an' he pull out thee canoe, I theenk."

We set our boat in toward the south shore of the bay and here we found the mouth of a stream. A few rods up this creek we made our landing, and in a little we had got boat and all out of the water and into a sheltered place under the palms, for day would soon be breaking.

"You're the darndest bunch!" said Ray, rubbing his eyes. "You'd think I hadn't paid for my lodging."

He had fallen asleep in the boat, and didn't awaken till Norris had almost rolled him out into the water.

"It's that cannibal-priest-voodoo-skunk again I suppose," continued Ray. "Where have you got him now?"

"We've got him cornered, surrounded on Crusoe's island," returned Norris.

"Surrounded," sniffed Ray, "like a gay porpoise, with water. And I'll bet when you catch him, you'll find he's only Crusoe's man, Friday."

This suggestion, although made in sport, startled us. Perhaps after all, the occupant of the canoe had not been Duran. It might have been only one of his numerous blacks, one more in his confidence than any of those on his schooner.

When day came, and that was but an hour after our landing, I began anxiously to scan that island through Marat's glasses. It was not long till I saw a rowboat put off from the island and move toward the south shore far down the bay. Unmistakably, it was a black in the boat, and alone, apparently, and his bulk was much too portly for the figure of Duran. And before the morning was half gone another figure appeared, coming out of the palms on the island. And my heart thumped with excitement as I strained my eyes at the glasses.

The figure (black of face) stood on the shore, looking out across the bay to the west. Was it Duran? I asked myself. Surely the form was not unlike his, but there were many real blacks in his employ who, at that distance would have looked much the same.

And then occurred a thing that settled the matter, and I thrilled all over. The man's hand went up to the side of his head, and the fingers toyed with the ear in that characteristic manner of Duran's, when he was in deep thought. There could be no doubt, I saw the hand moving up and down with the stroking. It was Duran!

I turned to my friends and gave them my news.

"Well, anyway," pouted Ray, "his man Friday was there; he went off in a boat."

"And now, what do you suppose he's doing on that island then?" asked Norris.

"He's burying his gold, of course," said Ray.

"Or maybe he's just after provisions," I suggested.

"And he sent that old fellow in the boat on his errands," offered Robert.

Carlos, appealed to, avowed that this explanation was not unlikely, since there was a bit of a hamlet far down the bay.

When the hot tropic sun had mounted to the zenith, Norris' restlessness seemed to be approaching a climax. It was with some difficulty we dissuaded him from a notion that had taken him, to make a trip back into the hills in search of that golden creek of his. And it was then there came a wet squall out of the west that drove us under the shelter of our over-turned boat till it went by. The monotony of that wait, too, was a bit relieved by the return to the island of that boat that had gone down the bay in the morning.

Before dark came I got Jean Marat aside and communicated to him an idea that had grown in my head that afternoon.

"Captain Marat," I began, "it is going to be very dark nearly all of tonight, and it will be hard to see, at that distance, when Duran leaves the island—if he does."

"Yes," returned Marat, "I have think of that."

"Well," I continued, "even in the dark it won't be safe to row over to the island. Duran might happen to be on the shore and so see us."

"Yes, jus' so," agreed Marat.

"I want to swim over," I said. "It's only half a mile."

"Ah!" said Jean Marat. "Thad might be. Yes—yes." (He pondered the thing.) "Yes, I swim too, with you."

It was the very thing I had in mind, this idea of his accompanying me, though I hesitated to include him in my suggestion.

"And then," Marat continued, "maybe we hear some theengs thad will help us."

Here, too, was some of my thought, remembering that night when he and I had rowed over to the *Orion*, in the harbor, and heard Duran say things that had enlightened us very much. Though some of the things he had said had not been at all clear, else Ray and I had been spared that period of captivity.

We were not long in giving our plan to the others. Norris, eager for activity, would like to be one of the party, but he himself found objections the moment his wish was expressed.

"It won't do to have too many," he said; "and then I can't understand the *parley voo* like Captain Marat."

"Besides," put in Ray, "there'd be an awful hulaboloo among the fish. They'd think it was a—" Norris had him in his grasp. "—A mermaid," finished Ray.

We did not wait long after night had settled over the bay. Jean Marat and I kicked off our clothes and, entering the water, headed for the island. It was chalked out that the others should hold everything in readiness, and if they should hear a signal, they would immediately row out and pick us up, to take up the trail of Duran again.

It was no great feat to swim that half mile of smooth water. And then it was with great caution that we crawled across that island beach. I must have been a curious spectacle for Jean Marat—black of face and arms and feet, the rest of me all white. The curly wig, of course, I had left with my clothing.

We passed in among the cocoanut palms, traversed a belt of hammock, and came to a piece of clearing. A light shone from a window of the hut. There were some bushes near the wall; these we got amongst.

Keeping our faces in the shadow, we contrived to look in. And it was somewhat a startling spectacle presented to us there. Duran's features—though stained like myself and Robert—were not so hard to distinguish in the light of the lamp. There was but one other occupant, a negro, old and portly of body. Duran's head bore a red kerchief, wound turban-wise, and his body was clad in a red robe—much like I had seen him wearing that night in the forest. He stood by the table, and in his hands he clutched a fowl, just beheaded, for the blood was running from the raw stump of the neck into a bowl.

When the dripping had almost ceased, Duran gave the chicken into the hands of the negro, who laid it aside. And then Duran poured rum from a jug into cups, and mixed in blood from the bowl; and now the two drank. And there showed that horrid, excited hankering of an old toper, in Duran's face when he brought the cup to his lips. Whether it was the rum he craved, or the blood, or the combination, or if he was really taken with a religious fanaticism, I have never been able to fathom. But that his emotion was real I could have no doubt.

A number of drinks round, and the black set himself to plucking the feathers from the fowl; and then it was not long till he had the bird in a kettle on the stove. Duran, after a time, inclined his head to a little box on the table, and presently it occurred to me that they must have the voodoo snake there as well. It was evidently a voodoo ceremony they were enacting, and I knew it could not be complete—if bonafide—without the snake.

Through it all, there was more or less talk between those two, and to that Marat was giving his ear. At times he moved over and put his head to the boards, the better to hear.

When at last the fowl was cooked, those two feasted on it, and ate little else. And then, in time, they dropped off to sleep; the portly negro seeking the floor, Duran slumbering in his chair, head and arms on the table.

Captain Marat and I now seated ourselves on the ground, a little away from that window to wait while those two within should sleep off their debauch. Marat told me something of the talk of Duran and the other. But there was nothing of new interest in it, since it referred almost solely to matters on which they were then engaged. Duran, however, had found occasion to descant on a purpose he professed he had, to bestow great riches on the black, how he would be required to remain faithful to Duran's service but a few days more, and he should be literally over-burdened with the gold that should be his.

Maybe two hours of waiting had passed, with occasional peeps in at that window, when Duran raised himself from his slumbers. He forthwith aroused the black, and divesting himself of the red gown, he addressed himself to the negro, who began putting together certain parcels of supplies in a pack. Duran took up a paddle, and the two moved out of the door, talking as they went.

Captain Marat and I crouched in the shadows, till they had gone toward the beach. Then we followed, moving from bush to bush. And we saw Duran embark in his canoe, going back the way he had come the night before.

So soon as the black had moved toward the hut, Marat and I entered the water and started for the shore of the mainland, where our friends awaited us. When we deemed it safe, I gave the whistle signal, and our friends came off in the boat and took us in.

"Thee *Orion* weel be here in thees bay before a week is gone," said Captain Marat. "Duran expect then to sail away, pay off hees crew, an' come back with new crew who know nothing about thee gold. And then he will take on gold cargo. And then for Europe. He tell that black man he take him with, and he will make him ver' rich."

"But he didn't tell that black where he was going to get his gold cargo?" ventured Ray.

Marat said no to that. But Duran had promised the negro that he should go with him, in two boats, and they two should transport all the gold aboard the vessel; and the new crew were to be told that it was all specimens of coral and other stones, for a museum in Europe. "And so," Marat continued, "Duran tell him if any strangers come round, he must not know anyone by name Duran, or Mordaunt, or anyone like that. And Duran tell him, too, thad when the *Orion* come, if anyone on the schooner come to the little island, he tell them Duran gives order thad no one of them is allowed on thee island; they must stay on the schooner."

"And why," began Norris, "do you suppose he don't want his own sailors on that little island?"

"Ask Wayne," said Ray.

"Now, Mr. Norris," I said, "you're just wanting to hear somebody echo the thought that's in your mind. Suppose you tell us what it is."

"Well," said Norris, "Ray said it last night. He's been burying some of the gold on the isle. And now he's afraid that if his men set their feet on the place, they'll get to looking for it."

"That's the way with people," said Ray. "If they hide something, they suspect that everybody that comes around can smell it."

"Ease on your oars," Marat admonished.

Norris and Robert were rowing. Intent on our discussion, they had forgotten caution, and were sending the boat forward at a rate. The night was quite dark in spite of the stars, and we might easily drive ourselves within hearing of Duran without realizing it. The night breeze rippled the bay, so that the canoe on the surface would not be visible till one should be almost on it.

"It's a mighty good thing," observed Robert, "that he doesn't make his trips in daylight. He couldn't help seeing that a good many besides himself have been tramping on that trail."

"He'd think a whole army was after him," said Ray.

When at last we came to the inlet, it was with some difficulty we found our way, so dark was it. It was Carlos who at last made out Duran's canoe, amongst the reeds.

"Well, he's got a good deal the start of us," said Norris, when at last we had got our boat in hiding and were ready for the trail.

"Perhaps it's just as well we're not too close," I offered, falling in behind Carlos, to whom we gave the lead.

"You don't believe he'd give us another chase in the schooner?" queried Robert.

"No," I admitted, "but he might pick a new trail, and throw us clear off again."

Single file, we moved forward. We were soon in the wood, where night birds and insects gave us their music. Out again in the glade; again into the forest. And at last, we came to where the trail dipped into the stream.

There was nothing to do but remake our camp in the old place, a little way to the west of the creek. There came renewed conjectures seeking solution of this mystery.

"Well, you'll find out my balloon is the only explanation," bantered Ray. "He carries one in his vest pocket, all neatly folded; he takes it out, blows it full of voodoo rum stuff, and—whiff—up he goes."

"Maybe there's some one of those lianas hanging from the trees that he swings out of the water on," offered Robert.

"That's so!" cried Norris. "A fellow might swing a big long jump that way without touching his foot to the ground. I'm going to have another good look there first thing in the morning."

Captain Marat had been taking stock of our supply of food.

"Someone have to go for more provision, if we stay much longer," he said. "We have hardly enough for one day."

So that after some hours of sleep Robert and Marat set off to return to the *Pearl* for fresh supplies. They planned to row across the end of Crow Bay before day should come, for there was no certainty that Duran's black on the isle might not have an eye out. It would not do to risk another daylight crossing.

Day had no sooner shot its earliest rays into the recesses of our forest, than Norris was over to the creek investigating the big vines that hung like so many ropes from the branches above. He finally came back to his breakfast, his face giving no signs of success.

"Never mind, Norris," said Ray. "If you're going to make that Duran out a monkey, you can hardly expect to find tracks—monkeys don't leave any."

"Well, anyway," insisted Norris, "that's the way he went, and we'll find that gold mine up on my creek—see if we don't."

For some unaccountable reason, I was not any more impressed by Norris' conclusions than by Ray's playful explications, and I was taken with a desire to be alone with the problem. So I urged the others to go and explore Norris' creek, and I would remain on watch at this place of Duran's strange disappearance.

When the three had gone, moving eastward along the foot of that towering stone wall, I began where the water came tumbling out of that hole in the cliff, and carefully examined the banks of the creek again, up and down, for half a mile or so. I reasoned that if he waded into the stream he must certainly have waded out of it again. Unless, as Norris had conjectured, he had swung himself over the bank by the means of some liana. I therefore imitated Norris and searched both sides for evidence of any such means; and with a negative result. Nowhere, so far as the forest followed the stream, was there a loose liana near the bank on either side.

And then it came to me that perhaps Duran had gone into the water at the end of the path, only to retrace his steps and leave the path some way on the back trail, thus to deceive any who should chance to come so far on his track. And so I scrutinized every foot of the path back to the edge of the forest, and some way across the glade. I even went off the trail, and fought my way through the growth as I went back, paralleling the path, and looking for signs.

But I got back to the creek bank and the music of the little cascade, no nearer the solution than when I had started. Hours had been consumed in my search. It must have been past ten when I squatted on the stream's bank, looking into the clear water, puzzling over this thing.

A beam of sun shone down through the water and illumined the creek's bottom. A round bit of rock or coral lay there, almost white in that liquid light. For a long time I stared on that spot, as if the solution were to be found there. I never before had felt so baffled.

And then I was startled! I could no longer see that stone—nor any part of the creek's bed. The water had in that moment become turbid. Something had muddied it. I leaped to my feet and hurried up to the fountain in the cliff. The water was coming out of the rock in that muddied condition. Now what could it all mean? I asked myself. And I set my wits to the thing as I continued to stare at the phenomenon. Presently the water cleared a bit. And then in a little it came as muddy as ever again.

CHAPTER XXIII

WHAT THE WATER HID

My thoughts flew. In a moment more I thrilled with an idea. Then I dashed into the water and got myself up to the little waterfall, made, as I have said, by a portion of the water coming round a rock and flowing over the edge of a flat shelf of rock.

I tried to look through that thin veil of liquid, failing which, I braved a shower and put my head through. In another moment I had my whole body behind that little cascade. I crouched, sputtering, under the rocky shelf. Then for eight or ten feet I crawled forward in the darkness. Directly, the passage made a little turn to the right, and the ground under my hands sloped upward. It may have been fifty feet, it may have been a hundred and fifty feet, that I had penetrated that cliff—my excitement had taken no measure of the distance—when I found that I could no longer feel the wall on either side. I was in a cavern of unknown dimensions.

I could hear the rushing of water, below and to my left. A feeling of exultation filled me almost to bursting; I had at last discovered Duran's secret. I came to a stop, fearing to lose my exit. How I wished for my flashlight! I had come away leaving it aboard the *Pearl*.

I do not know how long I had tarried in that spot, when a beam of light struck down from above on my right. And then came sounds of some being up there, and the light approached.

I retreated into the narrow passage by which I had come, ready to scramble out if there should be need. But soon the slant of the light beams showed me that the lamp had passed to the left, and I ventured forward again, and peeked around a projection of rock.

There was Duran's blackened face in the light of a lantern, which he was in the act of hanging on some form of hook in the cavern wall. The vault, I saw, was high, and at least fifty feet wide. It was down near the water that Duran was; and I saw him stoop and put his hand into the stream; and he fished out some sort of packet which he laid on the cavern floor. Time after time he reached down into the rushing water, and took out a packet each dive, till he had a pile on the floor that would measure a peck.

At last Duran sat himself on the cavern's floor, and he busied himself with untying knots and separating the objects he dealt with in two piles. And next he rose to his feet and set to transporting one of his piles to some niche that was out of the field of my eye.

Duran's next procedure was to gather the other pile into a sack. And this he took in hand and forthwith began to move back toward my part of the cavern.

I wormed my way down in my passage again, and when I had got a little way from the cascade, I waited and listened. But he must have gone back the way he had come. I ventured in again.

When I poked my head out of the passage into the cavern, there was no sign of Duran. But the lantern still hung where he had fixed it, throwing its light about that space.

I now ventured down to the scene of Duran's labors. There, completely spanning the stream, and reaching down to its bed, was a network of some sort of tough fibre, reinforced with slender bamboo. Near at hand, in a niche, lay, in a pile near a foot high, short sections of bamboo as thick as my arm. I took up one in my hand. Even prepared as I was for the discovery, its weight nevertheless startled me; it might have been solid brass.

"At last this smells of the gold mine!" I thought to myself. He would hardly miss one of these. And after hefting in my hand a half-dozen more, to satisfy myself that all were loaded, I retained that first bamboo cylinder and hurried to my exit.

As I passed out on all fours through that little waterfall, I got a fresh drenching. I waded on down the stream, and presently I heard a voice. It was Ray's; and he was over in our little camp.

It came into my mind to even up for some of the tricks Ray had played me. So I trilled out a low whistle, and when I heard them coming, I ducked myself in the creek. I held my breath for as long a space as I could manage, and then rose out of the water and made for the path, pretending not to see those petrified forms pedestaled on the creek bank. I went up the path and moved toward the camp, and when they hurried forward—"Hello!" I said. "Are you folks back already?"

"Say, now!" began Ray. "What in Sam Hill! Are you playing alligator, or mermaid, or—"

"Playing!" I said. "I've had no time for play." With one hand I was nursing the heavy cylinder that I now carried under my shirt.

"And what have you been doing?" demanded Norris, eyes big with perplexity.

And Carlos appeared no less mystified.

"I've been visiting the gold mine," I said simply.

Even Ray could not resist a look over to that spot in the stream where I had appeared to them out of the water.

"I thought I heard you whistle," he said.

"Dreaming some more," I suggested.

Norris got a long stick and began poking in the bottom of of the creek.

"Oh, not that way," I told him. "You have to say 'Open Sesame.'"

"Now look here, open up!" pressed Norris, dropping his pole.

"All right," I returned. And I produced the cylinder of bamboo.

"Well I'll—!" began Norris, hefting the thing. "Say, there's sure something heavy in that thing. Where'd you—?" And again his eyes turned quizzically toward the water.

"You know what I told you this morning," broke in Ray, taking the section of bamboo in his turn of scrutiny.

"Yes," assented Norris, "you said Wayne would have it all figured out—what became of Duran—by the time we came back. And that's one reason why I was ready to come back as soon as I found those two little colors."

And Norris showed me two little flakes of gold he'd washed out of the black sand in the creek-bed.

"But open up now, Wayne," he continued. "Tell us."

"Well you see," I began, "you, Norris, would have it that Duran had gone through the woods by the lianas; and you, Ray, insisted on it that he went through the air. Now none of us had thought of his going through the water—"

Instinctively we all looked into the creek, and there I discovered that the water had gone muddy again.

"Look there, see that!" I pointed. "You know how clear that water has always been. And now see how riled it is."

They looked intently as if expecting to see Duran appear out of the stream as I had seemed to do.

"Aw, say now, what are you giving us?" said Ray.

Norris and Carlos were already moving up toward the spot where the water poured out of the cliff. But before they were half the way, the stream cleared again.

And then I went on to tell them how I had discovered the hole behind the little cascade. And they were open-mouthed till I had completed my narration of Duran's activities in that cavern in the cliff.

"Well now, and to think—" began Norris. "Anyway that proves that the gold mine is on a continuation of the creek where I found the colors. That creek goes into the rocks up there and comes out into some kind of a basin, and then goes into the cliffs again and comes out here, like a train going through two tunnels."

"Brava!" cried Ray. "Now you ought to have told us that yesterday, and saved all that trouble."

Norris had to penetrate the little cascade and see the beginning of the passage into the cliff. When he came out, it was decided to wait for night and the coming of Captain Marat and Robert, with the lantern, before going into the cavern. For, since Duran was working by day he would doubtless sleep at night.

"Well," said Ray, when we got to the camp. "I want to see what makes that thing so heavy."

The cylinder of bamboo was plugged at the one end with a section of wood, the edges being sealed with raw pitch. We heated the thing at the fire, and then pried out the plug of wood.

"Hooray!" cried Norris and Ray together, as I poured the contents into a tin.

There was fine dust of gold mixed with many small nuggets.

"How many of those things did you say you saw in there?" asked Ray.

"I didn't count them," I returned. But I showed with my hands the dimensions of that space that was filled with them.

"And that's only the beginning," said Norris. "Say, Carlos, we've found your gold mine," he continued, seizing that black by the shoulder.

"Yes, we find him now," grinned Carlos. "Maybe I find where my father buried." And his face went serious again with the sadness I saw there, something that was doubtless hatred of Duran, his father's murderer, showed too. And I wondered—and conjectured—what was in Carlos' mind, and shuddered.

Marat and Robert came at last, in the dark, and they marvelled at the tale of success we had to tell them.

"But, Bob," said Ray, in the midst of the tale, "to think that Wayne would play a trick like that on me!—who nursed him through measles, mumps, chicken pox, cholera morbus, and a stubbed toe, and even fed him up, dozens of times, on all-day suckers!—to pop out of the water like that, and bow, and tell me he had been playing Jonah, and that the whale had just stopped behind to wipe his feet on the mat and would be in directly."

Everything, Captain Marat told us, was going well on the *Pearl*; and Julian, good lad, was content to wait indefinitely, while we searched for the mine.

Fortunately, Robert and Marat had brought the lantern, and Robert had thought to bring along the electric flashlights; and most of us were supplied with matches, protected from the damp in tightly corked vials. We were soon at the little cascade, and crawling, one after the other, pushed through the curtain of water.

"I say," began Ray, sputtering, "I feel fit to enter the holy temple now."

The lantern was set alight, and I led the way up into the interior of the cliff. My comrades feasted their eyes on the accumulation of gold-laden bamboo cylinders; and then they must investigate that net in the stream.

"Now I'll say that's a clever stunt that skunk played here," declared Norris. "Instead of toting that gold around some difficult path, he makes the creek carry it straight down here near the outlet. And he ties pieces of some buoyant stuff to each of the cylinders to make it float."

"Here's what he used," said Robert, who had picked up a small block of cork that he thrust into the lantern light.

"Sure, that's it," said Norris, taking it into his fingers. "He got his cork out of a life-belt, and he makes his little cork bricks do duty time after time. There's no telling how much gold they've floated down here."

"And what do you suppose he does with it when he takes it out of here?" asked Ray.

"He take eet to thad little islan' down in Crow Bay," offered Captain Marat.

"He's planning to take over there all that he's got mined," added Robert, looking to me for confirmation of his surmise.

"Yes," I assented. "And then he'll likely clear out, and keep away from this region till we've all had time to forget him, and the coast is clear again."

"That's it," agreed Norris. "But now we're on his trail again, let's see the place it leads to." And he turned up that incline, within the cavern, down which I had seen Duran come during the day.

The climb was rather arduous, as the ascent was somewhat sudden, though it was smooth going under foot. We went single file, all following Norris, who was in the van, carrying the lantern.

When we had climbed to a height of perhaps a hundred feet, we came to an exit of the cavern. We could hear the rustling of the leaves of trees in the night breeze, and stars showed above. The path continued on up, apparently on a ledge; and we must finally have attained a height of three hundred feet, when something like a plateau presented to the left. We took the path of least resistance, picking our way carefully among rocks and scattered growth of trees. There was but the one way sufficiently free of obstacles, and on this road we moved without hitch or hindrance, till we finally brought up sharp at the edge of a precipice. Further progress appeared impossible, wanting wings, or some mechanical means of descent. It was a black abyss of unknown dimensions that lay at our feet.

"It's down yonder somewhere we'll find our gold mine," said Grant Norris. "And how to get down, that's———"

"It's no trick to get down," interrupted Ray, "but I'm thinking you'll be all out of the notion for the gold mine when you land there."

My mind full of the notion to discover a stone stairway, or some other medium for descent used by Duran, I moved to the right, where a clump of cedars showed, outlined against the starry sky. It was here my spirit of enterprise nearly cost me my life, and did deprive me of the use of my limb and the companionship of my comrades for the span of a day. I got in among the cedars, and threw a gleam from my flashlight about the ground, an impulse prompting me to risk the chance that it might be seen by Duran somewhere below.

In that flash of light my eyes got on a small rope, hanging from the limbs above me, the other end gone somewhere down the cliff below. I got my hand on the rope and gave a gentle pull. It was fast above. I made a bolder pull. It gave several feet; and that unexpected and sudden release lost me my balance, and I toppled off the brow of the precipice, clutching the rope for dear life. Wildly I sought to wind a leg about the rope, for it burned and tore my fingers beyond endurance. I must have fallen forty or fifty feet, when I struck a bit of a ledge; but my fall was broken by brush and vines, and it was these vines saved my life, for they held me in some of their tangle till I finally brought up with a thump at the bottom.

I was a good deal shocked, but strange though it seems, throughout that fall I had not experienced a moment's fear for my life. There was a sharp ache in my right ankle. I wiggled my toes, and satisfied myself that there were no bones broken, but a step or two convinced me I was to be a lame brother for a greater or less period.

CHAPTER XXIV

IN THE HIDDEN VALE—A NEW ACQUAINTANCE

With crawling, I managed to get myself away from the foot of the cliff a piece, and I found I was in a space of open ground. And I then began to think how I was to publish my predicament to my friends on the top of the cliff, some hundred, or perhaps two hundred feet above. I felt in my pocket for my flash-lamp, and it gave me much comfort, on pushing the slide, to discover that it had not been put out of commission by the fall.

At once I began to send flash after flash up there. Almost directly, I saw answering flashes aloft. And then I spelled out, in code, a brief story of my adventure; and I asked that they throw me some grub, and then to stay away till the next night, when they were to return for news of some route by which they might join me.

I waited perhaps three-quarters of an hour, when a flash of light showed above. I answered with my light. And thus came Ray's signal. "Here it comes," it said. And then in a little, something umbrella-like appeared, gently oscillating between me and the stars; in the next moment quietly collapsing on the ground, near by. I took it up; it was a parachute, made of four handkerchiefs hastily sewed together. To the strings was made fast a packet of provisions; biscuit, cheese, and a cloth bag holding a mess of codfish cooked with vegetables. And there was a note from Ray. I read:

> "That was a smelly trick—to *ditch* us like that. If you only knew what a nasty time of it we've been having to keep Norris from sliding down there after you! He said if you could do it he could, and so on. Now don't go poking your nose in any alligator's private affairs. And *wire* us *soon*, and give us *all* the news of that *hades*, down there."

It always irked Grant Norris to know that anyone was before him in any adventure, and I began to fear that in his impetuosity he might make a try for a descent, in which event he hadn't one chance in ten to come off with as little damage as I suffered. So I signalled, then, to make no move toward seeking a way down till I gave the word, and I gave a terse hint of the great danger in such an attempt.

It was a matter of course that my friends would keep someone on watch up there; and it would be Ray and Robert, turn about; for they two, only, knew the code sufficiently well to take my signals.

I now took up the packet of grub they'd thrown down to me, and began to crawl farther from the cliff. I thus came into a wood, and it was with great labor, and great stabs of pain in my foot, that I traversed some hundreds of yards of the forest, at last to come upon the bank of the rivulet. It could be no other than that stream that tumbled through the cavern to gush out of the rock to make the little cascade.

Soon now I was bathing my swelling foot in the cool water, and I did not take it out for above an hour, and then I bound the ankle with Ray's parachute; and I sat me beside the creek, my back to a palm, feeling less discomfort, and so was able to give clearer thought to our situation. There was, of course, not the least doubt that this sink I had fallen into, was that secret retreat of Duran, we'd been searching for, and the source of all his wealth. It was the very place discovered by Carlos' father, who in an evil hour had communicated his find to the perfidious Duran. I was equally convinced that this hidden vale was hedged in on the sides, and closed at the ends, by sheer cliffs; and that that rope which had both entrapped me and then helped to save me in my fall, was some part of Duran's means of ascent and descent. It should now be my first aim to discover the other component parts and the workings of that mechanism, to the end that I might put my friends in a safe way to join me.

To accomplish this it was only necessary that I have an eye on the place when Duran should find it in his way to go out of the place in daylight. And that was a thing he was altogether likely to do, if he were to have more business in the grotto.

My ankle was so much eased that I could have slept were it not for the myriad mosquitoes that attacked me, the while dinning their horrid song in my ear. As it was I got an occasional short snatch of rest with dozing till a dozen or more wee living stilettos got home in my flesh, and brought me awake and set me to thrashing about with my palm-fan again. And once or twice I jumped awake with a queer notion in my consciousness, and that was that one or more of those mosquitoes had learned to crow like a cock, for I seemed to have heard such music while my head nodded.

I was glad when the dawn broke and sent the greater part of my pests back to their lairs once more. I made a meal out of the packet of grub, getting my drink from the creek. And then I searched about in the wood, till I found a stick having a crotch to fit under my arm; and so I made me a wooden leg for my lame side. I hobbled over to the edge of the bit of forest, where I could command that place where I had suffered my fall.

I gazed to the cliff top and waved, hoping to attract any of my friends who should be on watch. But no living sign showed there. And then, finally, I set myself to watching for signs of the enemy.

It was a tedious wait, though one not so very long. Less than two hours had passed when I saw a figure come out of the brush back up the vale a piece.

Though he was black of face, I saw it was Duran. I concealed myself more carefully in the undergrowth and watched his approach.

When he came opposite me, less than fifty yards away, I saw he carried a pack. It was doubtless no more nor less than another freight of the gold in bamboo. He passed on down the vale, looking neither to right nor left, never dreaming that any enemy eyes could win to a near view of any part of his retreat. As he disappeared, presently, round a portion of the wood, I had also a very good guess as to what was to be his employment down there, and had I had full use of both my nether limbs, I should have followed and witnessed his manœuvres. As it was I must content myself with picturing him in my mind's eye, at setting afloat in the little stream one richly-laden bamboo section after the other, and I could see them bobbing at the surface, as they moved in line to a hole in the rocky wall, and at last find lodgment against the reed net within the cavern.

My heart danced with anticipation, as I crouched there in the edge of the wood, awaiting the next scene of Duran's performance. And this, too, I knew as well as if I held a printed "synopsis" in my hand.

It was not without some tremor of apprehension, too, that I at last beheld the figure of Duran appear again on the back trail, for I was not at all sure that I had not left some traces of that violent entry of mine into this sunken pasture. And sure enough, when he arrived at the place, he came to a stand, and gazed on the torn vines and the rocky debris that had accompanied me down that cliff-side. His hand went up to his ear in that characteristic manner of his. And my breath came hard, in the more than half dread that he should discover my trail leading here to the wood.

It was the accident to my ankle that saved me, for having crawled away on hands and knees, I had left no tell-tale prints of shoes in the sod. He must have concluded that it was a bit of landslide had disturbed the growth, for he turned from his inspection finally with an air of unconcern.

Duran moved over to the left a piece, and then began to mount the cliff-side on a gently sloping ledge, which came to an end among the vines I had so violently disarranged. Here he got his hand on that little rope by which I had made a portion of my descent. For some time he carried on a species of struggle with the line. (Doubtless I had disarranged that thing too.) But at last things seemed to have come right; he began to pay out the line; and then I could see something unfold and drop down the cliff-side, which turned out to be some form of rope ladder. As I afterward learned, his halliard worked through a pulley bent on a limb of those cedars aloft, and was strung in and out among the rounds of the ladder, to be tied to the bottom round. When he was abroad, rope ladder, halliard and all was stowed up there; when he was home in this hidden vale, the ladder was pulled aloft, and the halliard made fast in hiding among the vines. The reason for this latter precaution I was yet to learn.

Directly, Duran was climbing above by his ladder, and then I saw his form disappear amongst those cedars on the cliff-top. And now he was gone to the cavern in the cliff to recover, and stow away, that new lading of gold. I caught myself wondering now what might be the employment of my friends, whether any of them might be in any part of Duran's path. And I hoped that they would be very careful not to allow him sight of them; for we were not yet ready to give him warning that we were so close on his trail. It was not merely to discover the concealed mine that we were putting ourselves to so much trouble, and danger as well, but we had a mind to unearth so much as might be possible of the golden product, which for so many years had been filched, piecemeal, from that deposit that belonged, by miner's right of discovery, to the Brill family. To give Duran notice of our presence would manifestly but serve to place obstacles in our way.

Five minutes after Duran had passed out of view, I hobbled on my crutch out a little into the open again, once more hoping to attract any one of my crowd who might be stationed up there on the cliff. And sure enough, I saw the head and hand of someone—it must be either Robert or Ray.

I forthwith began with my signalling. The facility shown in the responses, convinced me that it was Ray I conversed with. I told him of the rope ladder and the manner of its disposition, as near as I had been able to judge. Then I hinted the importance of some of our party following Duran, if he should go off with a burden of treasure this coming night. I ended the exchange with a caution to get back in hiding against the return of Duran, and discovery.

I crawled back into the cover of the wood again. When Duran finally came and had got down to the ledge, and with his hands on the halliard was hauling the ladder up to its nest in the firs, I saw the figure of Ray up there, doubtless watching the working of the rope mechanism. Duran went down that piece of sloping ledge, and marched off up the vale, the way he had come when I first set eyes on him that morning.

It was well past noon when he made his appearance again, and passed on down the vale with another burden on his back. He made a second trip with a second load before climbing up the cliff on his ladder. And I had another few words in code with Ray, while Duran was gone to the grotto.

For that day, it was the last journeying of Duran over that route, for when at last he went up the vale again, no more was seen of him in daylight. I hobbled along after, in time, keeping within the edge of the wood which flanked the stream. I had got myself some two hundred yards on the way, when the ground rose to accommodate a ridge of rock that went all the way across the vale, from the sheer and beetling crags of one side to those of the other. The stream broke, tumbling partly through, and partly over this ridge; and the country above was a bit more elevated than that part of this out of the world region with which I had already made some little acquaintance. The growth consisted of palms, live oaks, tree ferns, and other plants, tropical, for which I had no name.

I found an elevated situation on the ridge that gave me a fair view of this sunken region into which I had tumbled so unceremoniously the night before. Less than two miles above, showed the wall of cliff that closed the vale at its upper end. The forest growth hid from view any habitation or any other works of man that might be between.

Though a path marked the way Duran had gone, I durst not tread that road lest I unexpectedly meet up with him somewhere on its windings through the growth. The sun had been some time past the zenith when I took some more food, and then made a hurried trip to the stream for a drink; this, before taking up a position within some screening brush, whence I could command that path. I looked for Duran at the earliest, some time after dark. But I had learned to be prepared to expect the unexpected, as Ray would have put it. And it was well I did so.

I was almost dead for sleep, and it was a wonder I did not drop off completely. But I contrived to doze in cat-naps, with one eye open, as it were, till a short time before dusk, when I was startled erect by a footfall on a rocky bit of the path; and there came Duran, bearing a short gun slung on his back. And directly he had passed me, I picked up my crutch and started after. I watched him climb by his ladder, and saw him haul it up after him, and he brought up the halliard as well. So that now I knew I was indeed a prisoner in that hidden dell, till someone should let down that ladder again.

The way was now clear, I felt, for a free investigation of that region at the end of the path. And I must hurry if I was to go far before night should throw its black mantle over the scene; time enough to summon the others later.

So back I went, boldly, over the ridge. I moved as rapidly as my impromptu crutch and one good leg would carry me, till I passed round a turn of the path, and all but collided with a queer figure of a man. He plumped down on his knees and began to beg mercy.

"Oh, sor! Don't kill me, sor! I wasn't hafter spyin' on ye, sor! I was only afraid ye'd forget to bring me the morphine, sor! I—"

The creature opened his eyes, which had gone closed, likely in anticipation of the dreaded gunshot, that for some reason was now due to put a short stop to his miserable existence. He had taken me for Duran, it was plain, and the opening of his bleared eyes had shown him his mistake. Undersized, thin-lipped, and apparently toothless, was this slight specimen of a being; and his mouth, eyes, head, shoulders, and limbs twitched and jerked in abominable fashion. Indeed he fairly danced on the ground like those jigging toys that are set going by winding a bit of clock-work. I afterwards learned that it was only at times of great emotion that this extreme agitation of all the muscles on his slight bones were set in motion; but there was scarce a minute of the day that he was not at some form of grimace or contortion.

Taking courage of this being's evident fear, I demanded, "Who are you?"

"My nyme is Handy Awkins," he replied. By which I came to know he meant—"Andy Hawkins."

"I don't know 'ow you came 'ere," he said, the contortions of his body quieting considerably, "but I sye, ye won't tell the boss ye sawr me down 'ere?"

"On condition *you* won't tell 'the boss' you saw *me anywhere*, I won't tell him I saw you down here," I bargained.

His writhings now were those of joy. And he tried to set into a smile that slit of a mouth of his.

"Yer 'and on it!" he cried. "We're on the syme side o' the fence, ain't we? An' we'll be great Bobs together, you an' I, if ever we get out o' this 'ell of a 'ole—I don't care if you are a nigger. Eh Tommy?—I'll tell ye, I'm the only white man in this 'ere part o' the world, that I am, 'ceptin' the boss, and—" here he whispered the news—"'ee's only painted black, to fool the likes o' you."

CHAPTER XXV

WE CONSORT WITH A PICKPOCKET

I was not slow to perceive that this Andy Hawkins was, in some manner, an unwilling slave of Duran; and as such, might prove a more or less valuable ally to my party. Without giving him more information than that my party was a strong one, I got out of him something of his story. It seemed that something near two years back he had fallen in with Duran in one of the British islands.

"The police hofficers in that town," said Hawkins, "were 'aving a sharp eye on me. Some gents 'ad missed their purses, ye see." And Hawkins winked slyly. "I was runnin' short o' the blunt," (he meant money) "and I was gettin' a little of the rhino out of some o' Munseer Duran's niggers by way o' the three-shell game, when sudden along comes Munseer Duran and hoffers to turn me over to the police. But 'ee ends by taking me on for a job on 'is ship.

"Then the next day I was to go on board his ship, and 'ee sends one o' his sailors to me in town. I 'as all my worl'ly goods I could hide distributed about under my clothes—I 'ad to leave my portmanty, bein' as 'ow I was owin' my landlord a pretty penny, an' I was takin' French leave.

"Well, this nigger sailor showed me a man an' a kid walkin' down the street, an' said for me to follow them down that way an' I would come up with Duran an' the rest o' the bunch, an' be taken on the ship. So I follers the man an' kid, and they goes into the park by the edge o' the town.

"They goes out o' sight behind the bushes. And then next I know I 'ears a yell; and next, I see Duran an' some o' his niggers, an' 'ee 'ands one a long knife, and I see one nigger 'olding the kid. And Duran tells me to run for my life with the niggers. An' so we dodge into the woods out o' town. And we don't stop for ten mile, an' I'm almost dead, an' then that's in some thick bush near the water. And at night a boat comes ashore after us—kid and all.

"When we gets on the ship the boss is in the cabin. And 'ee shows me a printed bill that offers one thousand pounds for the capture of a man known as Handy 'Awkins, wanted for the murder of a respected citizen and the kidnappin' o' a child.

"When I read that bill my knees just let me down to the deck. I see 'ow it was; Duran knifes the man, steals the kid, and 'as me to run; and 'ee stays be'ind to 'elp put the blyme on me. And I 'ave never done no worse than to snitch a purse now an' then, when I was 'ard up; an' I never 'urt anyone in my life."

Although I experienced disgust for this ill-favored being, who was telling me his hard luck tale, I felt some sense of pity as well; and above all, I could have gloried in the spectacle of that inexplicable fiend, Duran, being slowly tortured—drawn limb from limb. And I fairly ground my teeth as I thought again of how I had seen him mixing with clean folk, and his blood-stained hands touching the fingers of mothers and daughters.

"'Ee took me ashore one night," continued Hawkins, "and 'ee tied a rag on my eyes, an' led me through bushes an' water, an' let me down by ropes. And 'ee set me to work with a nigger at the minin'; an' many's the time 'ee 'as laid the lash on me. An' w'en he see I 'ad no strength to work without the drug 'ee brought me some. An' there's times, if I 'adn't 'id some away, I know I'd die; for 'ee'd forget sometimes to bring the dope. Oh, I tell ye it's hall as keeps me alive!"

And with a sudden movement he produced something he held between his fingers, and which he threw into his mouth. He'd got the vile habit, he told me, one time when he was in hiding among some Chinese.

"Oh, it's been 'ell 'ere," continued Hawkins, "when the boss 'as been away a long time, an' the dope 'as all run out. Oh, I 'ave run round this 'ell 'ole, and tried to climb the rocks, and tore my 'ands; and once I like to broke my neck in a fall."

He told me that when Duran was away the only other inhabitant was a black, called Limbo. Hawkins said that it must be he was named for the place he lived in. The two were engaged in the gold-digging; and even when Duran was gone, the black kept spurring him at the work. For when the "boss" came back, and there wasn't a showing to please him, Hawkins said there was "'ell to pay."

"But I sye, pard," he went on, giving me a poke in the side, "Hi'm slick, Hi am; an' when your friends gets us out o' this, an' the boss is gone, you an' me'll come back, and I'll show you enough o' the yeller stuff, 'id syfe awye, to keep us in dope, and drinks, an' livin' 'igh all our d'ys."

Night had turned the place into a dark pit, and the mosquitoes were abroad on their nightly foray. I struggled to my feet, and got my crutch under my arm, telling Hawkins that my friends would be expecting to hear from me; and I began to hobble back down the dark vale. It was with some feeling of disrelish that I accepted Hawkins' shoulder, to assist me in steadying myself on this unwonted leg. Hawkins hoped that my friends were as high-class niggers as myself. "Leave me alone to know a 'igh-toned nigger when I sees one," he said. The irregular twitching of his shoulder proved rather a doubtful support, and more than once all but upset me. But he certainly made my progress more rapid.

"It happens my friends are all white," I told him, "except one; and he's less than half black, the rest of him being Indian."

"You don't sye!" cried Hawkins, coming to a sudden stop. "I'll be very 'appy to meet some folks of my own degree—meanin' no disrespect to you; you ain't just a common nigger, you know."

I disclaimed any disposition to take umbrage at his show of preference for the white race; and we continued our walk.

When we arrived opposite Duran's ladder, I detected the rattle of stones over at the cliff wall. I began to fear that Duran had returned, till I heard low voices, and then I got the conviction that it was my friends, who were coming down by Duran's rope stairway. I hurried over close, and called to them, directing them down the inclined ledge. And at last Norris and Ray stood before me.

"I couldn't keep this kid, Norris, back any longer," explained Ray. "I had to tell him how the ladder worked, and—"

"Who's your friend, Wayne?" said Norris.

Hawkins, who had held back, was now moving forward.

"This is Andrew Hawkins," I began. "He—"

"Yes, gentlemen, my nyme is Handrew 'Awkins," interrupted that individual. "An' right proud I am to make yer acquyntance," he bowed; "an' to bid you welcome to—to—this—this—"

"'Ell 'ole," I prompted him, by way of cutting short his disgusting performance.

"Yes, 'ell 'ole, right you are, my black friend, 'ell 'ole. And 'aven't I 'ad reason to know, bein' 'ere this two years or about?"

Ray and Norris were leaning forward in the dark, the better to see this grimacing, dancing being that accompanied me.

"Well, I say now, if this ain't a bloomin' countryman of mine!" broke out Grant Norris, seizing Hawkins by the hand, with a squeeze that caused that being to writhe and dance on the sod, with mingled agony, joy, and the contortions of his infirmity. When at last Norris turned him loose, he nursed his crushed hand, saying—"Ow, yes, God bless Queen Victoria and all others in authority."

From that moment the little pickpocket deserted me, and fastened himself like a barnacle to the big, hulking, patronizing Norris.

"What kind of a plaything have you got here?" demanded Ray, putting his hand on my improvised crutch.

And then I had to tell all the story of my descent into the sink. And Ray told how he and Robert were put to it, at the watching on the cliff top, to keep awake, and to dodge Duran on his trips to the cave. When at last Duran was observed to start down the path to Crow Bay, Captain Marat, Robert, and Carlos followed, leaving Ray and Norris to wait on my signals. And here was a strange circumstance; Duran had gone off empty-handed, leaving behind in the grotto, not only that stack of gold; but his bag and pack straps he left on the floor there as well.

"I guess," said Ray, "that he went to get a mule, or an ass, or something, to carry it for him. You see he didn't know about Norris being—"

Ray got behind me for protection, and cautioned Norris to be careful of my sore foot.

"Come on now," said Norris, "we're going to see where Carlos' gold mine is. Lead on Brother 'Awkins." And with that he seized me under the shoulders and threw me on his back.

Hawkins, like a little dog eager for the chase, trotted on ahead, twisting his shoulders, and bobbing his head in a manner without rhyme or reason. Ray, I could see, had curious interest in the miserable being's antics; and I knew he was priming for some sort of explosion, and wondered when it was to come.

When we had crossed the ridge, our way went through the wood, and I had to keep my head well down a share of the time, to avoid having my eyes put out by branches that overhung the trail. And then at last we came upon a clearing of some extent, in which stood an occasional cabbage-palm, left, it might be, for decorative effect. And as we moved forward, there loomed two or three structures of undetermined size or contour.

We now came to a halt, and Norris set me on the ground, and the four of us got our heads together to whisper.

"It strikes me," I said, "that we're a little too precipitate. Here's this black fellow, likely snoozing over yonder in one of those shacks. There's no one here to talk with him and explain our presence; even Hawkins, here, hasn't in two years, learned the language he speaks. Now, if he sees us, who's to say he won't tell Duran about us when he returns. And we're not yet ready to try conclusions with that—that—"

"Polecat, skunk," prompted severally, Ray and Norris, in the same breath.

"So," I continued, "we'd best get back in the brush; and depend on Hawkins to steer the black boy out of the way in the morning, till we have seen what we want to see. And then we'll get back to our own camp, till the time's ripe for our next move."

"And then clubs will be trumps," said Grant Norris.

"Hear—hear!" said Ray.

We were led by Hawkins to a sheltered place, and he soon had brought a pair of mosquito-bars from the shacks. Protected thus, it was not many minutes till I had dropped off. I opened my eyes once during that night, and that was to hear the crowing of roosters nearby. They were no doubt the same birds whose music I had heard faintly the previous night and confused with the mosquitoes. There were not less than three cocks out there vieing with one another, and each sang out perhaps a dozen times.

Ray, who lay beside me, got on his elbow. He listened silently for some time; then he said, "Say—don't it listen good to hear something talk good old United States again?"

It was soon after daybreak that Hawkins appeared, to say he had managed by their sign language, to talk the black boy into going far up the vale for a jag of dry wood. And then he told us where to find the gold workings, and other matters of interest. "When we're comin' back, I'll be singin', 'She died of the fever,' so'll you can 'ide out," said Hawkins.

"Well now, Hawkins," said Norris. "We'll soon have you out of this and back in civilization again, if you play square with us, and don't give that skunk any hint that we're here, and—"

"You don't need for to 'ave no fear, 'ee'll never know," declared Hawkins. "Hi'm slick, Hi am. Hi can 'old my gab—Hi'm old at that."

And away he went with his head and shoulders still cutting capers that rendered Ray dumb with fascination. And then finally, Ray broke out. "There goes our gold mine," he said. "We mustn't lose him! When we get back in the States we'll join a side show.—'Ladies and gentlemen: it is my privilege to present to your astonished eyes the one and only living rubber-man. Observe the wonderful effect, as the breath and pulse of life courses through him. The only self-inflating—why, the only dread we have is that he may chance on some unhappy occasion to sit down on a bent pin or a sharp tack. In our travels we found him in the tropical jungles, where he had been lost, and where he had subsisted for two years on the juice of the rubber tree. In truth, ladies and gentlemen, even now, the only sustenance he is able to take is the milk of the rubber plant, and—oh, I say now, ladies and gentlemen, who have kindness and charity in your hearts, if you have any old, worn out overshoes, garden hose, and—'"

Grant Norris had picked up a length of dead limb and was now manipulating it menacingly, with an eye on Ray. And then there came through the brush the voice of Hawkins, singing. It was a snatch of "Twickenham Ferry," ending with a—

"Oh! yo ho. Oh! yo ho. Oh! yo ho. Oh!"

"That means they're on their way for the load of wood," said Norris.

We waited some minutes, to insure the black boy getting out of view with Hawkins; and then we went forward, and out across the semi-clearing. There were four palm-thatched structures over there, with frames of pine saplings and bamboo. Beside the fourth, was the chicken yard of bamboo held together with tough grasses. In this corral were some hundreds of fowl, scratching and clucking much in the fashion of chickens back home.

"Chick, chick, chick, chick!" called Ray.

The fowl flocked toward the fence.

"I told you!" broke out Ray. "They sure understand United States."

"Oh, come on," pressed Grant Norris. "Let's get up to the diggings."

"Poor old Norris," murmured Ray, as if talking to himself, while he followed. "He'll be so disappointed when he finds out there's no gold mine."

Ray took shelter behind me as Norris, ahead, cast about for some kind of missile. We passed by a vegetable garden as we went; neat rows, carefully weeded.

I should say that my ankle was so far recovered that I had discarded my crutch and now limped on a cane. We soon had come up with the creek, where it flowed amongst the trees. A path showed the way along the bank, and the eager Norris pushed ahead, urging us to follow. I trotted after, at the best speed my lame ankle would allow, and Ray by my side. We hadn't covered two hundred yards, when another bit of clearing showed ahead.

"Hurry up," said Norris. "We'll be there in a second—Hurrah for the gold mine!"

CHAPTER XXVI

DOINGS ON THE LITTLE ISLE AGAIN

"Hurrah!" echoed Ray, with teasing, mock enthusiasm. "Hurrah!"

But we hadn't taken two more steps forward, now, when there broke out ahead of us the voice of Hawkins again, singing:

"She died of the fever, no doctor could save her."

Smash! went our enthusiasm, and we turned tail and skedaddled back on the path. We pulled up a moment at the edge of the open bit, and we heard:

"She was a fish monger, and where is the wonder—"

We hopped across the clearing, and still the song followed:

"For they all wheeled wheel-barrows through streets wide and narrow,"

"Crying—'Cockles! and mussels! alive, alive, O!'"

"That blooming idiot!" broke out Norris, when we came to a stand in the brush. "What business had he coming back so soon!"

"He just couldn't wait to sing us that song," said Ray. "'Cockles! and muscles!' But say—Hurrah for the gold mine!"

"Perhaps the black boy smelled a mouse," I offered.

We hadn't long to wait till Hawkins came pushing through the brush.

"I tell you wot, fellahs," he explained, "that nigger suddent got stubborn, an' wouldn't go no farther. 'Ee was just afraid, I guess, as 'ow the boss 'ud raise *ructions* if we 'adn't got enough work done when 'ee gets back. This last trip, the boss sure 'as got a big 'urry on; 'ee'd 'ave us workin' night an' day, if 'ee 'ad the light."

"How much, now, do you suppose he has got out of the diggings?" questioned Norris.

"Hit's a 'eap more nor I can guess," answered Hawkins. "Hit's a 'eap o' pounds we 'ave got out the two years I 'ave been 'ere. An' now, 'ee's a cartin' of it awye from some 'ole back in the rocks where 'ee's been keepin' it, 'ee don't let the nigger nor me go near the plyce. 'Ee says 'ee 'as got a trap there; an' 'ee'll shoot us if we foller 'im anywhere 'ee goes."

Norris had many queries to put the little cockney contortionist, but I soon pressed him to go, lest the black boy should come seeking him. And so he went, having exacted a promise that we would not go away from the region without him. In return, he contracted to play into our hands in circumventing Duran. "And Hi'm slick," he declared. "He cawn't fool Handy 'Awkins."

"And now—" began Norris.

"Now we'll get back to our little camp," I said.

"It's hard to go without a sight of the gold diggings," said Norris, half in earnest, half playing the youngster.

"The diggings will keep till the time's ripe," I said, assuming the paternalism forced on me.

"Hurrah for the gold mine!" teased Ray, keeping a wary eye on Grant Norris.

We were soon in the path, and presently scaled the cliff on Duran's contraption. We coiled the halliard under the brush on the cliff-top, as Duran had left it, and picked our way to the cavern entry-hall. A flash from my electric lamp revealed that all the gold-laden bamboo cylinders were gone from that niche, where we had seen them.

"I hope to Heaven our fellows saw what he did with that stuff," prayed Norris, when we had crawled out through the curtain of water into that outer world again.

"Trust Bob for that," I assured him. "He'll have the place spotted if he's had half a chance."

Everything was ship-shape in the camp-place amongst the brush. There was food in plenty, and though it was late, I was glad to round out my breakfast with some fruit and a nibble of cheese. We had nothing to do but to rest until the return of our comrades. And that event we were not to expect until some time between sunset and morning, for we had already seen that it was by night, by preference, that Duran traveled to and from that secret vale behind the cliffs.

It was a long and irksome time of waiting that day and night, for a good share of the night had passed ere they had come. Even now, so long since that time, I yawn to think of it. And I am thinking that I can do no better, to cover that space, than tell how our friends employed the time, while they were gone down Crow Bay.

It was soon after nightfall, Carlos—on the lookout—had heard Duran splashing in the creek, below the cascade, and he made out the ill-defined form of him as he moved away down the path in the murk. Carlos hurried over to the nook in the brush and made his report.

Duran's coming, of course, was expected—though he seemed a trifle early—and the plan of procedure had already been outlined. Grant Norris set off at once to again achieve that passage through the grotto and join Ray, who lingered at the cliff-top, where he had witnessed Duran's passage. Captain Jean Marat, Robert, and Carlos prepared to follow on Duran's trail.

But there was a circumstance troubled Carlos, and he had a word to say.

"Duran, he walk ver' light, an' it seem' he keep ver' straight," he began. "I think he do not carry anything."

"Let's go see!" said Robert.

And he and Carlos hastened into the cavern, where Robert threw his flashlight on the scene. There was that stack of gold-filled sections of bamboo, quite of the same size as they had seen it hardly more than two hours before. And more—on the floor of the cavern lay a canvas pack, with its leather straps.

"He hasn't taken a thing!" broke out Robert.

And the two hurried out to where Marat stood waiting on the stream's bank.

Robert gave him the news.

"Ah!" said Marat. "He go for help to carry thee big load away."

But Robert's mind was full of another idea, and he said, "Captain Marat, suppose you and Carlos go and see if you can see anything of him out in the bay. I'll stay here. And if you see him going off in the canoe, send Carlos after me. If you don't see him, wait for me."

"Ver' well," said Marat.

And the two set off in the murk. They moved rapidly, alternately trotting and walking, intent on covering as much of the space between them and Duran as might be. And as they went, Marat—and Carlos as well—began to have an inkling of the thought that was in Robert's mind.

When they got to the water they quickly satisfied themselves that Duran's sturdy little canoe was gone from its place. Soon they were in the skiff and out on the bay. Swiftly they moved down the shore, looking over their shoulders now and again, for the sight of some dark object on the quiet surface of the water. They had hardly gone a mile when they rested on their oars, and took one good long look down the bay. Nothing showed.

Robert, in the meantime, squatted on the bank of the creek, and waited patiently for perhaps two hours. A tree-toad trilled out, now and then, to mingle his song with the music of the nearby cascade. The tree-tops hung over the stream with never a rustle, for the night breeze had not yet risen.

At last Robert became conscious of a new sound, seeming to come from some point way down the creek. In another minute it had grown more distinct, and he knew it for the gentle and regular dip of a paddle. And presently, a black mass showed between the banks. And then a canoe poked its nose to shore, not forty feet from where Robert crouched by the tree trunk.

The canoeist secured the painter to a root in the bank, and forthwith moved to the cascade. In five minutes that figure appeared again, and Robert saw him stoop over the edge of the canoe and distribute something on its bottom. When he went back a second trip, Robert made a hurried visit to the canoe and satisfied himself that it was the gold-laden bamboo that found placement there. Four trips that figure made, all told, and then loosed the painter and re-embarked, moving quietly down the stream in the dark.

Now, Robert took to the path and sped on down the way the others had gone. He found them awaiting him in the skiff.

"He's got all the gold in the canoe," Robert explained. "And he's on the way."

"Thad w'at I been thinking," said Captain Marat. "He go roun' by one lagoon an' fin' thee creek. I think I have see where thad lagoon, it go in. We go there an' see."

So the three set the skiff in motion, skirting the marsh-grass, till they came to where a narrow channel opened inland.

"Another one leedle more down," said Jean Marat; "maybe he come out thad one."

They had got the boat to within view of the opening of that next channel, when an object shot out from behind the grass.

"Down—queek!" spoke Marat, in a hurried whisper.

All ducked their heads and lay quiet for some minutes. Then they ventured to peer over the gunwale, and saw the canoe as a dark mass, moving steadily away down the bay.

"He didn't see us," observed Robert.

"No," agreed Marat, "fortunate' he did not look round."

There was little doubt as to Duran's destination, so the three made the passage leisurely down over the same route they had rowed that other night. And they turned the skiff up that same creek of the mainland. This time they were determined on a bolder move than before. They meant to risk discovery, and land with the boat on that little island, though under cover of night. Carlos and Robert—who, like myself, still retained his black-stained face and hands—were to remain in hiding throughout the coming day, and observe, if possible, how Duran should dispose of that gold he had taken from Carlos' mine. The while, Captain Marat would hold the skiff over at the mainland, ready to pick them up the following night, when Duran shall have departed from the island again.

They waited till midnight, and then rowed to the isle where Robert and Carlos disembarked.

"Two flashes will be the signal," said Robert in a whisper.

"All right," returned Marat. And he rowed away.

The two crawled into the shelter of the brush. In time, they had gained the clearing in which stood the little hut. No gleam of light shone there. Creeping close, they could hear the snoring of one, and the heavy breathing of another sleeper within. This was enough. They got to the shore again, and found where the skiff of the isle was lying on the beach.

"Well, Carlos," said Robert, "suppose we have a snooze. There won't be anything going on till daylight."

"Yes," agreed Carlos.

And they crawled into a close piece of underbrush.

Carlos was the first abroad when day had come. Robert missed him when he opened his eyes; but he had hardly finished rubbing the sleep from them when Carlos appeared, to say that the negro was already setting off in the skiff for a trip to mainland.

"That Duran is sending him off on an errand again," observed Robert, "so he will be alone to bury the gold."

"Yes," said Carlos. "I heard Duran say to him that he must not forget to bring the drug. He say something about someone who do not work anything without he have the drug."

Robert puzzled a moment over this intelligence, and then, seeming to give up the problem, he said, "well, let's have a bite and then see what Duran's up to."

Presently they got themselves behind a shelter, whence they could look out into the little clearing. Duran was nowhere in view. They waited patiently some minutes, and were rewarded with the spectacle of Duran coming into the clearing from a point to their left, and bearing on his back a heavy pack. He passed the cabin and moved to its north side. In ten minutes he returned without his burden, going back the way from which he had brought his load.

Now, when Duran had gone out of view again, they scurried round to a point of vantage situate to the northeast of the hut. So when Duran appeared with his next load, they followed him with their eyes till he disappeared in a thicket that debouched from the wood on the north into the clearing.

In a little, Duran again appeared. And he had no sooner vanished to the south for a third freight of the gold, than Robert and Carlos were startled with the spectacle of a naked, lithe, black body springing from the ground, as it seemed, and who stole snake-like to the edge of the thicket where Duran had gone in and out.

Our two looked at one another in their astonishment. It was evident there was at least one other than themselves spying upon Duran and his doings.

On an impulse, Robert took up a cudgel and threw it hard to the place that naked black had gone into. He immediately followed it with another missile. That black body suddenly appeared, like a rabbit flushed out of his brush, and sped for the shelter of the wood.

When Robert and Carlos came to the wood's edge, by the north shore, they saw the black head of a swimmer making haste across the bay.

"I wonder where he came from?" queried Robert.

"I don' know," said Carlos. "Maybe from the *Orion*."

"Well, we gave him a scare," said Robert. "He won't come back."

They got to their point of vantage again, and watched till Duran had taken into the thicket a fourth, and last burden. This time they had above an hour's wait for sight of him again. And now he bore a shovel, with which implement he disappeared into the cabin.

"I guess he's through with his job," observed Robert. And such was the case, for no more was seen of Duran for some hours; and then he appeared, but to go down to the south shore, apparently to look for the return of his black. That portly individual indeed showed up, down the bay, his oars rising and dipping leisurely. Robert and Carlos watched the landing of the skiff. For cargo, there was a coffee-sack, holding some parcels of stores. And the desired drug the black brought, too, for Carlos heard him report as much to Duran.

It was already past the middle of the afternoon when those two disappeared again in the cabin with the coffee-sack. From then till dark, neither showed a face except the once, when—near dark—the fat black came out for an armful of wood. And then the coming murk encouraged our two to creep closer, and they had their appetites set on edge by the smell of fresh-made coffee. They peeked through the window to see those within having their snack.

Duran rose from the table at last. Robert and Carlos were down by the shore when the canoe was pushed into the water, and Duran began his return voyage up Crow Bay.

The flash of Robert's light brought Marat over; and it was an interesting report Robert had to make to him as they propelled the skiff again on Duran's track.

"Ah, thad ver' good," said Captain Marat. "We find where he hide it now without much pain."

Duran's canoe was in its place near the bay end of that path; and within the hour the three were received by their comrades in the camp.

CHAPTER XXVII

THE GOLD MINE

"It looks bad that that black cuss should be there spying on Duran," Norris said, when Robert and Captain Marat had told their tale.

"Yes," agreed Marat. "They weel be there some time to look for thad treasure he hide; but eet will not be so ver' soon, I theenk; for now they weel know thad someone find them out."

"That black bird wasn't from anywhere but the *Orion*," said Norris. "That schooner of Duran's can't be far away—down the coast a few miles behind some point, I'll bet."

"Say," spoke up Ray, who had hitherto been a silent listener, "and I'll bet that poor pickaninny will be telling the other pickaninnies what a narrow escape he had, and how he's sure it was I and Norris that got after him."

We began now to think upon the next move. Robert was for making a trip to the *Pearl*, to see how Julian Lamartine and Rufe fared, and give them the news; and incidentally, he would add something to our stock of provisions. But Norris maintained that, while he felt it too bad to keep Julian so long in suspense, he felt more that there was no time to be lost. "Some roaming, black voodoo may happen to get an eye on us," he said, "and then we'd likely have a regular swarm of them about our ears. And we've already seen evidence that Duran's sailors must be getting restless."

Captain Marat agreed with Norris. "Julian weel be ver' patient," he said. "And there ees no time to lose."

And then, while we three boys and Carlos busied ourselves with making a cache of a portion of our belongings, the two elders set themselves to discuss, in some detail, a plan of action.

It must have been near midnight when we moved, all in single file. On our hands and knees, one after the other, we scurried through that vale of water and passed into the cavern in the cliff; then up that steep slope within, and again down the more gentle, rocky slope without, on the other side of the high wall.

Each carried, mostly in his pockets, some little portion of the food that remained; and Norris had insisted on taking along his rifle with several rounds of ammunition.

"We're not looking for any of that kind of trouble," he said, "but if—"

"Yes," interrupted Ray, "it's sure to rain if you don't carry an umbrella."

We found Duran's rope ladder tucked up in the cedars, held by the halliard, which was taut, having been fastened among the vines on that sloping ledge down below. It took some tugging to tear loose the piece of vine to which the halliard was knotted down there; but at last it came away, and we got the ladder slung down the cliff-side.

When we all had got down to the ledge, we again hauled the ladder aloft, and tied the halliard to another piece of vine, so that Duran should not suspect that it had been tampered with. In twenty minutes we had made to that place in the brush where Ray, Norris, and I had passed a night.

For the rest of that night we got what sleep we could, taking watches, turn about. Andy Hawkins had left one of the mosquito-bars at the place, which served the turn of the sleepers. Day had not yet dawned, when Hawkins crept into the brush—Norris and I chanced to be taking the watch at the time.

"I'm right glad to see as 'ow ye've got back," he said, still at his bodily contortions. "The boss got back, an' 'ee routed us hout, an' seems to be a bit hoff 'is hoats. 'Ee ain't noway satisfied with the way 'ee's gettin' out the bloomin' gold. 'Ee says as 'ow there ain't a'goin to be much o' the stuff for any of us, if we don't get a big 'ustle on."

Norris put it to Hawkins that he was expected to help us this day to find the storehouse whence Duran took the gold that went out water-wise, through that hole in the cliff.

"I s'y!" began Hawkins, fairly dancing on the ground in his excitement. "I got me orders from the boss long ago; and 'ee marches the nigger an' myself hoff to the diggin's each day that 'ee's 'ere, an' if I so much as turns me 'ead to see w'ich way 'ee's goin', 'ee'll plug me carcass full o' cold lead."

And then Hawkins told how, long ago, he had searched a cavern that he had found in the cliffs, during Duran's absence, but had not got trace of Duran's depository. And then, more than a year back, Duran had cooled his zeal for further search, by warning him that if his curiosity got the better of him, and he went poking his nose about those cliffs, he would certainly fall into a trap, and pull some tons of rock down on his head for his pains.

When day broke, Hawkins made a detour, going back to the huts; and Norris and I aroused such of our party as were still asleep. Our first move was to seek out and establish our headquarters on the other, north, side of the stream. And then while we made a cold breakfast, our plans came to a head. Ray and Robert were to try to keep an eye on Duran, while Captain Marat, Carlos, Norris, and I should visit the scene of the mining, and incidentally, to have a try at a piece of proselyting.

The four of us crept through the undergrowth on this north side of the creek, for some hundreds of yards. A harsh sound, like the shaking down of a furnace, presently set our ears alert. We crept forward till we came in view of the source. And there in the edge of the creek-bed stood Andy Hawkins, hoe in hand, stirring dirt and gravel in a long box, into the one end of which water flowed from a dam in the stream. Beside him was the negro lad, wielding a shovel. Another object caught my eye, for, perched on the edge of the box was a monkey.

As far as we could see up the stream the rocks were denuded of soil, showing that operations in this small way must have been going on a long, long time. Norris breathed fast, and his eyes shone with excitement. It was by no means the first gold-diggings his eyes had looked on, but the tussle with nature for her treasures was no less meat for the keen spirit of this soldier of fortune than the smell of battle in any appealing cause.

Captain Marat and Carlos moved forward. Then the black boy discovered them, dropped his shovel in panic, and was about to flee. But Carlos spoke a word in a soft tone, and the lad stood, staring his wonder.

Carlos and Marat, together, engaged the black lad in talk; and Norris and I joined the group. A pair of mining pans lay nearby, and two wooden buckets stood on the ground. I could see shining, yellow particles of gold in the long box, called a Long Tom by the miners, as I learned. Norris scrutinized every detail, and poked among the gravel with the acutest interest.

At last Jean Marat turned to Norris and myself, and gave us some part of the black boy's story; more of it came to us, piecemeal, later.

He had a very imperfect recollection of the coming into this hidden vale. Indeed, he was a creeping babe when his father carried him there. The father, he said, was a cripple, with a very crooked leg, and who ever lived in great fear of Duran, and whose sole business was the digging in the creek, and separating out the yellow grains, and tending the chickens, and waiting upon Duran when he appeared.

The father told him nothing of the world without, but ever taught him to seek to please Duran and never ask questions; and that one day they would move from the place into another world, and live happy in a home of their own. It was some years after the boy had become strong enough for the work, that his father went to his sleep one night never to waken. It appears that the boy drooped with his loneliness, thereafter, and Duran brought him the monkey for a companion. And then, finally, he came with the grimacing white man (Andy Hawkins). Duran warned him, on pain of death, not to seek to learn any words of the white man's language, nor to make the white wise in any of his French speech.

Jean Marat said the black lad was struck with wonder at some simple things he had told him of the world; and he was greatly elated over Marat's promise to take him to witness what was described.

"Do you think he'll have the wit to hold his tongue?" asked Norris.

Marat spoke with the lad again, who listened with intentness, and nodded eloquently.

"He understand the importance to not betray us," said Marat. "We can depend on him."

The monkey had scrambled to the black boy's shoulder on our first appearance; and he eyed us, and seemed to scold, during the whole talk. It was the same animal, without the least doubt, that we had come upon far up on the higher cliffs of the mountain that overlooked this vale.

It was arranged that Hawkins should come to us in our covert, whenever the opportunity should offer, and bring some small quantity of provision. We did not scruple to take some sustenance of Duran's providing, since it was paid for out of Carlos' gold.

"Blyme-me if I don't fetch ye a roasted chicken," said Andy Hawkins, punctuating his speech with a violent jerking of his shoulders. "I can roast it right under the boss' nose, an' 'ee won't see it. Oh, Hi'm slick, Hi am."

And then, astonishing thing! He began to distribute among us, things that he had conjured out of our pockets; some rifle cartridges to Norris, a knife to Marat, my flash-lamp. And then another curious thing happened. The monkey, witnessing this distribution, scrambled down to the Long Tom, plunged in his fist, and handed up to me—who chanced to be nearest—a little gold nugget, the size of a bean. He looked up, watching me while I tied the little lump of gold in a corner of my handkerchief and tucked it into my pocket. He let me take his hand by way of thanking him, and took kindly to the fondling bestowed on him; climbing to my shoulder, looking into my face, and chirping some kind of monkey talk.

We finally tore Norris away from his explorations in the diggings, which he declared still held unlimited store of gold, and we got back to our new camp site. Carlos and I forded the creek, to go to seek out Ray and Robert. And we found them at the edge of the clearing wherein stood those structures.

They were just on the point of moving over to the path that went down to the lower western end of this sunken vale. For they said that Duran had just gone that way, carrying a pack on his back, having come out of the thick wood at the rear of the huts.

"Well," I suggested, "if you, Ray, will go with Carlos and have an eye on Duran, Bob and I can slip over into that brush and see if we can find the place where he gets his goods."

We found the way easy going in the woods for a piece; but when we neared the cliffs of this south wall of the vale, the undergrowth impeded us. With much going about, we finally won in to the cliffs; and after moving some way to the east, we came upon the mouth of a cavern.

"There!" said Robert. "How about that?"

But Hawkins had been all through that, as he had assured us, and we must seek elsewhere.

We finally concluded that we had better have taken the way in the other direction, along the cliff foot, and so we retraced our steps. The farther to the west that we went, the more dense the tropic growth. The damp heat here, too, was stifling, and our progress was most slow. We had struggled on, keeping close to the high, sheer, rocky wall for half an hour, almost, and finding nothing to our present interest, when a cautious whistle brought us to a stand. We moved out toward the sound and joined Ray, who informed us that Duran was on his way back.

"There's no telling where he'll come through here," I said. "Let us get back across the clearing."

When Duran appeared, after one look toward the huts, he plunged into that brush we had just come out of. In twenty minutes he appeared again, and again he stooped under a heavy pack. He but repeated that journey down the path that he had made so many times before. Carlos had continued on down the vale, Ray said, to discover where Duran went to set afloat the gold-laden bamboo.

I have forgotten how many trips Duran made this day, transporting that gold. As often as we sought to discover whence he took his freight, we came no nearer a solution of that mystery than on that first search in the back of that jungle. Once, when Duran climbed out by his ladder, to go to that cavern where he made temporary storage of the treasure, Norris took Andy Hawkins' place at the diggings, while that gesticulating individual went to act as guide to the rest of us in the search. But he proved as helpless as the rest. So when night found us all gathered together in our cheerless camp, we were conscious of a day passed with meager progress.

"Wherever that hiding place is," Norris was saying, "I'll bet there's a big heap of the stuff there."

"But he's been toting a lot of it away," suggested Ray.

"Toting it away!" burst out Norris. "Ask Captain Marat, here, what that nigger told him about the lot of stuff that's been mined all these years."

"Yes," agreed Jean Marat, "thad boy say ver' ver' much gold have come out of thee creek. I theenk not one ten' part have Duran take away."

It was not long till Andy Hawkins appeared. And true to his word, he brought a roast chicken.

"The boss was a bit dumpish tonight," he said. "'Ee was bloomin' tired, an' 'ee's sleepin' sixty mile to the minute right now."

While we feasted on the bird, Norris pumped Hawkins for details of Duran's doings; and it was indeed little that was enlightening that he got out of the fellow. But he got loquacious with reminiscences of his own past life as a pickpocket; and while Norris pretended to get much amusement out of that poor, misguided human's escapades in crime, we were not sorry when he made his way off to the huts to seek his bed.

On the morrow we began the day with much the same employment. But the day was not far gone when things suddenly took on a changed aspect.

Norris, who (true to his nature) found the suspense unbearable, determined on a bold move. It was when Duran was returning from his first trip with a load, Norris followed him into that jungle on the far side of the clearing. He meant this time to see where Duran went for his gold. The rest of us lay in the shelter from which we had watched Duran the day before.

It was not ten minutes after Duran, and Norris on his trail, had been swallowed up in the growth over there, that Duran suddenly appeared again, this time without his pack. And he seemed to be in excitement. And he made off, running down the path, directly disappearing from our sight in a turning.

"I'll bet he saw Norris," said Robert.

"Come," I said.

And I set off, followed by Robert. When we got across that ridge, of which I have spoken, we got a view down the open space. And there, nearing the top of his rope ladder, we saw Duran climbing.

In another moment he was hauling up his rope ladder; and quickly he got both ladder and halliard on the cliff-top.

CHAPTER XXVIII

WE ARE TRAPPED—THE BATTLE

We turned back, when Duran had passed out of our view on the cliff-top. Lest he should be watching, we still kept ourselves within the edge of the wood, till we had recrossed the ridge where the trees covered all of the ground. And there on the path we met the others and Norris, looking a little embarrassed, I thought. Doubtless, he was conscious that he had in his impetuosity discovered himself to Duran, and so spilled the soup, as it were. He did not mention it, and no one taxed him with it; but I know the thought punished him, and made him for a time a bit humble.

"He pulled the ladder and all up with him," I reported.

"And where is the polecat running to, do you suppose?" queried Ray.

And no one had an answer to that which he thought fit to give voice to. I doubt not, each one of us had pretty much the same thought, one that he dreaded to hear echoed by some other.

We were properly immured in this sink, of that we were all well assured. For we had Andy Hawkins' story of the times—in the two years—that he had made the round of those craggy walls in search of a possible escape.

It was a silent cavalcade that marched back to the clearing, and up to where Hawkins and the black boy were busy in the diggings. We gave them the news of Duran's precipitate flight, and Hawkins gave it little more thought than to "'ope 'ee didn't carry hoff the brown stuff," (meaning the opium) and "Hi'd give my 'and to know where 'ee keeps it."

Carlos, I noticed, had some private word with the black boy, and the two soon were gone into the brush together. The lad soon came back, and I egged on Jean Marat to question him as to what Carlos might be up to. For answer he led the two of us to where we found Carlos kneeling beside the skeleton of a human—it was in a patch of vines.

When finally Carlos discovered us, looking on wonderingly, he beckoned us. "My father," he said, in explanation. And he held up a gold cross that was on a chain that still hung on the ghastly figure.

And then Carlos got to his feet. "Duran—" he began, but the rest of the speech stuck in his throat. And I saw a look in his face that I had seen there before, and which boded ill for Duran.

With the black boy's help he had at last found the grave of his father. And such a grave! It went indeed hard with the elder Brill. The spoiler of his mine, and his murderer, had not even given him decent burial. We sent for the others; and then and there we dug a grave, and Norris was able to summon out of his memory a few words of the burial service. We left Carlos kneeling beside the mound. And when he rejoined us, much comfort showed in his face.

That bit of experience somehow drove, in large part, the gloom from our spirits, and we went about our further doings with more semblance of cheer.

Norris volunteered to go down and watch for Duran's possible return. I guessed his thought; that he felt that his bungling, in allowing himself to be discovered, had made him deserve this less agreeable task. The rest of us set ourselves to the business of searching out Duran's hidden storehouse. In spite of our zeal and numbers, the afternoon was nearly gone, and we no nearer the solution. We explored that cavern that Andy Hawkins had told us of; and moved forward in a passage that went upward in its windings. I marvelled at the singular freshness of the air, till—having traversed some couple of hundred yards—I discovered the reason. The cave had but the one gallery, and that ended in a chimney, just over our heads where we now stood, and through which showed the light of day. That little opening, in which a hat would have stuck, was high in the cliff-side, as we were to learn.

Ray and I hurried down the path in the dark, to Norris, to report our failure and to relieve him on watch. But he refused to budge from the place.

"I gave us all away," he said, "and now I'm going to make it up somehow. I'm going to make that skunk show us where he's got the stuff. And he'll do it, too, when I tell him a few of the things I've seen done to carcasses like him."

When he would not leave the watch to us, we decided to remain with him. He was not cheerful.

"You see," began Ray, then, "you'll have us to prove things by, when you're trying to convince that polecat. You'll say 'Isn't that so, Ray?' And I'll answer, 'Yes, that's so, Norris.' And then Wayne, here, he'll say, 'Yes, Norris, that's right, I know, because you never tell—'"

"Hist!" I interrupted him. "Listen."

Some little time back I thought I heard a thing like thunder, far back in the mountains. But it had been momentary, and I set it down as an illusion. While Ray prattled his nonsense, I seemed to hear it again. We cocked our ears, but heard not even so much as the trill of a tree-toad.

"Ah, say," began Ray, "What—" And this time he interrupted himself, to listen.

There was that quavering, rolling, rumble that we had heard weeks before. Each succeeding wave of sound seemed to join with, and accentuate, the preceding. And then came a decadency, like a wagon rolling out of ear-shot. And again—we could not tell just the moment we began to hear the sound—there came from afar that eerie rumble, swelling, slowly to die away once more.

"The voodoo drum," said Ray. "Some more voodoo doings—that's what he went for."

"Yes," said Norris, "and I'm afraid we'll have a *taste* of some more voodoo doings before we get through."

Neither of us cared to ask Norris what he meant. We continued to give ear to that weird music for long; and to each of us it seemed full of a portent; and each dreaded to hear another put it in words.

I do not know how many hours we three continued to squat there, at the edge of the wood; seldom talking, and then avoiding the thought uppermost in our minds. But at last it came, and we heard voices over by the cliff wall. They were coming down the rope ladder.

We rose to our feet, and scurried off in the edge of the wood, till we crossed the ridge and came to the beginning of the path. And there we crouched in the brush and waited.

At last came the stealthy, black figures, moving in silence, and in single file. We counted twenty as they went by us, and each carried some kind of gun. My heart pounded with the emotion; I have never before nor since experienced such fear as gripped me at sight of the martial array.

When they had passed, we got over across the stream to our friends, and gave them our ill news. The coming of those twenty dusky voodoos could have but the one explanation: Duran had brought them to hunt down, and destroy, the six of us. He would madden them with rum, mixed with the blood of fowls, and sick them on to us. And he made sure of us, since there was but the one exit from this vale; and there he doubtless had stationed some trusty black at the cliff-top, to keep the ladder and the halliard, till he should have need of it—when the work shall have been completed.

We trapped ones, got our heads together for some talk of our situation. How we lamented our lack of foresight, in leaving behind our arms and ammunition! Norris's lone rifle, with but a handful of cartridges, would but delay for a little the inevitable end. But for a time I had had my mind full of a wild thought. And I pulled Norris to one side, and opened the thing to him. My plan was so desperate that I hadn't the courage to tell it to anyone less bold spirited than he. It was no less than to employ that under-water way that Duran had used to transport the gold—to sink into the stream and be carried through that hole, and fetch up within that cavern; and so out to our camp in the forest, and return with the three rifles and the ammunition by way of the ladder—that was the plan.

Norris seized me by the arms. "The very thing!" he said, "——if it can be done. We'll find out!"

When we told the others of the plan, they took it without enthusiasm; declared it impossible—suicidal.

"You've no idea how far it is in to the cave," said Ray.

"We'll measure and find out," I answered. "Besides, it's our only chance."

There was no time to lose, for what we had to do must be done before daybreak; when we would have the whole cannibal crew stalking us.

We had a coil of half inch rope, which, with other things, we had taken from the shacks. This I took up, and Norris, Robert, and Carlos, made up the rest of the party. We moved down the stream in the dark, picking our way amongst the underbrush. At length we got out in the open, beyond the place of the ladder; and Carlos guided us to the spot on the bank of the creek, where he had seen Duran setting afloat the gold-laden bamboo. It was a wide pool about that hole, into which the waters disappeared in the cliff-side.

We found a piece of wood the size of a man's thigh. In this, all around, we drove a half dozen sharpened twigs; and we weighted the little log with stones, tied on; and at last bent on an end of our half inch rope. We then set it afloat, paying out the rope. And the log, neither scraping the bottom, nor yet floating on the surface, was carried on with the current into that hole.

I had my hand on the rope, and presently felt the impulse, as the log found an obstruction. It rested against that net of Duran's in the cavern; of that there was little doubt. We pulled back the log again, and so got the measure of the distance.

"Not over twenty feet!" declared Norris.

"And none of the pegs are knocked off," announced Robert, who explored the log.

"Now," I said, "I'm going. If after I get to the net, you feel two sharp jerks, in a little while repeated, you're to give me the rope. If I give five or six jerks, you're to pull me back; and if, after I touch the net you get no sort of signal, pull me out; and you, Bob, you know what to do."

None had better than Robert, the technic of artificial respiration.

"Now look here, Wayne," began Robert, "I'm going, too; and it's my turn to make it first."

And so here began a discussion, and if each, including Carlos, had had his way, all four would have gone that route. But at last we came to a decision, and Robert and I won, I to go first.

I selected a stone of sufficient weight to hold me down, so that I should not scrape on the roof of that passage; and I let them set the loop of rope about me, under the arms. I waded into the pool. I felt the suck of the water on my legs when I neared that hole.

"Keep your nerve and trust us," said Norris.

"Let her go!" I cried, and took a breath and held it, and ducked my head.

The current caught me. I experienced but a momentary pang of fear; and then succeeded a pleasurable sense of excitement. The next moment my feet touched something more yielding than rock, and that was the signal to lift my head to the surface. I was in the cavern. I slipped out of the noose, and gave the signal to haul away, and the rope went out of my hand. I crawled out of the stream.

It seemed little more than a minute, and Robert was beside me. I heard him gasping for his first breath.

"Who'd have thought it would be so easy," he said.

We took in the rope and hurried out to our old camp in the brush. We knew well where to lay our hands on the rifles—Marat's and Robert's and mine. There were some hundreds of rounds of cartridges for the larger guns—Marat's and Norris's—and many more of the twenty-two calibre for our little rifles.

We tarried not at all, but got back through the cascade into the cavern again, and so up and out, on the way to that cliff-top.

We moved cautiously, as we neared those cedars, where hung the rope ladder, for it was probable there should be a peril there, in the shape of a black, guarding the ladder, and it was in reason that he should have some kind of weapon. Our plan of action had been determined before we left Norris. We would surprise the fellow, pounce on him and secure him with the rope.

Then we would let down the ladder to Norris and Carlos, who would come up and help us lower the captive into the vale.

Our bare feet crept forward at a snail's pace, nearer and nearer to the cedars. A pebble rolled, and suddenly a figure rose up before us with a startled grunt.

And that instant it toppled over the cliff-edge with a guttural cry; and we heard nothing more.

In a minute we had the rope ladder unrolling, down the cliff-side. We threw down the loose end of halliard, and began the descent.

"I didn't expect we'd get him down so easy," observed Robert, seeking comfort in a grim joke.

"I wish it could have been as we planned," I said. I sickened at the thought of that mangled body somewhere down below.

We soon had our feet on the sloping ledge. Norris and Carlos stood there waiting.

"Did you have to throw him down?" queried Norris. And then, when I had related the circumstance:—"He must have been asleep," he said.

Having pulled the ladder up to the cedars, I took up the loose end of the halliard, and climbing as high as I dared venture among the vines, I made fast the rope so that Duran would not easily discover it.

Norris and Carlos had made some disposition of the black's body, for which I was thankful; for I had no wish to set my eye on the thing, even in the dark.

Norris and Carlos took over the heavy ammunition, and we set off up the vale. It was a silent file that stole cautiously through the woods, till we had joined Marat and Ray, who were greatly relieved to learn that our adventure had been carried through without unhappy accident. That it had cost the life of one of the enemy was accounted a gain. There had fallen an accession to our party, too, while we were gone; and Hawkins and the black boy had stolen away from Duran's party soon after the arrival at the huts.

"The boss," said Hawkins, "'ee butchered some chickens, and 'ee began to dose them niggers up on the rum."

The black boy had told Jean Marat a startling piece of news: no less than that Duran had promised his voodoo crew a feasting, on the morrow, on the hearts of his white enemies.

"They've a surprise in store for them, I guess," said Norris, when Marat had repeated the intelligence.

"Yes, I think," agreed Captain Marat. "We maybe feed them on thing' what give indigestion." And he continued to distribute about his person his share of the ammunition.

Day was not many hours off, and Norris and Marat put their heads together to discuss the plan of battle. At the first, we were to be on the defensive, and when the enemy had been given a proper reception, a vigorous offensive action was to follow with the purpose to quickly demoralize the blacks. Robert and I came forward with the suggestion that while Marat and Norris should crouch behind some breastworks of logs, that should be thrown up at the edge of the clearing, Robert and I would seek sheltered places well forward on either side of the clearing, and with our little silent guns we would throw lead into the feet and legs of any blacks who should spread out to either flank. And thus we would help to keep the enemy in a single mass during their attack, which would give Norris and Marat their chance.

Some parts of fallen trees were dragged near the edge of the clearing. And then a fire was made back among the trees, with the intent to give direction to the enemy when they should come. When we had all taken our places: I was at the edge of the clearing, close to the beginning of the path; Carlos crouched with me behind a tree, to lend me his eyes; Ray was doing the same for Robert on the opposite side of the clearing; Marat and Norris lay behind their breastworks; Hawkins and the black boy were at the back, ready to call, in any case of need.

You will never think that our situation was an agreeable one. I know I speak for all of our party—except perhaps, Norris and Carlos—when I say that we would gladly have escaped from that vale, and boarded the *Pearl*, to sail away without thought of return. And you will say, there was the rope ladder ready to our hand, and none to block the way. But not one among us had the hardihood to suggest retreat. It was Norris held us, of that I am sure; throughout, the thought of retreat never entered his mind; that must have been plain to us all. We had some things in our favor. Marat and Norris, each with his own heavy-powered rifle, had long ago forgotten what it was to miss; Robert and I, with our little guns, rarely ever lost our target.

After our fire had been set alight, not a sound had come from the huts. Night birds and tree-toads intoned peaceful notes. The night breeze rustled the tops of the taller palms. I crouched at the foot of my tree, getting much comfort of the sound of Carlos' breathing close by. Fortunately I had not to bear that suspense for long.

The first hint of dawn had hardly showed above the trees, when that score of blacks poured into view by the huts, each holding a gun. They moved forward, four or five spreading out on either flank. There was one who was about to enter the wood to my right. I drew bead on his foot and pulled the trigger. The black stooped, uttering a painful grunt. I did the same for the next near black fellow. He cried out with the pain. And the two forthwith limped back the way they had come. The others of the stragglers on my side showed themselves startled at this inexplicable conduct of their two fellows, and fell in to the main body.

A glance told me that Robert was having similar luck on his side. And there was evident consternation among those of the enemy who saw some of their comrades limping painfully away; for up to now there had been no sound to account for such conduct.

But now the quiet of that dawn was broken. Two loud reports rang out and set echoes going in the vale. Two more shots followed, and there lay four writhing black voodoos on the ground. The rest of the blacks let go one volley, and then broke and ran. One more among them fell before they gained shelter behind the huts.

Then Norris joined me where I crouched. "No one hurt amongst us, I guess," he observed, as he kept his eyes on the structures. When a head or shoulder showed there, he let fly at it with a ball. We heard an occasional shot from Marat's rifle on the east side of the clearing, where he had gone to join Robert.

"If you can drive 'em back into the cave we've got 'em," spoke the voice of Hawkins. "Hi'll take care of 'em then, Hi will." And he crept up and whispered something into Norris' ear.

"Good!" said Norris. "We'll get them there. Run round and tell that to Marat."

And the fellow set off through the woods to get round to Captain Marat.

For a time, the enemy let off an occasional shot on general principles, and without effect, but soon lost all ambition, apparently, and silence reigned. It was then I heard an exclamation from Carlos. "Ah! Duran!" he cried, and he set off through the brush.

Instinctively I followed him. Directly, we were on the path. When we had crossed the ridge, I saw Duran out in the open, legging it toward the cliff under the cedars, and calling out as he ran. Doubtless he called to the black he had left in charge of the rope ladder—he who now lay, a mangled corpse at the foot. He continued to call as he hurried up that inclined ledge. But no ladder came down to him.

Carlos was at the foot of the incline when Duran reached the limit of the ledge. On up that way sped Carlos, after him. My heart, my breath, my feet, all alike stopped, as I awaited the clash. And then it came. The struggle was short. The two tripped over the edge together. I saw Carlos grasp at some growth; it tore loose. And then he seized on a vine, finally sliding to the bottom. I rushed to him. He had escaped with a badly wrenched shoulder.

Duran lay at the rocky foot of the cliff in a heap, the death-rattle already in his throat. He had broken his skull.

CHAPTER XXIX

HOW THE ENEMY PERISH AND THE MONKEY DISCOVERS THE TREASURE

It was some minutes before Carlos could hold up his head, so badly shaken was he. I went all over him, and had soon satisfied myself there were no broken bones. He had been saved by the very mass of vines that had before preserved me from death. His fall had been but forty feet, and mine had been many times that; a fall, after a manner of saying, for, as will be remembered, I slid down the rope halliard the greater part of the descent.

I ran through the wood to the creek, and brought Carlos a drink; and it was then he got to his feet. We stood looking on the now quite inanimate form of Duran, for a little, neither of us speaking his thoughts. I could not tell by Carlos' stoic features what there was in his mind; but in mine there was admixture, of some sorrow, that the presence of death always puts into one when excitement is gone, but more of a sense of elation that Duran had come by his death in the manner he had. For whatever intent Carlos had entertained in his mind, he had not actually slain the man with his own hand. And there on the ground, too, lay a knife that Duran had tried to use on Carlos, who was without a weapon of any sort, his own knife being in the camp.

It was time we were on the way to join our friends. I had been hearing occasional shots, but when we turned away from Duran's body, all sounds had ceased. We crossed the ridge, and in a little had come to the clearing. There was no one in sight; so we went round within the edge of the wood back of the huts; and as we neared the cliffs my nostrils were filled with the odor of sulphur. And we had no sooner got to the edge of the little open space in front of the cave, than Robert was upon us and pulled us to the ground. He had us to crawl after him to where Norris and Marat lay, gun in hand, behind a fallen tree-trunk.

They had their eyes on the mouth of the cave, and looking over there, I saw a curious thing. A fire burned at the very entrance of the cave; and on the one side, Andy Hawkins lingered beside a pile of dried brush-wood and dead palm leaves. This fuel he cast on the flames, from time to time. Ray and the black boy soon came to view, back of Hawkins, with arms filled with more fuel which they added to the pile.

I now saw how it was; the enemy had taken refuge in the cave, and now our party were smoking them out. The smoke, I saw, was drawn into the cavern as into a chimney; and I remembered how, when I was in the cave, I had felt the draft of air going through. I looked up the cliff-side; and there, far to the left, I saw a wee column of smoke going up from a cleft. And then—there was that odor of sulphur again. Smoking them out! Ay, but how smoking them out? My flesh crept with the horror of the thing. This was the miserable Hawkins' doing. I remembered now that word he had let drop about his taking care of them if we should but drive them into the cave—and his whispering in Norris' ear. I felt sick.

"Are we doing right?" I said to Norris, beside whom I crouched.

"Right!" he said, turning an angry look at me. "Didn't they plan to eat our hearts this night? And didn't they attack us, twenty guns against four—the murderous, child-eating cannibals? And isn't smoking as easy a death as hanging? What do you want?"

I was effectively silenced. And then I thought, too, on the alternative. Suppose we retire and let the blacks out. Would they go their ways and let us alone? I knew better. They would simply set a strong guard on the only exit; and then collect many more of their voodoo comrades; and they would have our hearts for a voodoo feast in the end. So I gave in to this thing that was going on, distasteful as I found it.

I watched Andy Hawkins over there. That thin body of his squirmed with his infirmity, and made him seem to be in the throes of a heathen dance, as he plied the fire with the fuel. The volumes of yellow-white smoke continued to pour into the cave's mouth. It was burning sulphur, as I learned.

It may have been two hours that we lay behind that fallen tree, and the sun was mounted well on toward the zenith. Then Norris and Marat conferred, and decided that the enemy must be in a state beyond all power of striking back. So we approached the fire and pulled it away from the cave's mouth. But nearly another hour passed before we ventured in. Norris took the lead with a battery lamp, the rest of us following.

A little way within, we came upon a body that lay in a pool of blood. He was one that sought to rush out, and got a ball in his body. Then at various portions of the passage we saw three more blacks, all inanimate. And at the uttermost confines of the cave, just below that narrow opening out—the chimney, as it were—all the rest lay in various postures, where they fell, choked by the fumes.

"Well, they all got just what they earned," observed Norris. "The world would be better, if all of their kind were here with them."

"Yes," agreed Jean Marat, "but Duran, he ees not here. I am ver' sorry he ees not here weeth hees voodoo frien's."

I had not told of Duran's accident at the foot of the ladder. Now I told it.

"Ah! You don't say!" said Norris. "Are you sure he's dead?"

"Yes," I assured him. "His skull was fractured."

"We're in great luck," said Norris. "Now we've got the whole secret of this place among us. And Carlos, you had a narrow escape."

"Yes," said Carlos. "And my father, hees murderer, he dead."

We dug a long trench just without that cave; and it was well past noon when we had dragged out the blacks and buried them in it, with the five that had fallen at the clearing. We took a meal before we went down the vale, and placed Duran and that other black in another grave.

It was while we were dining (and it was a pair of Duran's chickens that made our feast) that Andy Hawkins told how he had come by the conceit of the sulphur fumes. It was one day that he had watched Duran, when he took a chicken tied by the legs, into the cave. Duran had then set a tin, holding the sulphur, at the entrance, and built a fire about it. An hour or two later, he had brought out the chicken, quite dead.

"I thought to myself then," continued Hawkins, "An' w'y does the boss be doin' of that thing? And then I got the idea. 'Ah, 'ee's a slick one, the boss is,' sez I to myself. "Ee's after findin' a easy way, maybe, to get rid of anyone as is in 'is way 'ere. And that might be you, Handy 'Awkins, and you'll better keep out of that cave!'"

We took possession of the palm-thatched huts; and made beds, of palm fans for mattresses, which was pretty much all the bedding that was required, though Duran had blankets enough to cover us all in the event of a chill night. Out between the structures was the kitchen; and this was no more than a kind of shallow box, sand filled, and elevated on four posts, to make the fire on; with overhead a roof—palm-thatched—for shade, and protection against rain.

Our day had been pretty full, and when supper had been disposed of, all were ready to stretch out at full length for a needed rest. It was not altogether such a cheerful company as you might suppose. Even Ray was more dashed in spirit than I have seen him in many a day. You might say that we had every reason to be in high feather, having so lately been delivered of a great peril; not to say that we were in addition well rid of Duran, who alone was in a position—rightly or wrongly—to dispute with us the possession of this gold-paved vale.

But if you think we should have felt blithe that night, it will be because you have never been in the presence of so much death. I know the thought worked continually in my mind, of that score and more of humans—however villainous they may have been—that but a few hours before had danced with life and vigour, and were now already beginning to rot in their graves. Only Norris and Hawkins refused to be downcast; Norris, because he had been accustomed to battle, and had learned through discipline to rebate his natural qualms; with Hawkins, it was his dulled moral sense.

"Now tomorrow," said Norris, "we must find that place where Duran has been storing the gold." (Duran's taking off had so far softened him at least, that he refrained from referring to him as "the skunk.") He continued, "I know blooming well he has taken out of this place only a small part of what has been mined."

And Hawkins (and the black boy, too, when questioned) agreed with Norris.

"Thad Duran was ver' clever," said Jean Marat. "He find one ver' good place to hide thad gold."

And now, it would never be guessed how we came upon a clue to that spot. It came about this way. Although we turned in early, we were that wearied that day came and caught us, every one, sound asleep. I was the first to wake; and it was with the feel of a wee hand upon my face. And when I opened my eyes, there was the monkey. And he held out to me one of Duran's sections of bamboo.

I sat up, startled, and took the thing he held out, and it was weighty, like those others laden with the gold.

The monkey observed me narrowly, as though to gauge the degree of my interest in the object he had given me. Then he took my hand; and without stopping to slip on my shoes, I allowed the little animal to lead me forth.

My heart thumped in excitement of anticipation; I was filled with a hope, as we went into the wood back of the huts, making direct toward the cliffs. He led me to where the vines, in a dense mass, went climbing up the rocky wall to a very considerable height. There he let go my hand and leaped upon the vines, and began to climb, looking over his shoulder, as if expecting me to follow monkey-fashion.

Then, seeing me hesitate, the monkey came down, and took me by the hand again. And, curious, I stepped forward, to find that where the vines sprang from the ground the wall ascended, for some six or eight feet, in a gentle slope that I could climb with ease.

When I got so far, and spread apart the vines, to my amazement I discovered that what I had thought was a part of the cliff wall, was no real piece of the cliff at all, but just a ridge; and behind it, and concealed by the mass of vines, was a bit of a dingle, perhaps fifteen feet across. The monkey and I descended into the place; and as my eyes became accustomed to the comparative darkness, I made out the low entrance to a cavern.

Stooping low, I followed the monkey in. Twenty steps, and I heard the squeaking monkey-talk at my feet. Then I felt another bamboo cylinder pressed to my hand; and I stooped to feel a heap of the bamboo, of unknown proportions. I took up several of the cylinders. All were heavy.

At last we had the thing we sought. And it took a monkey to find it for us! My battery lamp was out there in the hut; I did not tarry to investigate further, but hurried out; and, followed by the nimble monkey got back to my friends, who were now astir.

The black boy was kindling a fire on the elevated hearth; Norris stood looking on. At my approach he turned.

"Hello!" he said. "And where——"

He cut off his speech at sight of the bamboo I carried in my hands.

"Say, now!" he began again, and he seized and hefted the things. "Where have you been picking up these?"

By this time all the party were crowded round, and the monkey scrambled to my shoulder. I told the story of the find.

"Aw," began Ray, "he's just trying to make monkeys of the whole crowd."

They all wanted to fondle the animal, who, scolding, wormed himself out of their hands and scurried up a post to the kitchen roof.

"Now you know I told you, Norris," said Ray, "It would be Wayne that would find it."

"It's all right, Ray," I told him. "I don't mind your giving my name to the monk."

There would be no breakfast till they had seen the place.

"We've got to see how much there is there," declared Norris.

And off we went, the monkey again leading the way, over the little rising, through the curtain of vines, and into the cave. The lights illumined the place, and the sounds of amazement echoed. For there, on the floor, heaped on a tarpaulin, showed bushels of yellow, glinting gold-dust and nuggets. And there were beside it two greater piles of the bamboo cylinders, the one heap already gold-laden, as we found; and the other awaiting the filling. On the ground stood a tin holding pitch, for sealing; and there were small bricks of cork, and pieces of life-jackets, torn open to extract the cork. A ship's lantern stood on a projection of rock.

"I never saw such a pile of the stuff!" spoke Grant Norris, plunging his fist in the yellow mass.

Many hands went in to feel of the precious commodity, and nuggets of varying size were held to the light. Even the monkey must imitate the others, and enjoy the feel of the yellow stuff; and he insisted on pressing nugget after nugget into my hand.

Andy Hawkins had soon borrowed Robert's light, and with many jerks and grimaces he poked about in the nooks and crannies in search of something. I easily guessed what the thing was that he put above the gold in his interest; for it had been plain that Duran doled out the drug to Hawkins in a fashion that best served his (Duran's) interest. And, having an eye on Hawkins's doings, I observed him at last to pounce on and bring out a little parcel from a nook, his face lighting up with a gleam of victory. Later in the day, when I had told Norris of the circumstances, he bullied Hawkins into giving up the supply of drug, telling him that he (Norris) would perhaps be a better judge of dosage than the patient himself.

Before we left that cave, we explored the place, to find that it was but a small affair, going in not above a hundred feet. It was a joyous breakfast we sat down to at the huts, for we had now attained the thing we sought; and we had every reason to believe that no one living, outside of our little party, had any knowledge of this hidden vale with its gold mine, so long ago discovered by the father of Carlos. And all our talk now turned on how we should get all that mined gold out and aboard the *Pearl*, and not forgetting that unknown portion of the treasure that yet remained to be discovered on the isle out in Crow Bay.

"We can find that without much trouble," declared Robert.

"Yes," agreed Captain Marat, "We know ver' close where thad place ees. We take the schooner in to the bay, an' then eet will nod be so ver' hard to ged all of thad gold on board."

I observed that we seemed to be forgetting that black that Robert and Carlos had seen on the isle, and the schooner, *Orion*.

"Yes, I've been thinking of that," said Norris. "We'll have to be getting over there, or that crew'll be stealing a march on us."

In an hour we were off. Andy Hawkins and Black Boy were left behind, to keep house. We promised them they'd see us back the second day at the latest; and then it would not be long till they should have a sight of the world—again for the one, and for the first time for the other.

In that open bit, below the ladder, we stopped a moment beside the two mounds covering Duran and the black sentinel.

Grant Norris was looking down on that of Duran.

"Drop a tear on him," said Ray to Norris. "Think of all the fun and excitement he gave you."

"He was a queer composition," observed Norris. "I've met many queer cusses, but he's the first white cannibal I ever saw."

We soon had down the rope ladder; and when all had mounted to the clifftop, we pulled up the halliard, for we had no real assurance that that ex-pickpocket, Hawkins, might not take it into his head to climb out and wander off to our betrayal.

When we got to our boat, a pair of us sat ourselves in Duran's canoe, and soon we were out on Crow Bay. It was with some satisfaction that we noted the absence of any sail upon that water. Those black sailors of Duran's had apparently not seen fit to venture in as yet in quest of the treasure in the isle.

We crossed the end of the bay, and in time had joined Julian Lamartine and Rufe, aboard the *Pearl*.

CHAPTER XXX

THE CACHE ON THE ISLE

Julian was much relieved, but Rufe was overjoyed to see us.

"De Lord o' massy!" he began, "but I's glad to see you-all! Whah you been all dis heah time? I jes' been a-telling Jul'en, boy, dat shu'ah dem voodoo niggahs got ye. I hopes, now, you-all is gwine to gib up dat ol' gold-huntin'."

"Give up!" said Ray. "Say, Rufe, did you ever think Norris would ever give up anything? Why——"

"Look here, Rufe," broke in Norris thrusting a pretty nugget under the cook's nose. "Does that look like giving up gold-hunting?"

Rufe's eyes bulged. "Is dat sho' 'nuff gold?" he queried.

And then we began with our story. And Rufe must have us over by the galley door to continue the tale, while he hurried dinner, for he said, "I jes' knows you-all is nigh about starved out."

The black sailors were squatted in a circle, up near the bows, when we came aboard, and dice rattled on the deck, with snaps of fingers and sharp orders spoken to the bones for their better performance. Julian said it was the dice kept them contented, day after day and they were at the game continuously.

During the meal our plans for the following days came to a head. It was the purpose to sail the *Pearl* round to and through the tortuous channel into Crow Bay. The schooner would go out from the cove under the land breeze, sometime between nine o'clock at night and morning, and the trade wind—from the northeast—would take her into Crow Bay the next day. Three of us would row in the little boat, down the bay to that isle, to see that the coast should be clear. The afternoon was not idle, for Norris was full of preparation for the reception of all that treasure—gold-dust; and there must be bins made in the schooner's hold, for, "we'll have to dump some of it in, like grain," he said. "We haven't time to build chests for it all." And then Robert and I were tired of the stain on our skins, and must have it off.

Before night spread over the region, Norris, with his big rifle, and Robert and I with our little ones, were in the skiff, moving slowly out on Crow Bay. There was no sign of a boat on the bay yet.

"I guess they got scared out," said Norris, "and are still lying in some cove, waiting for word from Duran."

In these tropics you sweep the bright daylight landscape with your eyes, noting the graceful palms bowing to you over the beach; then you close your eyes, count a few hundred slowly, open them again, and—presto! all is black night, and the palms have melted into eternity, or are dimly silhouetted against the night sky. The narrow crescent of the new moon was among the tops of the palms behind us.

Within the hour, we made landing on the isle. We dragged our boat up into the brush, and then moved back through the wood to the edge of the clearing. A light shone in the window of the hut. We crept up and looked in. That same portly black was there, and he was in the midst of preparations to turn into his bunk. In another minute he put out the light.

We decided to go round the island beach for signs of any recent landing parties. We found the boat, used by the black of the cabin, in its usual place. Then we took to the beach, and with the occasional use of our battery lamps, we examined the sand floor as we went. We completed the circuit, seeing nothing to our interest. And then Norris was for at once going into that thicket where Robert and Carlos had witnessed the going in and out of Duran and that mysterious, naked black.

Robert led the way, which took us into the clearing to the north of the cabin. In a little, we had found a winding way, cut into the thicket. In the center of that jungle we came into a space having the dimensions of a small room. The floor was level—of sand. We threw our light around.

"Not a sign of anything here," declared Norris.

But Robert had another word to say. "Here it is!" he cried. And we joined him, where he was stamping with his foot. There was a sound—or feel—as we came down with our heels, of something hollow beneath.

We scraped the sand away with our hands, making a hole less than a foot in depth; and came upon something made of boards.

"So far, so good," said Norris. "The stuff is there without much doubt. We have nothing more to do, now, but wait till the *Pearl* gets here, tomorrow."

When we settled down beside our boat, close to the south beach, the night breeze was rustling the dry palm fans above our heads; the ripples broke on the beach with a soft playful sound.

"I guess Captain Marat will be getting sail on the schooner, now," I observed.

"I wish this same wind would get him here tonight," complained Norris.

"We ought to be glad we can depend on another wind to get him in tomorrow," I reproved the impatient one.

"Right you are, Mr. Philosopher," he returned with proper humility. "I'm a worse kid than any of you. But then, too, I don't mind saying, I don't want the interference of any more of these voodoo skunks till we get all the stuff into the hold of the *Pearl*. After that, let them come on—I'd just like another whack at some more of those blood-drinking voodoo cannibals." And he rubbed his hands with contemplation of the experience.

We took turn about on watch, though we did not think it worth while to keep any eye on the hut. It was three of the morning, when Norris roused me for my watch. I paced a little stretch of beach for a spell, to work off the sleep that clung to me.

Suddenly, I heard voices. I hurried in to the clearing. And sure enough, over near the hut, there were those who were chattering away with more or less abandon.

I rushed back to my comrades, shook them awake and gave them the news.

"Get your rifles," said Norris.

We hurried to the clearing. The voices now came from the shore to the west. We scrambled through the brush till we got in view of the beach.

There we made out in the dark a number of figures moving in a mass towards a boat. These figures hovered about the boat for some minutes, and then returned the way they had come, disappearing in the wood.

We three lost not a moment, but leaped to that boat. It was a ship's life-boat of considerable size, and clinker built; and between two of the thwarts there rested a chest of great weight, as we found.

"They're here sure enough," said Norris, in a whisper. "They're getting the stuff. Now it's for a fight!" and he patted his rifle.

"Wait!" I said, as he was about to lead the way after the blacks. "Leave the shooting to Bob and me, with our rifles—they can't hear ours."

And it was Robert, then, that suggested that we bore holes in the boat.

The planks were thin, since the boat was clinker built, so that we were not long in making a number of holes with our knives, near the bow, which was out of the water. We got in among the palms and brush and waited the coming of the blacks. I whispered Robert a caution not to aim above the knees; no need to do more than should serve our purpose.

We had time to spare, but the black figures presently pushed out on the beach, toting a heavy object among them. There seemed to be five in the group.

"Now," I whispered, and Robert and I raised our little rifles. As we pulled the triggers, there was no sound but two outcries. Then came two more howls, and down went the heavy thing they carried.

The blacks ran afoul of one another, in their frantic haste to get to the boat. They pushed off, scrambling into the boat, and we sent more silent, hot pepper after the legs that dallied. Norris could not resist; he jerked his rifle to his shoulders. But Robert and I pulled him down.

"Don't spoil it now," I said. "Let's not make a noise if we can help it."

"You're right," he said. "I'll maybe get my chance another time."

That boat was not over forty yards from shore now, and even in the dark we could see that it was sinking. And the blacks had evidently discovered their plight, and were leaping into the water and striking out for the north shore of Crow Bay.

When the last of the blacks had abandoned the boat, we had off some of our clothes, and rushed into the water.

It was up to our arm-pits where we found the boat. Though the water was within a few inches of the top of the coaming, we contrived with a few shoves to propel the boat some yards shoreward, before it sank, in five feet of water.

"Well, that's safe," said Norris, striking out for the shore. "We'll get that out with tackle."

Day broke while we examined that chest upon the beach. It was of rough lumber, roughly, but strongly made, having rope handles, and well padlocked. In the hut we found food, cooking utensils, an empty jug emitting an odor of rum, an ax, and a pair of shovels.

"That fat, black fellow who lived here must have gone off with the others," observed Robert.

Norris led the way into the thicket. In the spot we'd found in the night, a tight box of great size was sunk into the soil. Its cover lay on one side. On this cover stood an open chest, a quarter filled with the gold-laden bamboo cylinders. Down in the great box were three more of the chests; and these we found to be empty. All were fitted alike, with rope handles, staples and hasps.

"Well, anyway," said Norris, "we'll make good use of these boxes. There's all that stuff up in the cave." He ran on, with enthusiasm, on the things we would do.

"All right, all right," interrupted the usually taciturn Robert at last, "but when's breakfast?" And his hand went in where his breakfast should be.

"That's so," admitted Norris. "We've forgotten breakfast."

The odor in the hut was too much for our stomachs, so we eschewed the place for all that it had a stove, and made our meal down by our boat.

The morning dragged tediously. It was less than two hours of noon before the day breeze sprung up, so that we could hope for the coming of the *Pearl*. We crouched in the sand on the northeast shore of the isle, watching anxiously. And at last the sails of the schooner appeared, coming from behind the point near the inner terminus of the channel. We rose to our feet and shouted with joy.

"Hold on!" I cried, when I had taken a second look. "That's not the *Pearl*, that's the *Orion*!"

"Good God! Yes, you're right," said Norris. "What does that mean?"

We retreated into the shelter of the trees. And I sickened with a horrid sensation. It was as much anxiety regarding the *Pearl*, as fear for ourselves; and we had no proper defence, from which we could stand off a dozen or more armed black devils. The *Orion* changed her course and bore down direct for the isle. We stood, paralyzed with our surprise and dread, gazing on that vessel as it bore down under the freshening breeze. For ten minutes we stood thus.

"Shall we take to the skiff?" said Robert at last.

None answered him. I had just noted a strange thing. The black sailors on the *Orion*—now almost directly north of us—had none of their interest centered on the isle. I turned my eyes back the way the *Orion* had come. And there were the sails of another schooner coming from behind that point.

"Look!" I cried.

"The *Pearl*!" said Grant Norris. "That tells the story: the *Orion's* running away from her."

He danced with joy. And we three struck one another in our ecstacy of relief.

The *Orion* rounded the isle, and the *Pearl*, coming in chase, was soon opposite us, and near enough to hail. We rushed down to the water. Our friends, at the rail, waved to us.

"All is safe!" we called. "Drive the *Orion* out if you can!"

"Aye! Aye!" came back Ray's voice, and the chase continued.

Round the isle they went. We followed with our eyes, walking the beach. The *Orion* scudded off a way down the bay, to the east; then went about on the starboard tack and made for the channel, where she had come in. At last she disappeared behind that point again. And then the *Pearl* left the trail, and again set her bowsprit toward our isle, at last dropping her anchor some two hundred yards to the northwest.

In a little, Captain Marat, Ray, Julian, and Carlos came to shore in the boat.

"Well, you gave us a proper fright," I told them, "driving that schooner in on us that way."

"Norris didn't get scared, did he?" bantered Ray.

"Yes, he did," declared Norris, speaking for himself. "And the skin all up and down my back is wrinkled even yet. This little place isn't like that up there in that rock sink, with all those holes to crawl into when you're getting licked."

"I'll tell you, Ray," I interposed. "The thing that made most of those wrinkles in his back was thinking what must have happened to you and the *Pearl*—seeing that schooner coming in in place of the *Pearl*. Now tell us how you chased the *Orion* in here."

"Ah," began Captain Marat. "I guess thad *Orion* lay all night in thee passage. We see her there when we come in."

And now the party must visit the gold-cache in the thicket.

"Well," observed Julian, "this is interesting, but I want to see your gold mine behind that waterfall."

"The waterfall isn't much for size," returned Norris, "but it's a wonderful accident of nature; and I will say Carlos's father had a remarkable head on him to discover what it hid. But wait till you see his gold mine, and the stuff in the cave, that's come out of it, and you'll have an eyeful."

"Yes," added Ray. "And you'll see a monkey in there that's always filling Wayne's pocket full. That monkey and Wayne are in cahoots."

Our first care was to recover the gold-laden chest that went down with the boat. By diving, we got a hawser through the two rope handles. And when the tide was all in—and that was about two o'clock—we warped the schooner over to the place; and with block and tackle on the foresail boom, swung above, we had soon lifted the chest aboard. Many hands made light work of the other boxes.

With careful sounding, as we moved under reefed mainsail and jib, we got the *Pearl* to a good anchorage near the upper end of Crow Bay. And as there were still some hours of daylight, we took the empty chests in two boats, and sought out the bayou that took us into the mouth of the creek whose waters flowed from the gold mine.

Julian this time accompanied the party; and I got renewed thrills, to see how he marveled at the wonders that blazed the trail, from the little cascade that screened the entrance, to the placer mine, and the shining gold horde in the cave.

CHAPTER XXXI

WE RUN THE GAUNTLET—HOME BOUND

"Too bad we can't put in a week, getting some more gold out of this creek," said Norris. He was plucking little bits of the precious metal out of a pan of gravel he'd just washed. "There's no end of the stuff here still," he complained.

"Well, but aren't we coming back some day?" observed Robert.

"Just like some folks," said Ray. "The more they get, the more they want."

We had gone to the diggings to break up the Long Tom, to make boxes for floating the horde of mined gold through the hole in the cliff. The little bamboo cylinders offered too slow a means to satisfy our impatience.

Our party divided, some remaining in that outer cavern, to receive the boxes, as they floated to the net, and empty them into the chests outside; the empty boxes being towed back again, by ropes, to be new-laden with the gold. What with making our three little "under-sea-boat" boxes, and finding proper floats for them, we did not get much of our precious freight through that first day. Jean Marat, Robert, and Carlos slept in the boats on their side of the cliffs; the rest of our party, including Andy Hawkins, and the black boy, took cheer among Duran's huts within. We gathered round a fire after we'd had our supper, and it was a blithesome party, of which the monkey was a part, perched the greater part of the time on either my shoulder or the black boy's.

There was some exchange of yarns, most of them of Norris's telling. And Andy Hawkins had some experiences to tell that were a bit off color. It came to riddles at last. And here Norris shone again; and Hawkins was not at a loss for one or two. Norris insisted that we must each offer one riddle at the least, and out came the one about, "Why does a miller wear a white hat?" and others of later coinage. Norris held back Ray for the last. He must have been sure Ray should break up the party.

"Now your turn, Ray," said Norris.

"Aw, I don't know any," pouted Ray.

"Make up one," insisted Norris.

"Well," began Ray, drawling his words, "Mary had a little—Now don't interrupt!"

"Who is interrupting?" said Norris. "But you might give us something new."

"Well, if it don't suit you," shot back Ray, "you tell it."

"Go on," said Norris.

Ray continued: "It followed her to school—one day. The teacher dropped his book, and bent down for it. But—but—" (Ray seemed to have got to the end of his powers of "make up") "but—but—but—"

"Well, go on," pressed Norris. "But what?"

"The teacher, of course," said Ray, frowning. "What do you suppose Mary brought the goat to school for?"

We turned in early, meaning to rise with the sun for the next day's labors.

I dreamed I was at the railway station, back home in Illinois. I heard the roar of a train approaching. Then came an explosion. I opened my eyes. A tropic storm was on us, there was thunder, and the rain came down in a deluge.

I started up in excitement, as I thought of that little hole in the cliff, the only outlet for all the water. What if this terrific downpour should continue, and the water back up in this walled basin! But at second thought I remembered, and it was only the water that fell within our basin that we had to fear; for the stream met the same sort of obstruction to its inflow, above, as that which retarded its outflow, below. With that comforting thought I presently fell asleep again.

The day broke fresh and cool. The creek had soon discharged its excess waters, and our labors went forward without hitch, till the last of the gold-dust had been sent out through that watery portal. And that was late of the afternoon; so that when our party had said a goodbye to the gold valley, and stood by the cedars at the cliff-top, the region was all in shadow.

We unbent the ropes from the cedars.

"No use to chance some others finding their way in," said Norris. "And we can make another ladder when we come back."

Norris must have had Hawkins blindfolded, before we made that passage through the cavern. There was no assurance, as he afterwards explained, that the pickpocket might not pick up with more of his ilk, who would wish to seek out the place.

Andy Hawkins thanked him for the precaution. "Hi never want to be able to find my way back to that 'ell 'ole again," he said.

It was quite dark when we doused for the last time through the little waterfall. Robert awaited us with one of the boats, and it was not long till we were on the deck of the *Pearl*.

While some were below, stowing the precious cargo, others were in some preparation for a lifting of the anchor and getting on sail at the very first waft of the land breeze. Norris threw off the jacket of his big gun, and looked to the priming.

"You must never think," he said, "that those black devils are going to see us get away with the gold without some sort of attempt to head us off."

"Yes," added Captain Marat. "I theenk they try sometheeng."

It was in that narrow, tortuous channel the attempt would be made, if at all. It would be above a mile of ticklish navigation, following the curves, and avoiding the points. And there were heights from which they could rain shot on us as we passed. We got out all the mattresses; of one we constructed a bulwark for the helmsman, another covered the skylight, others were propped up at convenient places on the deck. It was conjectured that the attack—if one there was to be—would take us on the starboard, since doubtless the sailors from the *Orion* would land on that side of the channel, also since it was that side offered the better vantage ground. Norris brought his gun to that side of the ship.

The moon, which was in its first quarter, was due to set about ten o'clock. We hoped that the land breeze might come soon enough to get us through before its light should have gone. We needed the view of the channel, and some sight of the enemies' lurking-place would doubtless be to our advantage.

True to its practice, the land breeze rose at about nine. Up came the anchor, and with a rattle of blocks, up went the sails. The moonlight glinted among the wavelets directly in our wake, as we moved down Crow Bay toward the isle. We passed the isle on the left. Arrived at the wide opening of the channel, the sheets were run out till the booms hung over the port bulwarks. Robert was at the wheel; Captain Marat with his rifle was in the bows, from where he gave his orders; Norris, Ray, and Carlos, were at the gun, Carlos holding Norris's rifle; the rest of us, including two of the sailors, lay behind mattresses within reach of the sheets.

The breeze was brisk enough, and soon we were in the narrows, the *Pearl* in the shadows cast by the western shore.

"T'ree points to port! Ease on the sheets!" came Captain Marat's order.

The *Pearl* swung her bowsprit round a bit.

"Steady! jus' there!" called out Captain Marat again.

It was the first bend in the tortuous channel. It was deep in the fairway, we had only to avoid the points.

We had made another turn, and were near half way down the channel, when the flash and rat-a-tat of a score of guns sounded on the heights to our starboard, and the lead rained like hail on our deck. Marat's and Norris's rifles answered. Norris, for some reason withheld the fire of the big gun.

"Anyone hurt?" called Norris.

There was no answer.

"Keep behind your mattresses," he cautioned.

He swung the big gun round, as I could hear. As much as a minute passed with no sound on shore. Then came another volley from the enemy. The two rifles replied again. There came another pattering of bullets from the enemy. Norris spat out an oath. The next moment Ray called to me, saying that Norris was wounded. Leaving the fore-sheet to the sailors, I scurried over to the gun, and we began to uncover Norris's wound.

"It's nothing bad, give them the gun first," he said.

Carlos seized the carriage and began to train the gun while random shots continued from the enemy.

"Hold her right on the edge of the bank," said Norris, his voice husky with the pain.

"Now," said Carlos.

Rufe applied the fire.

"Boom!" The thunder echoed in the hills. From the shore came horrid yells, of pain or fright, but never another shot.

"We got them that time," said Norris, with a sigh of satisfaction.

And now we turned to Norris's wound. The ball had passed through the fleshy part of his shoulder, and was not deep. We soon had on a bandage. After a good swig out of the water butt, he declared he was ready for another fight. Though after one attempt to stand he was content to recline on the deck. But he insisted on our re-loading his gun.

The moon had set when we passed out over the bar, between those two flanking lines of surf.

"There's a schooner!" called Robert, come from the wheel, where he had been relieved by Captain Marat.

To the east, the vessel showed, all sails set, scurrying away.

"The *Orion*!" cried Grant Norris. "Give her that shot!" he commanded.

Again the gun boomed. But it was a clean miss. Of this I was glad, for there was no occasion for further bloodshed; though I would not have betrayed the thought to Grant Norris, suffering as he did from that shot of the blacks.

We got Norris down under the cabin light, and properly cleaned and dressed the wound. While we were busied thus, Captain Marat had brought the schooner about and set her bow toward the west. In an hour everything was ship-shape, and Norris propped comfortably on a mattress on deck, with the rest of our party squatted about him. Rufe was busy in his galley, for none having had any lust for food at the proper supper time, and now the suspense having snapped, we had developed keen appetites.

"Dey ain't no use you-all tellin' me how yo' feels," Rufe called to us. "I jes' got dat same feelin' in *mah* insides."

The relief was general; all who were not chattering, were whistling or humming. And the sailors, forward, were mingling their voices in a negro melody. Even the monkey caught the infection, and scampered about like a playful child, times springing from shoulder to shoulder; and once he snatched a biscuit from Rufe's galley and thrust it into my hand, to Ray's pretended disgust.

"I told you the monkey and Wayne are in cahoots," he said.

But before we came to Jamaica, the animal had transferred his chief liking to Ray. None could long resist Ray.

The black boy never tired of roaming about the schooner, which to him was the wonder of wonders, never having so much as seen the picture of a ship, or anything calculated to give him overmuch yearning for the world without those rocky walls of that sink in the mountain. Julian, who had conversed much with the boy, told us that he could not understand the value of that gold on which we put so much store. To him it was nothing but so much dross that had given him so many lame backs with the delving for it.

Andy Hawkins sat there grimacing and jerking his shoulders, and telling such ears as would listen, of the bottles of soda water he would be drinking when he got to the shops. Strangely enough, strong drink had no charms for him, though he made no concealment of his slavery to the drug that had already marked him for an early grave.

"The last time I was in London," he said, "I put four bottles of 'Utchinson's Sarsaprilla sody-water down be'ind my collar; and if Hi 'ad them now, Hi think Hi'd be able to put down a heven dozen."

"You believe in getting full even if you don't get drunk, don't you?" said Ray.

They were uneventful days, those of the voyage back to Kingston, in the Island of Jamaica. It was before noon of the twenty-fifth of September that we let go the anchor in the harbor.

Captain Marat and Grant Norris had been having some conference with Carlos Brill, and at last called us all together.

"We've been talking with Carlos about the gold," said Norris. "Although the mine is his, he will not hear of any arrangement other than share and share alike—after the sailors have been paid a substantial bonus, and Hawkins and the boy have received a proper payment for their labors and sufferings."

There was an echo of protest. We felt that, as owners, Carlos and his sister should retain at the least a third of their patrimony.

"No," spoke Carlos. "No! We never get the mine if it not be for you. I feel in here" (and he put his finger to his chest) "what is right, and I can never be happy if I cannot do what is right. I speak for my sister, too, she will think jus' like me."

The final upshot of the whole discussion was, that he would allow that his sister should receive an equal share with the rest, instead of brother and sister having a single share between them as he intended. What our gold amounted to I will not put down—this is no business volume I am writing; let it be enough, that no one of our party had need to want for any material comfort thereafter, even should he live the length of two average lives.

The news of the arrival of the *Pearl* had, somehow, passed quickly into the city; and we had not finished our noon meal, when a boat came aboard, and we dropped our ladder, and received on deck some Kingston friends. There were Monsieur Cambon, with little Marie Cambon, she whom we rescued from the voodoos.

"She could not wait," said Cambon. "She must go and see 'the good American boys'." And Monsieur Duchanel, the old friend of the Marats, came out of the boat, too. He brought a message from Madame Marat to her son, Captain Marat. Jean must come to shore early, bringing with him all of the party; for she and Madame Duchanel were already about the preparation of a feast to the returning argonauts. Melie Brill sent a word, too, to her brother, Carlos, who must not disappoint her for an early sight of him.

"You all seem cheerful, and in good health," observed Monsieur Cambon. "But I see Mistar Norris, here—he have some accident?" Norris still wore his arm in a sling.

"Oh, no," said Ray. "It was no accident, it was all on a program; only all the program was not carried out, as, I guess, there are some voodoos left that could tell."

And then we had to recount something of that parting clash with the blacks.

"Come, Marie," said her father at last. "We must leave these boys to get ready for the party."

The child had discovered the monkey, and they two were making friends, by inches.

"Oh, bring the monkey with you!" cried Marie, as she went over the side.

And so we dug out all our best bib and tucker for the fete. Duchanel sent aboard a pair of men from his establishment, for a guard to the *Pearl*, since all our party were expected ashore. And the sailors were given shore leave, except only the regular watch.

It may be imagined what the party was, that evening, with the Cambons, the Duchanels, and the music of the little orchestra in that very park of a lawn, lights hung between the trees, and the cooling drinks and sherbets, and the wonderful cookery of Madame Marat, assisted by Madame Duchanel. Andy Hawkins felt a bit out of place, and kept himself a good deal in the background. Once during the evening, Ray got me by the elbow and pulled me toward a clump of the shrubbery.

"Hawkins has been sending someone on an errand," he said.

We peeked round a bush. On the ground sat Hawkins, grimacing at a pop bottle in his hand. He set it to his lips, and drained it. It was the second; the first—empty—lay beside him. In front, ten bottles, untouched, awaited his attack. He drank out a third, and with some access of squirming, a fourth. The fifth he barely tasted of, and he groaned with his defeat. He set the bottles on the ground, put his hands to his stomach and belched gas.

"What's the matter, Hawkins?" said Ray. "Sick?"

"Oh, I s'y," returned Hawkins. "Hi ain't no good no more. Four bottles puts me under the tyble."

"Are you full," said Ray, "or just intoxicated?"

"Oh, Hi feel just like my 'ead was goin' to blow hoff, or somethink," said Hawkins.

For near a week we lay in Kingston Harbor. Carlos and Melie Brill established themselves here, and they took the black boy under their care. Andy Hawkins found the place to his liking, and would remain till the spirit should move him to a trip back to London. The poor chap never got so far, for fever did for him before five months had gone. Grant Norris had some interest in Kingston, and would make it his home for the time.

During those six days, we made the division of the gold, weighing it in the hopper of a grocer's scale, set in the hold, under the open hatch.

At the end of the time, Madame Marat came aboard, and we set sail for New Orleans—and for *home*.

And then one day we passed through Lake Bourne and the Rigolets; the next morning we were towed in the basin to the very heart of the city. Soon we saw our chests of treasure carted off to the mint.

"Ah!" said Madame Marat, as we all entered her door, "how good it is to be home! And to think!" she spoke, looking aghast, "no dust! Thee air good and fresh! And—" (she sniffed) "thee smell of thee coffee!"

The door to the back opened, and the grinning Rufe appeared.

"Ah! thad why you delay so long," she said.

At Rufe's own suggestion, Jean Marat had given Rufe the key and permitted him to run ahead, to sweep, dust, and air the home, and get the fire going. The thing touched her good heart, and she patted the happy darky approvingly on the back.

Julian's grandfather was sent for, and there was a joyful reunion.

The leave-takings—always, some way sad they are—I omit. The three of us—Ray, Robert, and myself, made a quiet entry one night into our good old home town in Illinois. My father, who had returned from the southwest some days ago, on wired word from me, met us at the train; and he took us to the Reid home, where a little spread had been prepared.

It was when Mrs. Reid put her arms round Ray that I missed my mother most. But this good mother had a kiss for Robert and myself. Robert, you must know, was a full orphan.

There was consternation in the bank the next morning, when the three of us presented each a paper bearing amounts in six figures. They seemed to think that the receiving teller's cage would not do for such a transaction, but the business must be done in the directors' room, on the long table.

That afternoon the three of us went for a long row on the old Mississippi. We had things to discuss alone. It was Robert who finally opened the subject that was troubling us most.

"How much are we going to tell the world?" he said.

"Well," said Ray, giving his oar a vicious pull, "there's a lot of things I don't intend to tell, and———"

"But," I interrupted, "if you tell some things, and keep back some, people are going to wonder why."

"And," added Robert, "they'll fill in the blanks with all sorts of wild stuff that won't be very flattering—that's the way it goes."

And the discussion went on, till finally Ray put it flat, thus:

"Well, now then, Wayne, it's up to you to write the thing—write a book. Then if anyone gets curious and wants the story, we can say: 'All right, go and get the book.' Gee! It'll save a lot of talk—and a lot of fool questions."

THE END

---

[1] *Sang mele—said to be 127 parts white and one part black.*

www.ingramcontent.com/pod-product-compliance
Ingram Content Group UK Ltd.
Pitfield, Milton Keynes, MK11 3LW, UK
UKHW042148281224
453045UK00004B/235